MAXX FRAGG, V.P.I.

By S.A. Check

Ink Smith Publishing
www.ink-smith.com

ISBN: 978-1-939156-67-9

Ink Smith Publishing
710 S. Myrtle Ave Suite 209
Monrovia, CA, 91016

CHAPTER 1

Tucked between the shadows and the night, standing in a darkened corner of the room, Maxx Fragg watched the young couple huddled on the couch. They had no idea what he had in store for them. He almost felt sorry. Almost. He watched as Travis stroked Debbie's hand and whispered something in her ear. Maxx locked eyes with her as he moved across the apartment. He saw the desperation mixed with fear in her eyes and he grinned. He liked it that way. Pulling a pair of gloves from his belt, Maxx cinched them tight around his wrists. The rush of adrenaline rose up from his chest. This was far from his first job but he still got a thrill each time. He clicked off the lamp and the room went black.

Debbie gasped. "Can't we leave a few lights on?"

"I prefer to work in the dark. It helps me concentrate," Maxx said. It really didn't matter but he felt it intensified the experience.

"I think I'd rather see what's coming." Travis pulled a cushion on his lap, clutching the fabric.

"Why? You expecting a pillow fight?" Maxx dropped the equipment bag slung over his shoulder.

Debbie jumped. "What are you going to do with that?"

"What I'm being paid to do. My job." Maxx nodded across the room to his partner, who shook his head in disapproval. Bending next to the couch, Maxx slowly unzipped the bag. He was close enough to see the goose bumps on Debbie's arm rise with each click.

"I don't care what it takes. Just get that thing out of my house," Travis said.

"Don't worry. You'll be ghost free in no time." Maxx knew his clients needed to believe he could make it better, take away their fears. If only it was that simple. Everyone wanted to name the night, put a label on their personal horrors. He wished someone could shut the door to the monsters in his own closet.

Travis and Debbie wanted to leave as soon as Maxx and his partner got to the apartment but Maxx convinced them to stay. There was no showmanship in coming back to a ghost free home based just on his word and some lines arching across a digital readout. No, they needed the full hands on experience and Maxx made sure they had front row seats.

"Maybe this wasn't such a great idea?" Debbie's hand twitched against her boyfriend's knee.

He brushed his hand through her hair. "We contacted *them*, honey. They say he's the best at this sort of thing."

She sighed. "I know. It's just not what I expected. It's all so...clinical. They didn't even draw a pentagram."

Everyone had their own pre-conceived notions of how to get rid of a ghost. Maxx heard them all, séances, sprinkle salt along the door, burn sage, hire a bunch of meddling kids, craft some pottery together. He'd probably find it all funnier if he actually believed in any of it.

Maxx pulled a long metal rod from his bag. Standing next to the couple, he pushed a switch on the base, holding it high over his head. The staff hummed and vibrated like a radioactive tuning fork sending palpable energy out into the air around the room. Maxx swung it over their heads and they both instinctively ducked. They were like two kids watching their first fireworks display and Maxx was the guy lighting the wicks. He stepped around a small table. There wasn't much furniture in the apartment, a sign they hadn't lived there long. He read the digital display on the club's handle.

Satisfied, Maxx brushed his hand through his spiked hair, trying to express some fake concern. "You've definitely got a presence here. Readings are off the charts."

Pulling a notepad from his tactical vest, he scribbled down some notes. Maxx drew a smiley face with a frown and tears streaming down both cheeks. Underneath his sketch he wrote Travis.

"Well, I have to admit, I've never seen anything like this," Maxx lied. Everyone wanted to be special, even in the worst of ways. No one wanted to hear that they dropped a wad of cash on a specialist just to have him say they really didn't need to. The bigger the problem, the more satisfied his clients were with the result, meaning a bigger pay day. "You're lucky you called us when you did. Have you ever seen anything like this, Tane?"

Taking his cue, Maxx's teammate finished unloading some equipment and crossed the room. His six foot eight inch frame exerted considerably more effort to move around the furniture as size fourteen army boots left hefty impressions in the plush red carpet. Bending to clear a ceiling light, Tane looked at the readout.

"Holy crap! That's impossible. We need to evacuate the whole building."

Maxx elbowed him in the side and whispered, "Over doing it a little there, partner."

"Oh. I mean, yeah, those are some numbers. I think we should call in our other group, you know, the Black Oops Guys."

"You mean our Black Ops Special Detention Squad?" Maxx turned his back to the couple, pulling Tane around with him. "I think we can handle this one on our own."

He gave his partner a quick jab in the ribs. "I can't believe you."

"Ow." Tane rubbed his side. "Quit hitting me, Maxx."

"You're going to blow this whole thing," Maxx said.

"Guys?" Debbie asked from the couch. "Everything all right?"

"We're good here," Maxx said. "Whatever you do, don't leave that couch." Unbelievable. They practiced the script at the office right before they came over. Just once he'd like to get through a gig without having to cover up his partner's mistakes.

Debbie raised her hand. "Would it be okay if I just darted to the lady's room first? I really need to-"

"It's too late for that. The process has already started," Maxx said.

"But…" Debbie persisted.

Maxx secured the detecting rod back in his bag and withdrew a long barreled shotgun with a plastic cylinder attached to each side. "You can put your hand down now."

Pumping the stock, a neon gel flowed through the tubing running the length of the barrel. Maxx hit a button and the liquid energized, bubbling as it flowed the course of the weapon. The couple simultaneously pulled their feet up off the floor.

Travis and Debbie had reached the right mix of anxiety and excitement. It was time for Maxx to set up the final act.

"Don't worry, folks. You're entirely safe as long as my partner and I are here. You wouldn't want to miss the show, would you?" Maxx asked.

"They're professionals, Debbie. It's okay." Travis tried to reassure her with a half-hearted smile.

Debbie dug her nails into the couch. "I guess."

Maxx motioned to Tane. They needed to get through the rest of this job without any more problems. Debbie appeared on the verge of crying and Maxx knew Tane's concentration shattered at the sight of a girl's tears.

"Okay, Tane, let's do this. Set up the call."

Grabbing a small black cube from his bag, Tane positioned it on the ground next to the stone fireplace. He worked at centering it inside one of the bricks.

They both agreed that attention to detail was crucial to pull off jobs but Tane took it to an O.C.D. level at times. Maxx looked out a set of patio doors and down to the lights of the city below them. Row after row of neon skyscrapers lined the landscape stretching out to the horizon under a dull purple evening sky. The streets below pulsed with endless lines of traffic, diverting and streaming along paved circuit boards, individual bits of data following personal programs. At times, staring into its expanse, it was easy for Maxx to forget it was all fake, a virtual world built out of memory bytes and data chips. Like the advertisements said, within the world of Other Syde your only limits were your own imagination. It was somewhere Maxx could shut the door on the outside world, if only temporarily.

Maxx realized Tane was still fiddling with the cube. "Anytime this life?"

Tane adjusted it one more time and stood up. He stepped back and started to bend down again but stopped. "Ok. Ready."

Maxx's pulse quickened. His heart thumped in his chest as he braced the modified water cannon against his shoulder, flipping off the safety. Three blue targeting dots zigzagged across the room. He focused the glowing triangle just above the black box Tane had set.

Maxx leaned into the sights. "On your call."

Tane nodded and pressed a button on his belt. The box squealed to life, belting out a high pitched wail. It caught Tane off guard and he almost fell backwards.

Maxx felt another kick of adrenalin, that time from the embarrassment of his partner tripping over his own feet.

"Sorry, Maxx." Tane scrambled, fumbling for the weapon strapped to his back.

Maxx tactically advanced, scanning the room as he approached. The job was heading south and fast. Getting caught was always part of the thrill but Maxx wasn't letting that happen tonight.

Debbie held her hands up to her ears. "That noise is unbearable."

Travis wedged pillows against each side of Debbie's head. "Does it have to be that loud?"

Maxx maneuvered to the side and waved for his partner to take a position opposite him. They stared at the expanding mass of light surrounding the cube, both of their laser targets focused directly above it.

Maxx shouted to the couple. "We should see something any minute now. They can't help it. It's like a ghost bug zapper."

The job became easier when their clients had something tangible to focus their fear on. The entrance remained his favorite part.

Staying on target, Maxx waited.

He shouted over the screech of the bait cube. "Tane, are you sure you properly tuned the intensifier?"

Tane kept his eyes on the mark.

"Tane!"

"Oh…the what?"

Maxx waved his hand in small circular motions. If he wasn't his best friend, Maxx would seriously consider replacing him.

"The intensifier. Is it set to the proper frequency? We should be getting some type of reaction by now."

Tane lowered his weapon and casually walked up to the device. Kicking it on its side, he hurried back into position.

"I got it, boss. The sub atomic strato-structure was off balance. We should see activity any second now."

Maxx clenched the stock of his gun. They looked like amateurs.

A rush of blue light exploded from the chimney, flooding the living room.

Travis' voice jumped up two octaves. "Keep it away! Keep it away!"

Clawing over top of his girlfriend, Travis scrambled to the edge of the couch and pulled his way to the floor.

Maxx shouted, "Debbie, keep him there and don't move. It reacts to sudden movements…and screaming like a girl."

She grabbed Travis' collar and twisted him back to the couch. Gripping him around the waist, she pulled him down and locked him in place with a full nelson. His face forcibly stuffed into the back of the couch, she called back to Maxx, "Okay, I got him. Just get rid of that thing."

Maxx's eyes adjusted to the light burst. Hovering above the fireplace, a billowing green wraith snarled at them. Its unhinged jaw dropped down to its chest. Wailing out a blistering scream of its own, wisps of jade fog flowed from its mouth out into the living room. A viridian glow oozed from its skin and gossamer hair stretched out, like tendrils feeling for prey. Blackened eye sockets slowly scanned the room. The apparition's arms stretched out and lengthened along the walls, each hand ending in razor sharp claws.

Maxx hinted a small nod of approval. What Tane lacked in the performing arts category, he made up for in the detail he crafted into their targets.

"Get Ready." Maxx dropped to one knee and took aim.

His partner mimicked his movements. "Eady and Rable."

Maxx sneered. "Fire!"

Maxx braced himself as a stream of blue energy spewed from the nozzle, splattering against the wall just next to the creature. Tane fired the same pressurized current. It exploded against the ceiling. The rampaging wraith darted between the beams. Soaring over the terrified couple, it disappeared through a door leading into the apartment's adjoining kitchen.

Maxx raised a finger to his lips. "Shhh."

Travis' muffled cries filtered out between the cushions. "What is that thing?"

Maxx pushed Tane towards the kitchen. Cabinet doors slammed open and shut in the other room and an alarm chimed as something exploded. Smoke billowed from around the door and Maxx swore he smelled burned popcorn. The ghost shrieked as a white liquid seeped under the door's base, soaking into the living room carpet.

"This is bad, folks. It's hungry and I don't think it's looking for a pot pie," Maxx shouted. He nudged Tane's shoulder. "What are you waiting for? Get in there."

"Me?" Tane didn't move.

"Yes, you, use the hand-held spectro-nullifier and keep it contained." For a guy that spent his entire high school life immersed in online gaming, Maxx knew Tane wasn't a fighter by nature.

Maxx whispered in his ear, "We've been through this a hundred times. It's not like we can actually get hurt in here. Remember, it's just a computer program. Think of it like a level on *Planet of Punishment* and kick some ghost butt."

Maxx reached for the handle just as a flaming microwave shattered through the door, shooting out between the two ghost hunters. The burning appliance rolled across the living room floor, sputtering and sparking its last breaths inches away from Travis and Debbie.

Maxx grabbed Tane and waved back to Debbie. "We were just coming up with a battle plan." Pushing Tane into the kitchen, he said, "Come on. Man up."

Maxx yanked the door shut behind his friend. More wood and glass shattered inside. He leaned down to get a look through the impromptu window the flying microwave made. Corn flakes sprayed out through the hole, covering Maxx in broken crumbs.

"I think it's getting tired." Maxx ducked to avoid a gush of water spewing out the hole. "What are you trying to do in there? Drown it?"

"This isn't easy, you know," Tane shouted back. "Hey, hold still. I could use some help in here. No! Do not squirt that."

"You're doing great. Just stay out of arm's reach." Maxx retreated back to the couch and bent down near Debbie.

"This is worse than we thought. That's a class Zulu entity in there. They don't go down without a fight and I think we made it mad. We're going to need to go back to our office and get some heavier equipment. Can you two stay still for like an hour until we get back?"

Debbie sat on a pillow on top of Travis' head. "Are you crazy? You came here and ticked the thing off and now you're going to leave?" Her cheeks were already red from wrestling her boyfriend into submission. "You get that thing out of here. I don't care what you have to do."

Maxx nodded. "Okay, you're right but we're going to have to try something we've never done before. This is going to cost you extra."

Travis pushed his face free. "Pay them whatever they want. Don't let it get me, Judy."

Debbie bounced on the pillow as she screamed at Maxx. "I don't care what it costs. Get it out of here!" She punched Travis in the side. "Who's Judy?"

Cha-ching. Maxx ran back to his partner. "Hold on, buddy. I'm coming."

Two steps from the kitchen and a flying blur shot out over top of Maxx, knocking him back into the living room. The creature floated over the couple, drool slipping from its rolls of teeth. Holding a long silver butcher night, it wore one of Debbie's cooking aprons.

The ghost fixated on the petrified couple. "Fooooooddddd."

Travis slipped Debbie's grip and tumbled over the back of the sofa. Debbie grabbed a throw pillow, using it as a shield.

Maxx focused on the knife. They never added props to their ghost. They both agreed that it cheapened the effect. The cooking apron was *way* over the top. Maxx didn't want this turning into a comedy hour. He heard Tane stumbling out of the kitchen and turned towards his friend.

"Why is our creature from beyond wearing a cooking-"

"Maxx! Look out!" Something hit Maxx from the side and he tumbled to the floor. He spun around on his back, expecting Tane, but no one was there. That voice was so familiar. He knew it as well as his own but that was impossible. Maxx noticed the knife handle sticking out of the wall behind him, the blade embedded in the plaster.

"Jason?" Maxx twisted around.

No one else was near him. Maxx *knew* that voice. It was Jason. But how? His brother died six months ago.

Maxx laid on the carpet in stunned silence. He'd thought about Jason's death every day since it happened. He'd give anything to change that day.

"Next time I won't miss, Maxx Fragg."

Maxx spun towards the couch. The ghost looked straight at him. Its face had narrowed and warped, the wide eyed maddened look they gave their computer generated ghost replaced by one of anger and contempt.

"Who are you?" Maxx jumped to his feet.

Tane, covered in assorted condiments, raced in from the kitchen. He noticed the knife in the wall. "Something weird is going on here, Maxx. This wasn't part of the script...I mean plan."

Ketchup dripped down into Tane's eyes and Maxx saw the anxiety building in his friend's face. Maxx looked back at the floating ghoul, still hovering over the terrified couple. Its features had returned to the ghost-bot they programmed for that job. He needed to pull it together. They had a job to finish. They could figure out what went wrong later.

Maxx fired his weapon. "Now!"

The fluid ray struck the ghost-bot in the back. It screeched and lashed out blindly. Tane let loose his own energized stream, connecting with the wraith's shoulder. It squirmed and thrashed, trying to break free from the glistening tethered lines. Maxx cocked his head toward Tane. Just get this part right, was that too much to ask?

"We don't have anything that's going to hold this monstrosity. There's only one way to get rid of it," Maxx said.

Tane's jaw dropped. "You can't be serious."

Maxx felt his faith in his friend returning. "It's the only way."

"But..."

"There's no time to argue," Maxx said.

"You want to stross the creams?" Tane's eyes widened.

Not missing a beat, Maxx edged along the wall.

"Do it, man. *Cross* the *streams*!" Of all places to blunder, leave it to his friend to pick the punch line. Maxx couldn't let it bother him. It wasn't on purpose but he still wanted to finish strong.

The two faux ghost hunters slowly angled their barrels toward the other. The radiant shafts intertwined and convulsed, swiftly joining into the other and driving towards the ethereal horror. The molten blast smashed into the ghost's chest, ripping it in half. The creature slowly dissipated into the surrounding atmosphere, dripping remnants of amorphous skin into the plush carpet. Maxx knew the routine was schlocky but everyone seemed to respond pretty well to it. He figured they needed something they could relate with to keep them anchored.

Satisfied that their clients benefited from the full effects of their up close and personal ghost encounter, Maxx relaxed. "Area is clear. Target contained and perimeter secured. Power down." He exhaled an exaggerated sigh to drive home the fact it was safe.

Both beams went dark. Tane wiped away the considerable sweat pouring over his face. The perspiration mixed with the ketchup made him look like a professional wrestler after a cage match. Even though the entire routine was usually pre-planned, Maxx sensed a feeling of relief from his friend every time they finished a job. Tane hit a button on his belt and the bait box stopped wailing.

"That was intense," Maxx said.

Debbie sat on the couch while Travis peeked out from behind a cushion. Maxx had seen it all, women in control, men embracing their hunter/gatherer nature, both afraid, and both finding a renewal on their lives after what they believed to be a near death experience. The only thing that continued to surprise him was the randomness in each person.

No matter the outer guise, when faced with true terror, a person's inner self always shined through.

He offered Travis a hand up from the floor. "I think it's safe now."

Maxx swept the room using the same metallic rod he used earlier. It was post game and he was ready for the commentary and the naming of the M.V.P.

"No spectral debris. It's gone," Maxx said.

Travis sat down next to Debbie. "That wasn't so bad."

She stared at him in disbelief. "Some hero you are."

"Come on. I tried to drag you back there with me. I wanted to protect you." Travis reached for her hand.

"Maybe you thought I was Judy." Debbie pulled away.

Great. Maxx knew where this was heading. The last thing he needed was to get stuck in the middle of a domestic dispute. Maxx interrupted. "Look, folks. It's done. You won't have any more problems. That's our guarantee."

Tane finished packing up their equipment and came up beside Maxx. He handed him a slip of paper.

Maxx looked it over and handed it to Debbie. "If you could just transfer the credits into our account?"

Maxx's arm shot up and smacked Tane in the head.

"Hey!" Tane rubbed his eye.

Debbie turned her attention from the bill. "What was that? Are you sure there aren't any more ghosts?"

There was only one reason Maxx lost control of his in-world avatar. There were times he wished the program wasn't directly attached to his central nervous system. He needed to hurry this up.

"What? That? No, that's something we do after a successful job. It's like a high five. We do it all the time. Now about the payment, with the extra risk, I'm thinking double. Call it hazard pay."

Debbie typed something into a device beside the couch. "Okay, it's in. I don't know how to thank you two enough. Who would have ever thought we'd have ghosts inside a virtual world?"

Maxx holstered his energy cannon and headed for the door. It was only a matter of time before his next spasm. He couldn't believe she was doing it to him again. They'd discussed disturbing him when he worked in-world.

"You never can tell. Thanks for the business and remember to tell your friends if they have any problems to call the Maxx Fragg Virtual Paranormal Investigative Agency for all their para-cyber needs."

Maxx pulled the door closed as Debbie's voice filtered into hall.

"Who's Judy?"

CHAPTER 2

"I feel like a giant hot dog."

Waiting at the elevator doors, Tane wiped ketchup from his eye.

"I was thinking more like a wiener, Mr. Stross-the-creams." Maxx punched his friend in the shoulder. "I can't believe you."

Maxx unexpectedly lurched forward, slamming into the shaft door. "Ow."

"What is up with you, Maxx?"

Maxx shouted at the ceiling. "Okay, Mom. Hold on a minute." At least he made it outside. The last time she played Geppetto to his virtual Pinocchio, he was trying to close a deal with a client. The embarrassment aside, the lady thought Maxx was possessed. He convinced her he just forgot to take his meds.

Maxx hummed along with the elevator music as they rode down to the lobby. His body started vibrating. His hands and fingers blurred and his face distorted as the muscular man with black spiked hair morphed into a far less intimidating teenage boy.

"Nice flattop by the way." Maxx pointed at his friend's head. "Where'd you come up with that?"

"What? It's cool. I got it from some guy in a movie I downloaded last night. I'll burn you a copy. The whole town turned zombie and all he had was a ball bat, a weed whacker, and half a gallon of gas. His zombie girlfriend was totally hot. She's the one from those cologne commercials, *Can of Man*." He flexed his arms and sniffed his armpits, deepening his voice. "That's manly."

Tane's head shimmered, mimicking the transformation Maxx just performed. His hair turned from sandy blond to bright red locks. Several freckles appeared on his cheeks.

Maxx chuckled. "You know, Tane, a little extra creativity in your own disguises might not be a bad idea. For a computer genius, sometimes you have crap for an imagination. How'd you ever make it through art class?"

Tane ruffled his new red top. "I wrote code that randomly placed colored pixels into pre-formed boundaries to give the appearance of hand drawn reproductions. I sold that program to a small photo editing firm. It financed our limo for the prom, which you never did thank me for."

"I wondered how you did that. What was that girl's name? Lani? Lily?"

"Lilith," Tane corrected.

Maxx knew her name but got a kick out of how defensive his friend got when he brought up the topic. Tane's computer skills were on a whole other level than the average hacker, especially for an eighteen year old. He wrote programs like most people wrote shopping lists. Maxx called him the Curt Cobain of code. But, as awesome as his tech skills were, Tane's personal skills left something to be desired.

Tane thought Lilith was going to be the true love of his life, like every other girl before her. What he didn't count on was an overly suspicious dad, who happened to also be a federal agent in charge of a computer crime division. Tane thought Lilith was cheating on him, talking to some other dude on HeadRoom, so he embedded a key stroke recorder in one of his emails. Her dad's security software picked it up and two guys in suits showed up at Tane's door. Luckily he was just shy of turning eighteen and got a smack on the wrist, cleaning garbage along the highway for two weeks. The kicker of it all was she wasn't even cheating on him. It was her Cousin Merle from Toledo.

"You know, State Route 119 has never looked cleaner," Maxx said.

Tane's face reddened. "C'mon, Maxx. I'm trying to forget that part of my life."

"So, what was up with adding the knife to Count Spookula?" Maxx asked. "I wasn't expecting him to throw it at me."

"I didn't put a knife in the program. I figured you were just improvising in the living room. The ghost-bot acted funny in the kitchen too," Tane said.

"How?"

"Do you really think I'd program it to douse me in ketchup and mustard? It shoved a loaf of bread in my face and called me a buffoon."

"Who uses the word *buffoon*?"

"I know."

They exited the elevator into the main foyer of the apartment complex. A small common area with a half dozen chairs circled a small wooden table. The young man behind the front desk eyed them both as they lugged their equipment across the lobby.

Maxx casually waved as they passed. "S'up."

The clerk asked, "What's will all the bags?"

"My buddy and I are virtual burglars. We just cleaned out the top three floors." Maxx smiled.

"Whatever. This job blows." He turned back to the small television playing cartoons behind the counter.

"Maxx! What if he would've called the O.S. Corps on us? We don't need any more problems with those guys." Tane checked for flashing lights through the glass doors leading to the street.

"Relax. You have too much faith in people."

"And you don't have enough."

Maxx stopped at the revolving door. "Hey, Tane, were you...I mean...did you see anyone up there besides us and the clients? Someone else in the living room maybe?"

"The ghost-bot?"

"No. Somebody yelled before the ghost threw that knife and then pushed me out of the way."

"It was probably Travis."

"I don't think so. Travis was hiding behind the couch most of the time. I tell you, Tane, it sounded like Jason."

Tane stopped. "Your brother?"

"Yeah, I know it sounds crazy but I could swear it was him."

"But, you know, Maxx, he's…"

"Dead. Yeah, I know. You're right. It must have been Travis. He probably crawled back behind the couch and that's why I didn't see him. But why did the ghost call me by name and change its face? It doesn't make sense. You know I don't like surprises on jobs."

"We pulled it off, right? Ice and Neasy," Tane said.

Maxx bit his tongue. Tane's speech quirks made him self-conscious and Maxx tried not to get hung up on them. Tane suffered from spoonerisms where he mixed up the first letters in certain words. He tried speech therapists, self-hypnosis, even light electro shock therapy, but nothing worked.

"Just go over the program again. We don't need any more hiccups," Maxx said. "I don't want to mess up this gig. It's too sweet. Ghosts in a virtual world, it doesn't even make sense."

"People need to believe in something, Maxx."

"They're nothing but analog sheep to our digital wolves, buddy." Maxx's body spasmed again. "Look, Tane, I need to go. Can you head back to the office and kill Debbie and Travis' spook program?"

"No problem. I told Lady Ariana I'd link up with her before I faded out of town anyway."

"The dude who says he's a British ambassador's daughter?"

"What? She's real! Her family is just having a rough time stuck in that town in South Africa. All those sanctions with her passport and the exchange rates are very tricky. She promised to pay it all back. Quit being such a skeptic."

"As soon as you quit being such an easy mark."

Tane shrugged. "You seeing Emi tonight?"

"Yeah, she's picking me up in a little bit."

"That's every night this week. You two are becoming an item."

"She's just a friend."

"You'll never know until you ask, Maxx."

"Whatever. You coming down to The Wash after you fade back?"

"Yeah, I'll be there." Tane placed his hand on Maxx's shoulder. "Those people were really afraid up there tonight. Yang and Yin, you know?"

"It's make-believe, Tane. We made a nice chunk of cash tonight, so try to have some still tomorrow. Don't get cold feet on me."

"I know but-"

"They'll be talking about it for months with all their cyber-snob friends."

"How do you know they're snobs?"

"Just stop over later and we'll plan the next job. I don't want any glitches. It's bad for our reputation."

"I'll take care of it, Maxx. Glo nitches."

"That's what I want to hear."

Maxx concentrated and faded out of the hotel's lobby. Tane's hand fell from where it had rested on his friend's shoulder.

"They didn't seem like snobs," Tane said before vanishing too.

Chapter 3

"Don't make me rip that thing off of you!" The voice was female, angry, and Maxx guessed about six inches from his face.

He felt the pillow under his neck and gripped the leather arms of his chair. Transferring back from Other Syde was always a little disorienting and it took a minute to regain his bearings. Having someone screaming in your ear while it happened didn't help.

"You're missing supper. Again."

Maxx looked up into his mom's curly brown hair wrapped softly around her face, just touching the wire rims of her glasses. The smile lines curving around her cheeks showed only traces of concern. Maxx grew to recognize the look well over the last six months. A lecture loomed in his immediate future.

"We've talked about you spending all your time in that computer world. It's not healthy. You're going to be nothing but a bag of bones. Not to mention you're responsible for the garbage, which is three bags deep in the kitchen."

Huh, that wasn't bad as far as lectures went. She'd gone total mother hen since the accident. Pealing the adhesive pad from the back of his neck, Maxx felt the tingle trickle down his spine as it disconnected. Wires ran to an input jack in a nearby computer tower. Maxx typed something into a digital keyboard below a wall-mounted flat panel screen. Signing out of the Other Syde program, he stood up and kissed his mother on the cheek.

"I know, Mom, computers bad, garbage good. Stop worrying about me."

If his mom had her way, Maxx would wear a pillow suit and a bubble wrap jacket every time he stepped out the door. She didn't understand the virtual world, let alone the cutting edge technology used in Other Syde. Maxx got that part of it. She couldn't protect him there even though he explained time and again that he couldn't get hurt in a computer world. Worst case scenario would be a bruised ego if he managed to get himself kicked out. He'd already come close a couple times but she didn't need to know that.

His mom stared at the wires and computer equipment and shook her head. "You're going to have to grow up sometime, Maxx. Come downstairs. Supper's ready." She left his door open and walked into the hall.

Maxx grabbed a pair of shorts from a fresh laundry basket. Grabbing a tablet from his nightstand, he crossed off the name Debbie and Travis Everhart and circled the next name down, Steadready. The money from the Everhart gig would help pay for the new laptop and faster processor Maxx had been eyeing. He drew a cartoon ghost on the page, sketching in evil eyes, and thought about the ghost-bot back in the virtual apartment. Nothing like that had ever happened before. Aside from Tane's occasional fumbling of lines, their scripts played out solid. Maxx liked being in control. He needed it. That was one of the reasons he loved spending so much time in Other Syde. It was his night light to reality and he didn't want anyone messing with the switch.

Tossing the pad on his bed, he shouted down the hall, "What's for dinner?"

"Just get down here." His mom's voice boomed back up the stairs.

Maxx picked up a photo from his dresser. He couldn't get that voice out of his head. It was Jason back in that apartment. But how? And why now? It'd been months since Jason died. Everyone told him it would get easier with time but Maxx didn't buy it. They weren't the ones responsible for Jason's death. He was. Plopping back down in his chair, Maxx pulled up a webpage on his computer, the words

HeadRoom centered on top as he navigated to a profile page. A boy's photo, slightly older than Maxx, appeared in the corner as he typed in the dialogue box.

Hey bro, I miss you. Things here are as good as they can be. I just got back from another gig in Other Syde. I got this newbie couple to pay us double for the job. I know you'd disapprove and tell me that scamming people isn't right. I can almost hear you saying that. Craziest thing, I could have sworn I heard you inside the program. You pushed me out of the way before getting shiskebobbed by my own ghost-bot. I know it wasn't real but it was kinda nice having you watching my back again. Anyhow, I just wanted you to know that I'm still thinking about you. Always. Mom's yelling for dinner and I think Dad's home. I better go. Catch you later. Miss you.

Maxx hit enter and watched the screen go dark, replaced with the blurred image of his own face.

He plucked the screen with his fingers. "Jerk."

Maxx detoured to the bathroom and splashed some water on his face, his impromptu shower for the day. His jumble of black hair remained in a constant state of chaos, shadowed over his light olive eyes. He traced a finger along a scar that ran from the top of his ear down to his neck. The doctors told him it fully healed but it still hurt, especially at night. Tane said it was psychosomatic. Maxx knew what it meant but always asked what his scar had to do with starting fires with his mind. Tane told him it could be worse and be in the shape of a lightning bolt. Drying off, Maxx made his way down the stairs and smelled the boiling tomato sauce as soon as he hit the dining room. He could almost taste the garlic bread he hoped came with it.

Maxx's dad sat at the head of the table, his large frame stuffed into a short sleeve dress shirt and dark blue tie. A once athletic physique had given way to age and disinterest and the bottom buttons strained against a bulging gut. One of his dad's favorite sayings was how promising his future looked before they had kids. Of course that was before Jason died. He never said that any more. His dad stared intently at the steaming plate of pasta, his thick rimmed glasses resting halfway down his nose. Maxx's mom stood at the oven, pouring a ladle of sauce over another plate.

They both looked up when Maxx walked in.

"Well, look who decided to join the land of the living." His dad's fork hovered in front of his face. "Let me guess. You were playing in La La Land again all day."

Maxx picked the chair farthest from his dad, figuring he'd take all the distance he could manage. His mom placed a plate of spaghetti in front of him and patted his head.

"You need to get something in your stomach, Maxx. I made plenty."

"Thanks, Mom. It's Other Syde, Dad, not *La La Land*. And no, not all day. I had to finish a paper for one of my cyber classes too."

Shoveling in a mouth full of noodles, his dad grunted.

"And what do you get for that, a virtual degree? Are you going to work at a computer fast food restaurant? Would you like pretend fries with your make believe shake?" his dad asked.

Maxx twirled his own fork full of pasta and slurped the stray noodle strands into his mouth.

"Somebody already came up with that idea, Dad. Nice try though. You know the guys that run Burger Byte in Other Syde are millionaires? One's only twenty-five and the other is old, like thirty some. They're both set for life."

Except for a few details, the conversations between Maxx and his dad pretty much went the same over the last three months, ever since Maxx enrolled in the local community college's cyber curriculum. It wasn't an easy sell to either of his parents but Maxx convinced them he'd earn the same degree as his classmates but without the mess of the unwanted social interaction. His mom caved first and his dad figured it was easier to give in than argue. Besides, tuition was dirt cheap compared to other brick and mortar schools and he already had his first semester paid for from the proceeds of his ghost hunting business in Other Syde.

"Does anyone here know how to have a conversation without a mouth full of food?" his mom asked.

Wiping his chin with the back of his hand, his dad apologized. "Sorry, hon. That B.S. world of yours is just a game. When it's done, what will you have accomplished?"

Maxx downed a glass of green soda. "It's O.S., Dad, not B.S. And for the millionth time, Other Syde's not a game. It's a virtual *world*. There are thousands of people in it every day. It has its own commerce, politics, and entertainment industry. It trades on Wall Street and has an exchange rate higher than ninety-five percent of current blue chip stocks. It's the *future*. You either have to get on that bus or suffer the tread marks."

His dad's face reddened. "Well, I still don't see why you can't find a part time job or something. You can't stay locked up in this house. You're pale as a ghost."

Maxx chuckled at the ghost reference. "I've made more money running my business in O.S. than I could with twenty part time jobs. I go in when I want, dress how I feel, and all from the comfort of my own room. Who's fooling who?"

"Dammit! You're eighteen years old. You don't know squat about the world or what it takes to support a family to keep a roof over your block head. I've earned what I have from sweat and hard work. There's no computer program for that."

They sat in mutually uncomfortable silence until his mom chimed in. "Your dad is right, Maxx. It's a big world. You should go out and see it sometime. Besides, I just saw on the news they found two more people dead hooked up to that slick skin you wear. They say it rots your brain and makes your heart stop."

"Its *syn-skin*, Mom, and more people die from smoking, cholesterol, and lightning strikes than from using O.S. People just hate change. If they don't understand it, they're afraid of it. Sheep. Plain and simple."

Feeling triumphant with that last remark, Maxx resumed stuffing his face. He didn't want to push the cyber classes issue too far. That remained one of his best decisions to date. His term paper showing the advantages of standing while internet surfing to improve circulation earned him an A in his physical education course and was proof enough that he made the right choice.

His mom rubbed the top of his hair, which he would hate more if he spent any time fixing it.

She asked, "Well, do you at least have a computer girlfriend in B.S.?"

"That question is wrong on so many levels," Maxx said.

Cleaning up the remaining sauce with a piece of bread, his Dad asked, "What about Emi? You two seem to hit it off. Where's she at tonight?"

Maxx carried his plate to the sink. He needed to wrap this up before the invasive relationship questions came. "She should be here any minute. She had a couple errands to run. We're going to meet up with Tane at The Wash."

"Stupidest name for a restaurant I've ever heard." His father followed him to the sink. "Look, Maxx, you're a smart kid, just like your brother..."

Maxx jerked away. He should have seen it coming. "I'm not Jason." Every conversation turned back to his brother.

His dad stepped closer. "It's been six months. We all miss him. You can't live in the past, Maxx."

"I know, Dad. I'm okay." Maxx moved toward the door, safely out of hug range.

"You're not okay." His dad followed him. "You stay in your room and only come out at night. You barely speak to your mother and me. We don't even know you anymore."

"I got it under control, Dad. Look, Emi's probably outside waiting. I need to go." Maxx made a break for the back door.

His mom stopped washing dishes. "We're worried, Maxx. Just sit down and talk to us. Please."

Maxx's hand rested on the door knob. "I'm fine. We'll talk later. I promise."

His dad's arms fell to his sides. "You can't hide from life, son. It always finds you."

"Right. No running from life. We'll talk tomorrow night, for sure." Maxx half-ran out to the back porch and pulled the door shut behind him. He jumped down the three steps to the sidewalk and made his way around the side of the house. He heard his mom yell from in the kitchen.

"Maxx, the garbage!"

Maxx jogged across the yard towards the street. He knew there were only so many bullets he could dodge until his parents finally cornered him but at least it wouldn't be tonight.

CHAPTER 4

From the old oak tree in his front lawn, Maxx watched as a white van parked across the street. Other than the front cab, all other windows were tinted dark, giving zero visibility inside. Sneaking across the street between two parked cars, Maxx stealthily edged his way to the open driver's side window.

Maxx lowered his voice. "License and registration, please."

The young girl behind the wheel jumped off her seat, spilling coffee down her arm.

"Oh my God! Maxx, I told you never to do that!" She wiped some foam from her cheek before placing both hands on the window ledge. "Get in the van, little boy."

Laughing, she grabbed some napkins from the dash and dabbed the coffee splashes on her sweatshirt and dark brown hair, which hung down passed her shoulders. She bunched the wet wad of paper in her hand and threw it on the console.

"But I'm not supposed to take rides with strangers." Maxx raised his hands and stepped back.

Seeing Emi immediately brightened his mood. She was one of the few reasons he ever emerged from his cyber sanctuary. Tane would always hold the number one best friend spot but he talked with Emi in a way he never could with Tane. He felt comfortable with her and challenged at the same time.

"Get in, doofus. You don't want to leave Tane alone at the Wash, do you? Don't you remember the last time?" Emi asked.

Maxx climbed in the passenger side. The smell of spilled coffee filled the van and he felt a tinge of guilt. "You didn't get burned did you?"

"I'm okay. Thanks," Emi said as she started the van.

"You have a little something..." Maxx reached across the van and wiped some remaining foam from Emi's nose.

She smiled. "You're always looking out for me. Of course you're usually the source of my aggravation too."

"I resemble that remark." Maxx looked down at his phone. "Tane texted like ten minutes ago and said he was there."

"Maxx! You know he can't be left alone long." Emi put the van in drive.

Heading towards town, Maxx watched the last rays of daylight fade as the streetlights hummed and flickered as the van passed under them.

Emi pulled down the visor and using the mirror, she brushed the hair from her face. "You know if you didn't keep pulling him into your cyber city all the time playing ghost hunters, maybe he could get used to people."

"Not you too, I already got the Ward and June lecture tonight. I don't need another one. Look, I know Tane better than anyone. He's better off with me in O.S. No one makes fun of him there, well besides me." The only reason Maxx hesitated on his decision to forgo a standard higher education was the prospect of leaving Tane alone at Union City Community College. He tried to get Tane to enroll in cyber-school with him but his parents would never go for it. Maxx hated his friend being out of his immediate protection but at least he kept a pipeline to the daytime drama that seemed to survive after high school.

"Don't trip a circuit, cyber boy. I'd hate to say anything bad about your little electronic sandbox. Look at me. I shoot lasers at bad guys." Emi aimed her finger at him. "Pew...pew."

"Do you need me to fill out your paper work today?" Maxx asked.

"I'll do it later. They're the same forms every day."

"I'm just trying to keep you honest." Maxx grabbed a clipboard stuffed with papers from the dashboard.

Emi lunged but he jerked it away.

"Give it here. Don't be a tool," she said.

Maxx leaned to his side to shield the clipboard and unclipped a pen from the top. "Let's see. Was the subject seen exiting the residence at any point today? That would be a yes. Was the subject observed to have physically exerted himself in any form on this date? If so, describe in detail. Okay…"

Emi made another grab for the binder but Maxx countered by placing the board flat against the passenger window. The van swerved as Emi cut the wheel to avoid hitting a parked car.

"Give it back!" she yelled.

"Hey, eyes on the road. Good thing this isn't your driving test." Maxx scribbled on the form. "Subject cut down several trees in his yard with only a dull homemade ax and built a brick wall for no apparent reason before carrying multiple stacks of shingles up a thirty foot ladder and resurfacing his neighbor's roof."

"Are you trying to get rid of me, Maxx Fragnelli?" Emi asked. "I didn't tell your family to live next to an insurance scammer."

"He's a wad. Did I ever tell you that he kept every baseball that landed in his yard? Every single one! Besides, who ever heard of I.A.D.?"

"I don't know what surprises me more, that you remembered the name of the illness or that you played baseball. I figured you spent your formative years in front of a video game saving the world from zombies." Emi made a final half-hearted attempt for the notes and finally gave up.

"One, my athletic prowess is often underestimated. Two, its heavily documented that video games improve the player's hand to eye co-ordination. Hey, maybe I have I.A.D. too. What's the payout on that?"

"Imbecilic Asinine Dorkness? Oh, you've definitely got that. I think we'd have to pay that claim," she answered.

Maxx drew a smiley face sticking out its tongue on the form and showed it to Emi before tossing the clipboard back on the dash. He caught her checking the rear view mirror and glanced behind him.

"Are you checking for potential witnesses for your near miss back there? Is that a siren I hear?" he asked.

"Shut up." Emi stuck her tongue out at him before checking the mirror again. "Are you afraid Mr. Klingensmith is going to take away your title of king of all con men?"

"Him? Not a chance. How hard is it to do a little internet research for diseases with hard to prove symptoms and come up with Intermittent Anger Displacement? He's an amateur at best."

Emi's Dad was a private investigator the next town over and the bulk of his cases came from insurance agencies looking to debunk claims made by their clients. He wanted Emi to join in the family business and gave her these *starter assignments* to give her a taste of the work. Needless to say, she hoped for something more out of life.

"Have I told you how bad I hate this job?" Emi asked.

"Once or twice."

"Well, today I got to videotape an overweight shirtless man riding a lawn tractor from the back of the van in ninety plus degree heat." Emi frowned.

"See, and you say you have no fun," Maxx said.

"My friends work at Silky Smoothie at the mall and I get this."

"You have friends?" Maxx wedged against his door to brace for the impending punch.

Emi swung and missed, connecting with the side of the seat instead.

"Ow."

"Calm down, slugger. I'm only kidding. You know Tane and I are glad to include you in the ranks of the outcasts."

They pulled up to a stop sign and Emi looked each way twice before pulling through. Maxx knew why and appreciated the gesture.

He tapped his fingers on his leg. "So, how's the whole divorce thing going with your parents?"

"Well, Dad moved into an apartment above the insurance agency. He's in therapy for understanding mid-life crises or something like that and my mom just got a tummy tuck. How's it sound like it's going?"

"Is she still dating the Pilates guy?"

"Don't even go there."

"Sorry." Maxx sat up a little straighter in his seat.

The conversation dwindled and Maxx focused on the passing homes and businesses outside. He knew the bumps in the street by heart and could close his eyes and visualize the scenery with each turn in the road, a by-product of having lived in the same town his whole life. Rolling over a pair of speed bumps and rumble strips cut into the pavement, Maxx opened his eyes as they drove passed the new super discount store, Mega Mega Mart. It opened three years ago and made a serious dent in the downtown shopping district. The only businesses that remained along the town's main thoroughfare were scattered small independent clothing stores and novelty boutiques. Most of the window fronts were vacant. Maxx feared he'd already spent too much time growing up in the middle of the squalid collection of shops and the people who frequented them. His fate wove into the dying town he called home and the crush of its limitations became his own.

They passed the old movie theater. Maxx remembered the Saturday matinees there with his brother, sitting in the balcony stuffing tubs of buttery goodness in their faces. It closed last month. They couldn't compete with the eight movie screens the cinema complex at the mall a town over operated. Maxx missed the feel of the old torn theater seats and the sticky floors that came with generations of movie goers. He could still hear Jason laughing when they'd go see some schlocky horror flick and make fun of the plot holes big enough to drive a truck through. Another memory Maxx added to the growing list.

Emi broke the silence. "You know, I worry about you too. All this cyber ghost hunting stuff is taking up more and more of your time. You're in Other Syde more than you're in the real world. You can't take advantage of the system your whole life."

Maxx touched his forehead against the window. "Just watch me."

The van wove down the quiet streets and pulled into the parking lot of a small diner. *The Wash* shined in pink neon letters high above the block building. Emi parked in a space near the back.

Maxx reached for the door handle. "I saw Tane's bike on the rack out front. We'd better get in there."

Emi grabbed his shoulder. "Hold on a second."

He paused. "Yeah?"

"I told my mom that I'd visit her next weekend. She totally pressured me into it, not my idea. She thinks we need to bond. The Pilates guru will be there and he still creeps me out." Emi took a deep breath. "Anyway, I thought maybe I could use some backup. You know, maybe someone to help me stay anchored in sanity. You interested?"

Maxx turned toward her. "Are you asking me to meet your parents?"

She yanked her hand away, crossing both arms over her chest.

"No. Not like that. I mean…I just thought that, as a friend, you could help me out and come along."

Maxx grinned. "Wow, meeting the parents? That's a big step. I don't know but I'm flattered."

Emi opened her door. "Just forget it. It was a dumb idea. I just thought…forget it."

Maxx stopped her. "Hey, come on. You know I'm a perpetual smartass. I won't make any promises about being on my best behavior but I'll go. It sounds like fun. But what if she doesn't like me?"

Emi's foot touched the pavement and she stopped. "I wasn't expecting her to like you. I just needed someone to deflect questions. You'd be more like live bait."

"Then call me Mr. Chum."

"Thanks." Emi flashed a smile. "We'd better get in there." Shutting the door, she walked across the parking lot.

Maxx watched her go, heading towards the front of the diner. His thoughts drifted back to when Emi first appeared in his life. For the first couple weeks, Maxx watched her van parked across the street and the occasional camera flash or tell-tale blinking red light of a video recorder. Maxx welcomed the challenge and figured a disgruntled client from O.S. had tracked him down. He never considered the possibility she was taking pictures of his neighbor.

It didn't take him long to run the license plate on a hack site and find out it was registered to an insurance company. That's when the fun started. Nightly police checks called in by anonymous neighbors. Stink bombs discreetly let off under the van. Random food deliveries by angry pizza boys demanding payment.

That's where she messed up. She caved and agreed to pay with a credit card to a red faced Pizza Pronto driver who ran her card through a portable scanner in his Honda. Maxx intercepted the transmission and got her name and card number.

A couple of internet searches later and Maxx had everything he could want to know about his pretty paid voyeur. He discovered where she lived, her parents, where she went to school, grades, even social networking sights she frequented. He figured the next visit from a fake police officer who sang happy birthday to her in the middle of the street proved the last straw. The next night, during a thunder storm, Maxx ran the garbage to the cans outside. Emi tackled him from behind and they both sprawled out across his front yard. She pinned him down by his shoulders against the wet grass.

"Look, I know you figured out what I'm doing and probably don't like it but guess what, neither do I. Either knock off all the crap with my credit card or you can tell all your friends how you got a black eye from a girl. Got it?"

Maxx could still see her face, rain dripping down her nose. She was angry but in control. He admired that. Out of nowhere, Maxx felt a spark, a feeling he hadn't realized was missing until it returned. He wiped the mud away from his face and grinned. She burst into laughter. They both laid there, Maxx still underneath of her, rain drenching them both.

"Really? A singing cop? A little much, don't you think?" Emi asked.

"Roger the Insulting Mime was already rented out," he said.

Emi laughed and Maxx remembered that same warm feeling rushing over him. He brushed his wet hair back from his forehead and motioned to the door.

"Let's go in and dry off. You like lasagna? My mom just made some. She's always telling me I should bring home a nice girl."

"What makes you think I'm nice?" Emi followed him onto the porch.

"Any girl that can throw a tackle like you just did, my Mom will love." Maxx opened the back door.

"Wow, you must really like your neighbor to cause me this much grief."

Maxx turned. "My neighbor?"

Emi smiled. "Yeah, you didn't think I've been watching you this whole time, did you?"

Maxx's mother called from the kitchen. "Do I hear someone? Is that a girl? Maxx?"

***

"Maxx!" Emi called from across the parking lot.

Maxx was back inside the van. He saw her waving frantically near the side of the restaurant. He'd been zoning out a lot more since he started spending time in Other Syde. The nightmares were a whole other issue.

"I'm coming." Maxx jumped out and ran over to her. He could tell by her face that something was wrong.

She pushed him towards the entrance. "What were you doing in there? Hurry up, they've got Tane cornered and he's spazzing."

CHAPTER 5

"I'll fake your brace!"

Maxx watched Tane getting forced to the back of the Wash as his friend belted out a warning. He knew it was a shallow threat at best.

The building housed a fifties style diner and internet cafe. Joey Zippo inherited the diner from father, Joey Sr., and pretty much figured the restaurant's best days died with his papa. Joey's nephew suggested his uncle catch up with the times and helped him buy his first dozen recliners and computers. It caught on fairly quick, currently housing close to fifty computers, ports, or wireless access points and plenty of comfortable spaces to crash. Joey took credit for the idea, bending any ear that would listen about combining the two things kids' now-a-days loved, fast food and the internet. Young minds stocked the cushioned chairs, most of them wearing syn-skin patches and totally oblivious to each other.

Five guys had Tane boxed in the back corner of the diner. Trevor, the lead stooge, stepped into Tane's face. They were all guys Maxx knew from back in high school, the cool kids, the social A-listers. Maxx had hated them since grade school but felt trapped in their social network web like every other kid all through school. Another aspect of small town life Maxx hoped to escape.

Full of muscles and attitude, Trevor jutted a finger into Tane's chest. "Shut up, geek. You ain't breaking no faces and you ain't going anywhere until we get our money back from that bogus hack."

Even from across the room, Maxx could see the sweat dripping off his friend's forehead. Maxx pushed through the crowd of customers waiting for an open recliner.

"What are you talking about, Trevor? I didn't sell you bogus goods. You wanted tickets to see Cyber Train in concert inside O.S. That's what you got. Front reat sows."

Trevor's pack of carnivores broke out in laughter as Tane's nerves were getting the better of him. Maxx zigzagged his way through the dining area, heading straight for the group surrounding his friend.

"Front reat sows, huh? They scanned the codes, moron. They were fake. We're out three hundred bucks and you're fixing it. Now!" Trevor grabbed Tane's shirt and twisted him into a head lock, wrenching his grip around Tane's neck. "How's this feel, st-st-stutter boy?"

Maxx pushed past two boys battling an on-screen ogre with a plastic battle axe and cross bow. The group tightened in around Tane to avoid the interior surveillance cameras. Tane stood an easy eight inches taller than most of them and could probably have thrown Trevor across the room but instead Maxx watched him close his eyes and cringe.

"It's not a stutter!" Tane winced as Trevor cinched up his hold. "There's no way those tickets were bad. I got them straight from…Maxx."

Trevor twisted even harder. "We'll deal with spike head later. I want the cash transferred back. Plus a hundred bucks."

"No refunds!" Maxx shouted, finally forcing his way into the human perimeter. He pried Trevor's arm away from Tane's neck. "There was nothing wrong with those tickets and you're not getting any money back."

Trevor bumped chests with Maxx. "Who do you think you are Fragnelli? I say the tickets were bad and you need to cough up the cash."

Maxx matched stares with him. This wasn't their first run in. They'd been in each other's face since the playground. Cut from the stereotypical high school jock mold, Trevor rated his social status on how many people he could intimidate. His cropped flat top hair and endless wardrobe of varsity wrestling t-shirts accentuated that fact.

Maxx pointed to a nearby chair. "Don't you think it's time to put the letterman's jacket in the closet?"

"How about I stuff you in the closet?" Trevor shot back.

"How about we pull up the video from the concert and see if we can pick you and the dateless wonders out of the crowd? I put you right in front of one of the streaming net cams."

Trevor shrugged. "I don't care if we were there or not. Maybe I just didn't like the show."

Backing up the concert tickets was no big deal, but the fact that the mondo-jock had actually put his hands on Maxx's friend was unacceptable. "Really? Well how about this? The club was strictly over twenty-one, so maybe I send your grinning faces over to O.S. Security and some of their agents can pay you a visit the next time you're in Other Syde."

One of the other boys spoke up. "C'mon Maxx, we don't need that kind of trouble."

Trevor stood his ground at first but gradually stepped back into the comfort of his friends. "Forget it, geek wad. It's over. I just wanted to have some fun with the big dork there."

Maxx looked over his shoulder and saw Emi waiting near an empty table across the room. "Tane, why don't you go over with Emi? I got this."

Tane hesitated. "I could've handled-"

"I know. I don't want Emi over there by herself." Maxx gave his friend a gentle nudge and waited until he was out of ear shot. "I've warned you guys about leaving Tane alone. You each just donated twenty bucks to my personal online charity. I'll have Tane take care of the transfer later. And if I see you pull that crap with him again, I'll wipe your accounts clean *and* get you kicked out of O.S. and that trendy little club of yours."

Maxx felt his face flush. Another thing he didn't miss about high school was dealing with morons like these on a daily basis.

Trevor pulled out a twenty. "Here, man. Just take the money. Don't mess with our O.S. accounts. We're sorry. Tell Tane we're sorry."

Maxx looked down at the cash. "I'm not touching that. I'll transfer it out later. Put it away."

Maxx preferred the invasiveness of taking the funds directly from their Other Syde accounts. They may have ruled the school hallways and locker rooms but their best days were already behind them and Maxx ruled king when it came to their virtual lives. All of his friends maintained a HeadRoom account. It ranked right up there with having a cell phone and breathing. Back in the day, Maxx hacked their profiles to wreak havoc by changing more than one current relationship or romantically seeking status to bring down even the heavyweights of the social structure ladder. Other Syde opened up a whole new world of manipulation for him.

Satisfied with defending his crown, Maxx strutted over to his friends and plopped down in a chair. He touched a metal box on the table and a digital menu appeared.

"So what are we having?" Maxx asked casually. Faked indifference was a growing specialty of his.

Tane pierced the projection with his finger. "That was not cool, Maxx. How could you give me bad tickets? They nugee'd me." Tane rubbed the top of his head to stress the point.

Maxx leaned around the scrambled image. "The tickets were bad but there was no way they knew that. I upped the original ticket holders to VIP / backstage, so they weren't complaining."

Emi asked, "But how'd you know to put a camera on them?"

Maxx flicked a couple of the images on the floating menu.

"I didn't but I knew they were bluffing so I had to one up them. Are you guys ready to order?" He was waiting for his own heartbeat to slow down but he wasn't about to let his friends know that.

Tane begrudgingly swiped his finger over a couple of choices. "Well how about a eds hup from now on?"

"I promise a heads up from now on. Scout's honor." Maxx crossed his left arm over his chest. He took a long breath and checked to make sure Trevor and company had retreated to their own corner to lick their egos. "What do you want, Emi?"

"I just want water."

Maxx scoffed and ordered for her. "It's on the five stooges over there. I'll order your favorites."

"Thanks, Maxx. You really know how to treat a girl."

"I know. Did Emi tell you she's asked me to meet her parents?" Maxx hit a button and the menu disappeared.

Tane's face lit up. "Really? It's about time you two-"

"You're such a jerk. Not you, Tane. I asked him to go as a friend. Maybe I should have asked Tane instead?" Emi asked.

"Are you kidding me? He has to stop every ten miles to waz."

"I do not." Tane looked around to make sure no one was paying attention to them.

"And he has the table manners of a drunken Viking," Maxx said.

"Oh please. He's always a perfect gentleman. Maybe you should take some notes."

"Mebbe mi mould make mome motes."

"OMG! It's like talking to a third grader."

"Uh, guys?" Tane pointed as their waitress rollerbladed over, balancing a tray of glasses. "I think our drinks are here."

The girl on the blades noticed Maxx and her smile brightened. "Hey Maxx, how are you? I never see you anymore since we graduated. Where are you going to school now?" She shot Emi a quick up and down stare.

"Hi Maggie, I'm good. I've been busy. I have this whole cyber business I started up. It's taking up most of my time. I'm doing pretty well."

Maxx had a crush on Maggie Fenmore all through junior high and into high school. She never even acknowledged his existence until recently. Tane was well aware of Maxx's feelings toward her. Maxx could almost feel the tension between Maggie and Emi and he swore someone just cranked up the thermostat. He never acted on Maggie's new found interest in him. He intended to but then everything happened with Jason and his life spiraled in another direction. Since then, Emi fell into his world and his feelings for Maggie dampened. Maxx noticed both girls staring at him. He needed to figure out a way to survive this social tightrope he stumbled onto.

"I didn't know you worked here," Maxx said.

"Yeah, I started last week. My folks said I had to find a job or they weren't paying for no more school."

"Any more school," Tane corrected.

Maggie shrugged. "Yeah, whatever, so here I am. I only do this a couple nights during the week so it doesn't interfere with my weekends. Speaking of, my friend, April, is having a full on bash at her house Saturday night. It's gonna be epic. You wanna come?"

Maxx shifted in his chair. A former cheerleader, blond, and knock out gorgeous, Maggie was what he always pictured his dream girlfriend should be and she just all but asked him out. He glanced at Emi, her eyes still fixed on him. His net just got pulled out from under him and he could hear the circus clowns laughing.

Maxx figured a non-committal answer was his best shot. "This Saturday? Yeah, maybe, I got this thing in O.S. but if I finish up early I can swing by."

Maggie wrote her number on a napkin. "You mean that Other Syde computer game everyone plays?"

Maxx flipped the napkin over to be sure she wrote actual digits. A year ago, he'd have given his left arm for this. He noticed Emi rolling her eyes.

"It's not a game, Maggie. You've never been there?"

"No, I tried one of those life simulators before. I kept forgetting to eat and peeing myself. I don't get what anyone sees in them."

Maxx chuckled, "It's not like those lame sims. This is completely different."

"Whatev. Not for me. Maybe I'll see you Saturday night then." She skated back towards the kitchen, leaving Maxx with a parting smile and Emi with a sneer.

"Oh, Maxxie, maybe we could get together Saturday night and I can pee myself." Emi fluttered her eyes and blew him a kiss.

"She's nice. Knock it off. I need to network, you know?" Maxx tried to turn the attention to Tane. He felt his footing on his imaginary rope still slipping. "You know, Tane, if you busted Trevor in the nose just once, he'd never bother you again."

"Yeah, whatever, it wasn't nuthin'." Tane sipped at his soda.

Emi covered Tane's hand with hers. "Violence doesn't help things. You're better than that."

"Yeah." Tane gulped down another drink.

Maxx ripped the paper cover from his straw. "Okay, let's get back on track. Are we ready for the Steadreadys tomorrow night? No more bugs in the system?" He blew into the open end of his straw.

The paper projectile struck Tane under the eye and he winced. "It's all set up. I already memorized my lines."

Maxx turned to Emi. "This guy can write code like Nathaniel Daniels but he has the social skills of Elmer Fudd."

Emi wrinkled her eyebrows. "Don't be mean. Who's Nathaniel Daniels?"

Both Maxx and Tane dropped their jaws in mock astonishment.

"Nathaniel Daniels," Maxx said. "The guy that invented Other Syde? He's only like a legend in computer programming."

"Hold on, let me wipe that drool off your chin." Emi reached for Maxx's face with her napkin.

He swatted at her wrist and leaned back. "I can't believe you've never heard of him. Even if you don't stay up on your tech, and shame on you for that, you had to see something in all news coverage about his disappearance?"

Emi casually sipped at her drink. "Well, first off, not everyone, and by that I mean almost no one, stays up on their tech like you." Emi emphasized the word tech by scrunching her fingers into quotations. "And secondly, I don't watch the news. It's all sensationalism and doom. It just depresses me."

"But-" Maxx protested.

"Weren't we talking about Tane?" Emi cut him off.

"You're right." Maxx conceded. "Moving on. So, Tane, how was Princess Abbadabba last night?"

"It's Lady Ariana and she's doing better. The money I loaned her will get that whole passport thing sorted out. She's hoping to make it back to the states by next month. We're going to hook up in Texas."

His friends sat in silence.

"What?" Tane asked.

"Do you really think this girl is real, let alone royalty?" Emi asked. "You know, I have a friend that would love to meet you. I could give you her number. Maybe she could come out to eat with us?"

Maxx was glad in a way that Emi had attended a different high school. It separated her from the baggage of knowing your classmates since kindergarten. She didn't know that he threw up on Susie Walters during gym in the second grade or he tripped and face planted into his cafeteria tray in junior high. Emi and her dad lived in Franklin, the next town over, which made her a Franklin Owl. Only twenty minutes away but he didn't know she existed until a couple of months ago. Her mom moved to Newton City after her parents separated.

Tane fumbled with his plastic cutlery. "Thanks, Emi. That's nice but, well…oh look, food's here."

Maggie rolled up and placed their orders on the table. Tane didn't waste any time digging into his food. As she left, Maggie gave Maxx a parting wave.

The air around him definitely got thicker when Maggie and Emi occupied the same space. He casually crinkled up the napkin with Maggie's number and stuffed it into his jeans pocket.

"I want to give the Steadreadys a cyber-ghost hunting experience they'll never forget," Maxx said.

Tane's mouth was crammed full of food. "We're ready."

"Can I come this time?" Emi looked up from her salad.

Maxx pretended to search his pile for the perfect fry. "Uh, it's not that we don't want you to. It's just Tane and I have the whole thing kind of scripted out and we'd have to switch it around for a third person."

"Whatev. You two big babies go play ghost hunters by yourselves then. I didn't really want to go. It sounds boring." She flung a tomato across her plate.

Tane tilted his head toward Emi and raised his eyebrows at Maxx. Maxx shook his head no and his friend repeated the motion, this time more aggressively.

Maxx conceded with a small nod. "Okay. Look, let me work you into a script. It won't be tomorrow or anything but you can come with us on one soon, okay?"

Emi waved her fork near her mouth. "I guess. I mean, if you think you need the help."

Maxx shook his head and shot Tane a look. Figuring out the opposite sex was more complex than any programming algorithms his friend ever tried explaining to him.

Maxx pointed a fry in Tane's direction. "So how exactly are you planning to get to Texas to meet this internet diva? You don't drive."

"I'll find a way. Love crosses all boundaries, Maxx." Looking triumphant in his statement, Tane brought the menu back up and started pre-scanning the desserts.

CHAPTER 6

Maxx waved as Emi drove by the front of the Wash. As much as he enjoyed spending time with her and Tane, he needed his own space at times. Between spending his nights in O.S., scripting out jobs with Tane, the cyber classes he took, and a few hours of sleep, Maxx figured he could use the walk home. He caught Emi's reflection in the side mirror of the van and wondered if he made the right choice. He could still flag her down. She waved as she pulled out into the street. A bell rang behind him.

Tane pedaled passed on his bike.

"I'll meet you at the office tomorrow night," Maxx said. "I want to run through the details for tomorrow's job before we go."

"Dood as gun." Tane waved over his head.

A hint of summer remained in the air, making the evening perfect for the short trip home. He'd never admit it to his mother but he could use the exercise. Spending so much time in O.S. took a toll on the body, coupled with consuming all the Mr. Pew soda he could stomach to stay up all night. The evening wind whispered across his face. He closed his eyes, drawing in a long breath.

Maxx crossed the parking lot and started home. He thought about Tane back inside the Wash and being bullied by those walking turds. It wasn't that different when they first met back in elementary school. Tane was big for his age even then and the gentle giant always found himself as the center of conflict. The other kids got a kick from saying nasty things to someone Tane's size and knowing he wouldn't fight back. Even then, Maxx hated going along with the crowd and decided that sticking up for Tane was more to his liking. The two became inseparable. Neither of them was interested in playing sports and both loved all things electronic. Maxx proved no match to Tane when it came to writing computer programs but what he lacked in technical skills, he made up for in social engineering.

Maxx timed his steps to miss the cracks in the cement, having to pull every third step short to keep on track. It wasn't superstition but he enjoyed the order of pacing his gait. Maybe it was a little self-diagnosed O.C.D. too but he'd never admit that. He watched the pavement as he walked.

They were in fourth grade. He and Tane invented a revolutionary new gadget. It was a voice command box that could control every device in the house. Of course, the only two commands it recognized were on and off and really worked as a breaker switch between the plug and receptacle but Maxx spun it into the biggest thing since the microwave. They made close to two hundred dollars selling the invention door to door before someone pulled the plug on their business. One of their customers used the *Vocalometer* on their home security system and a burglar figured out all he had to say was off. It turned out that the burglar was the guy's son and was standing there when his dad bought it. Their parents made them return all of their profits anyway. Maxx's brother, Jason, told that story at every holiday meal. It was also one of Maxx's first lessons about the vulnerability of society.

Maxx jammed his hands in his pockets and felt the napkin Maggie wrote her number on. Instead of focusing on her, his thoughts turned to Emi. Since he met her a few months ago, Maxx felt something new. She accepted his quirks but had no problem voicing her opinion either. She made Maxx feel a way no other girl had before. He was attracted to Maggie but didn't know much about her outside of her looks. Emi was a friend. She was someone he wanted to know more about and the more he discovered, the more Maxx felt drawn to her.

Maxx caught sight of his porch light a couple blocks down the road. He hadn't realized he stopped walking and was standing at an intersection in the road. The breeze he enjoyed earlier vanished. Everything around him seemed still. He traced his fingers along the bottom edge of the stop sign, looking for a hold on reality in the rigid lines surrounding it. This was the spot that changed his life, transforming his existence from teenage ignorance to a living nightmare. Tears formed and he closed his eyes, still clinging to the metal traffic plate as memories raced back to him.

It happened so fast, a fraction of a second. He remembered a car horn blaring and tires locking, skidding on the asphalt. Metal crushed into metal as one life unexpectedly intertwined into another. The windshield exploded and tiny pieces of his broken world showered over him. He felt a sharp pain as something cut his neck. He turned towards Jason but he wasn't there, only air. Maxx remembered the sensation of flying, weightless as his body turned end over end and the sight of Jason's car flipping below him. Whether Maxx actually reached for his brother or he just imagined it, he still wasn't sure. The next thing he remembered was the taste of dirt in his mouth and smell of fresh cut grass as he skidded to a stop and then nothing. Maxx's world turned black, in more ways than one.

He once read that everyone has two or three truly pivotal points in their lives, events that shape the persons involved based on their decisions and the consequences. So many things could have gone different that day. Any number of choices could have put them a few seconds ahead or behind and they'd have missed that other car. He remembered his cousin, Francis, trying to comfort him by telling him that everyone's destiny had already been set into motion no matter the path we choose. Maxx didn't believe it at the funeral home any more than he did standing at that intersection. Fate was the sucker who dipped two quarters into the fortune telling machine along the midway and held its breath waiting to read the card. Maxx's future was his own and he'd decide his own road. He traced the scar along his face with his finger. His body healed but, somewhere in that intersection, Maxx lost faith in humanity.

Brushing away the tears, he crossed the road and stepped up on the next sidewalk. His house was just up the block and Maxx knew what was waiting for him. His parents were good people, just old and out of touch. He wished he could be more sympathetic to them, especially his mom. He promised himself to take it easier on them. The light was on inside and he could see their silhouettes in the living room. Maxx leaned against the porch railing and gathered his thoughts. He wanted to be calm and rational about the pending conversation. He would explain where he was coming from and, in turn, listen to what they had to say. They'd debate his current behavior like mature adults, point and counter-point, and they'd understand that he just needed some extra space to sort out everything out. Reaching for the door, Maxx felt confident and relaxed.

***

"Have you finally gone senile?" Maxx shouted.

"Don't talk to your father that way, Maxx. It's just a suggestion." His mother picked up a pamphlet from the floor.

"The National Guard? Me? Serious? What makes you think I'd want to turn G.I. Joe?" Maxx stood toe to toe with his father in the living room. The intellectual debate he expected degraded into a shouting match about ten seconds after he walked in. Maxx was pretty sure N.A.T.O. wouldn't be using this as a model for achieving world peace. His dad still had him by a few inches but Maxx stretched up to meet him at eye level. Maxx knew he had to hold his ground. For God's sake, they were using visual aids this time.

"There's nothing wrong with a little discipline." His dad grabbed the brochure from Maxx's mom and shook it in Maxx's face. "I went into the Merchant Marines right after high school. That's how I met your mother. I got to see the world, the real world. You need a change, Maxx. Go meet some new friends and find new hobbies. I'll take you down to the recruiters tomorrow and we can start the paperwork." His dad folded his arms across his chest to signal the end of the discussion.

"What do you have against Tane? You couldn't ask for a better friend. And what about Emi? You always say, meet a nice girl, Maxx. Well, I did. She wants me to meet her parents next weekend. I can't believe you're okay with this, Mom." Joining the military caught him by surprise and Maxx wasn't ready for this argument. It'd been a long night with the mess at the Wash and his rush of memories at the intersection. He needed a tactical retreat to his room and to shut out the world.

Instead, his father pushed a little more. "Maxx, we're not letting you wither away in that computer world you built around yourself." He smacked the pamphlet against his hand.

"Mom, so you think I'm a useless lump too?"

"That's not what your father said. Maybe we could go back to the counselor?"

"Am I that much of an embarrassment? The stay at home cyber-classes reject freak?"

His mom reached out to him. "Maxx, no one thinks you're a freak."

Maxx stepped away. "And no way am I going back to that counselor. I can't look at another ink blotch or express my feelings with water colors. It's all bullshit."

Maxx's mother walked across the living room, arms outstretched. "We could go somewhere else. You pick."

"You know Jason always wanted to join the Air Force," his dad said.

Maxx threw his hands in the air. "And there it is. I can't be Jason, Dad! I'm not him! He was the good son. I'm the problem child, remember?"

Maxx headed for the stairs. He knew when his dad laid out the Jason card the only option was putting distance between them.

Half way up the steps, his dad called after him. "It's not your fault, Maxx. The guy was drunk. No one blames you."

It was the same voice his dad used at the funeral, a mix of exhaustion and despair. Maxx paused. "Yeah, everyone keeps telling me that but Jason is still dead and here I am. Doesn't seem too hard to figure out who's to blame."

"Maxx!" He heard his mom coming up the steps after him.

He kept moving towards his room. "I'm fine! I got some stuff to do in O.S. before I go to bed."

Glancing down as he crested the top step, his dad crumpled up the brochure and threw it across the room as his mom covered her face and cried. Maxx slammed his bedroom door shut and locked the inside deadbolt.

Leaning against the door, he took a deep breath. "They're only trying to help you, dork."

Kicking over his trash can, Maxx plopped down on his bed, burying his face in the pillow. He growled into the fabric and rolled on his back. He grabbed a photo from the table next to his bed. It was Maxx kneeling next to an old Ford Mustang, scrubbing one of the whitewall tires. Jason washed the hood and they both stopped to pose for the camera. His brother worked for two summers to buy that car and planned on taking it with him to college. The weekend car wash was a ritual. Jason had the 'stang reconditioned close to how Maxx imagined it looked when it first rolled off the assembly line. His brother loved that car and Maxx loved the time they spent together working on it.

He remembered the insurance pictures he saw after the accident, the mangled mess of metal and memories. Two years of hard work and tender attention to detail destroyed in the flash of a brake light. Maxx rested the photo against his chest and closed his eyes.

What little interest Maxx had in high school prior to his brother's death vanished after that. He even quit talking to Tane for almost a month. Not wanting to face the other kids at school, the district allowed him to enroll in their cyber program. They even made him an honorary member of the debate team even though he never attended a single match. His parents told him he'd regret not going to graduation but Maxx couldn't face the sideways glances and behind the back comments from the other kids.

Over the summer, Maxx spent most of his days researching the internet for online scams. He ran a small re-shipping operation out of his room for a couple months. It didn't take long for Maxx to realize that he could scam the scammers and just kept the merchandise, reselling it on internet auctions. What were they going to do? Call the cops? The only reason he stopped was his parents got suspicious of all the overnight delivery packaging they found in the garbage.

That was when Maxx discovered the Other Syde. He followed its progress on the internet for months and the software's anticipated release date. He bought his first syn-skin weeks before the official launch from some of his overseas resources. He still remembered the first time he entered O.S., Maxx knew he found something special. The virtual world was populated by hundreds of thousands of consumers looking for something they lacked in their normal lives. Maxx fell in love.

For the first time since the accident, he felt excited at the possibilities the next day would bring. He ran pyramid schemes, sold knock off merchandise, ran a virtual pet sitter service, and worked as a cyber-psychic. That's what led him to cyber ghost hunting. Maxx figured if Syders were stupid enough to fall for virtual fortune tellers then why not kick it up a notch and add actual ghosts to the mix. A couple internet searches for folks who were already into the paranormal then Tane would hack their profiles and add a virtual ghost into the mix, some well-placed ads for their services, and it all fell into place.

He rubbed his thumb over his brother's image and set the photo frame down. Grabbing the legal pad from his bed, he scanned down the list of clients on the sheet.

"You people want ghosts. I'll give you ghosts."

CHAPTER 7

Maxx always wanted the traditional tree limb just outside his bedroom window to jump onto or a wooden trestle attached to the house that he could scale down in the middle of the night. Unfortunately, he had neither. Grabbing two well-placed metal handles that he screwed into the roof years ago, Maxx performed his best super hero crawl up the shingles. Scaling over the roof peak, he scurried down the other side of the house. From the edge of the main roof, the three feet jump to the porch roof proved a cinch and he navigated down the trellis at the corner. While not the most direct route, it served him well over his formative teenage years. The property line between his parents and the neighbors consisted of an eight feet high hedge that his dad trimmed with pride ever since Maxx could remember. Using it for cover to make it down to the road, he spotted Emi's van patiently parked at the curb.

He ran around to the side, deciding he didn't want a repeat of last night and Emi ending up drenched in hot coffee. Hopping in the passenger side, he smiled. "Good morning."

"It's quarter after six, Nosferatu." Emi grabbed a bottle of water from behind her seat and handed it to him.

"Thanks. See, I told you I'd be early."

"I can't believe you just woke up. Did you even brush your teeth?" Emi peered into his mouth.

"As a matter of fact…" Maxx let out a huge breath directly into her face. "Minty fresh. It says so right on the tube."

"Oh my God! You have no couth whatsoever. I'm friends with the wolf boy. Raised by a pack of wild beasts until he was ten, the wolf child now lives among us pretending to have been civilized by caring but naïve human parents." Emi shifted the van into drive.

"Aaaawwooooooooooo." Maxx howled at the ceiling.

"Let me guess, Silver Oaks?" Emi asked.

"Yep, I told my grandma I'd stop and read her all the tabloid headlines. She's getting behind on whose sleeping with who and the Botox nightmares they all endure."

Maxx hadn't figured on sleeping the day away. He wanted to get up early, well early for him, and work on a Sociology paper due next week. Instead, he woke up to Emi's text asking if he'd be ready on time. He spent most of the night surfing the internet and playing Planet of Punishment, as usual. He couldn't even say when he actually drifted off.

Leaving Maxx's neighborhood, the van stayed straight for several blocks before veering onto an entrance ramp leading up to a four lane highway. Emi accelerated off the ramp and merged with traffic before reaching over to turn on the radio. Maxx loved teasing her about her driving skills but she was actually an extremely cautious driver.

She glanced down at Maxx's lap. "Aren't we forgetting something?"

"Is my fly down?"

"You're disgusting."

Maxx buckled his seatbelt and settled in. One of the few advantages to living in a small town was they could get pretty much anywhere in fifteen minutes. Maxx often dreamed of packing up and moving to Newton City, about a two hour trek away, and was amazed when Emi told him she used to live in the city but found the easy living of suburbia more to her liking. Exiting the freeway, Maxx pressed his head against the open window ledge, letting the rush of air catch his face. He glanced at Emi and involuntarily smiled. She caught him and smiled back as the van pulled into the nursing home.

The building was one story and an ugly brown brick, the main entrance positioned in the center of the parking lot. The sign over the door read *Silver Oaks* in painted peeled letters. The grass looked to be about a week overdue for cutting.

Emi dropped Maxx off near the front and said, "Go ahead. I'm going to park and then I'll be in."

As soon as he opened the door, Maxx remembered how bad he hated the smell of the place. Not that it wasn't clean but it carried an overly anti-septic odor that took him back a step every time he walked in. He was met with the usual smiles of the handful of residents that looked up when the doorbell chimed, hoping maybe it was one of their own relatives come to pay a visit. He always felt a little guilty that he wasn't actually there for them and grinned as he made his way through the lobby.

His grandmother stayed in a private room at the end of the hall. She lived with Maxx and his family since he was three. His mom swore she would never see her mother put in a home and that her place was with her family. He admired his mom for that. It wasn't until his grandma's heart condition and diabetes progressed that she needed around the clock care. His mom kept up the best she could and refused to give in but after Jason died, his grandma made her own decision to move to Silver Oaks. She said his family needed to be there for each other and she didn't want to burden his mother with her care. Saying it was only temporary, she promised to be back by Christmas.

She waited for Maxx at her door, her smile instantly warming his heart. "Maxxy, I knew it was you. I know the sound of those feet. Get over her and give me a hug."

Grabbing him around the waist, she squeezed, burying her face into his chest. Maxx wrapped his arms around her and rubbed her shoulder. Choosing to avoid as much direct human contact as he could, his Gram was one of the exceptions to that rule. Every time she hugged him, he felt his anxiety fade away.

"Don't break a rib, Gram. Have you been watching pro wrestling again?"

"Quiet or I'll put you in one of those head jams."

"How are they treating you?" Maxx helped her back into her room. "Where's Emi?"

He threw out enough of his own topic diversions to know when he heard one. "I made her drop me off and park the van."

"Maxx, you're terrible. That's no way to treat a lady. Come in and sit down."

She shuffled across the tile floor wearing fuzzy pink bunny slippers, a present from Maxx last Christmas which she wore faithfully every day. She sat down in a recliner in front of the room's only window and caught her breath.

"Your mother was here this morning. She baked me some sugar free brownies. There's still some left."

Maxx looked at the plate wrapped in aluminum foil.

"Uh, no thanks. I just ate dinner."

She smiled. "I don't blame you. They're terrible. Don't tell your mother I said that. Bless her heart, she tries."

Maxx laughed. "I promise."

"She told me about the fight with your father last night. He's only trying to help, Maxx. He's never been good at expressing his feelings."

"I know, Grandma."

"But he's always treated my Katie well. He's a good provider and an honest man."

"I know, Grandma."

"I bet you'd look handsome with a crew cut."

"Stop it, Grandma."

"We all miss Jason, Maxx. He was a good boy."

Maxx turned as Emi came into the room. His grandma tried to get up but wobbled.

"Hold on, Mrs. Burwell, I'll come to you." Emi crossed the room and smothered her with a hug.

"My goodness, Emi! You'll squeeze the life out of me. Such strength for a girl."

They both giggled and Emi rubbed her hand across her cheek.

"I have to keep my strength up to deal with this one." She bobbed her thumb at Maxx.

"See Gram, I told you I brought the hot chick with me," Maxx said.

Emi punched him in the shoulder though Maxx knew she didn't really mind being the butt of a couple jokes for his Grandma's sake.

Maxx knelt down beside her chair. "Seriously, are they taking good care of you in here? Do you need me to bust any heads?"

Maxx caught the lady across the hall stealing his grandmother's puddings last month and he blew up on one of the nursing assistants when they insisted she made the story up to get extra desserts.

"I'm fine, Maxx, fine. It's nice of Emi to drive you here to see me, being that you won't get a driver's license yourself. You know I still have a valid license."

"What? For your wheelchair?" Maxx pulled up another chair beside the recliner. The driver's license story was one of her favorites and he knew where this was heading.

"Oh, that man. He always loved to tease about things. Did I ever tell you about the time he taught me how to drive?" She looked up to the evening sky.

Maxx snuck a look at Emi, who moved towards the door. He shook his head up and down. "No, G-ma, I don't think I ever heard that one."

"It was the summer after I graduated high school and he was home on leave. That crazy fool bought a brand new red convertible. It was a five speed and he took me out into the middle of nowhere..." She smiled and placed her arm on the sill.

Maxx saw Emi waving to catch his attention and she whispered, "I'll be out in the van."

He nodded and turned his attention back to his grandma.

***

Standing by the entrance to the nursing home, Emi pulled an inhaler from her pocket, taking two quick puffs. She'd hated that plastic tube since grade school, doubly so that it interfered with her dreams of dancing. Her parents saw it as an obvious sign she should abandon any intention of trying to make it professionally. Her dad made it clear that her future was tied into the family business of private investigating. His dreams had Emi attending law school and running a practice out of his office. Her mom wanted her to be an elementary school teacher, like she had intended before meeting Emi's father. Emi loved them both but the divorce cemented both of their desires for their little girl's future without taking her own wants into account. They thought a professional dancer was the aspiration of an eight year old standing on stage in her pink tutu and not something a young lady should pursue as a realistic profession.

Climbing back into the van, Emi wound down the front window to let a little air in while she waited for Maxx. Flipping on the radio, she relaxed her head against the seat. Maxx loved his time with his grandmother and she didn't want to intrude on it. It was one of the few times Maxx looked truly happy. Part of it was for his grandma's benefit, she knew, but Emi had been with him long enough to realize when he played a part and when he was genuine. With his grandma, it was pure. Maxx had become an unexpected anchor in Emi's newly divided world. She wished he would open up to her about his brother's accident but decided he would when he felt ready. Maxx didn't look at her like other guys. He listened and didn't pretend to know the answers. They were two broken parts unsure how to become whole. She could live with all his smart ass comments, knowing he used them as a shield because of his brother and she could relate to that.

Her hand drooped between the front seats and brushed against a small leather bag wedged beside the console. A yellow folder jutted out marked *Hopes and Dreams*. She glanced at the front door for any sign of Maxx and then pulled out a brochure from the New Brighton Fine Arts Academy and a formal application to apply. Emi stared at the photo on the cover. Rows of dancers glided across the stage. She imagined herself among them. When she made her stand and told her parents she was going to school for dance, they laughed. She was given two options, go to college for law or elementary education and have it paid for, or nothing. It wasn't much of a second option.

Maxx tried to enroll her in a virtual dance school in his computer world. She appreciated the thought but there were some things that a computer couldn't duplicate, no matter how advanced. Emi feared the end of high school had also meant the end of her dreams. She wished Maxx could have come to at least one of her recitals and watched her onstage. She imagined him sitting out in the audience, sandwiched between her divorced parents, watching her perform. When the lights dimmed, he would stand up and applaud, calling to her.

"Hey lady, move that thing!"

Emi's eyes opened. The same voice called out from behind her.

"We've got an ambulance coming in. You're in the way."

"Yeah, yeah, Maxx. Just get in the van." She sat there and waited to hear the passenger door open.

"Look lady, I ain't messing around. Move the van."

Realizing it wasn't Maxx, Emi jumped up and stuck her head out the window. A large, mustached man dressed in an orange jump suit stood beside the van and glared at her as he threw his arms in the air. She fumbled for her keys, jamming them into the ignition.

"I'm so sorry. I thought you were a friend just being an ass. I mean, hold on, I'll move it." She threw the van in reverse and asked out the window as she passed the angry orange man. "Who's the ambulance for?"

He waved to his partner in the waiting ambulance to finish backing in and answered over his shoulder. "Mrs. Burwell. Chest pains."

"Oh, God." Emi whipped the van into another space and ran back into the building. Rushing into the room, Maxx stood frozen in the corner as two nurses tended to his grandmother on the bed. One squeezed a blood pressure cup around her arm while the other injected a syringe into an IV in her wrist.

"Maxx?" Emi stayed focused on his grandma.

He answered from the corner. "We just started reading and she said that her chest was hurting and she was having trouble breathing. I called for a nurse." He turned to the nurse closest to him. "How is she?"

The woman, in her late fifties, kept one hand on his grandma's wrist and pumped the blood pressure cup with the other. She stared at her wristwatch. "She's okay. It looks like her heart went into an irregular beat for a minute but its back. Her pressure is good and her breathing's normal. We can call the desk and cancel the ambulance. We'll call her daughter and let her know her mother had another episode."

Emi moved next to him. "She's okay, Maxx."

Still clinging to the wall, Maxx asked, "G-ma? You okay? You scared the crap out of me."

His grandma laughed weakly. "I'm just getting old, Maxx. Ain't nobody found a cure for that yet. I'm fine. I need some rest now. All this excitement makes me tired. You and Emi go on and go."

Maxx timidly approached the side of the bed and took her hand. "I'm not leaving you."

She patted his arm. "I'm going to sleep. This is the third time this month I had one of my episodes. I'm fine. Come back and see me soon and bring me some chocolates."

One of the nurse's spoke up. "She's not allowed chocolate."

"I'm eighty nine. I can have whatever I want."

Maxx squeezed her hand and kissed her on the forehead. His face was pale. Emi took his hand and led him to the door.

"You okay?" she asked when they made it out into the hall.

"Yeah, I can't stand seeing her like this," he said. "I just…never mind. What time is it?"

Emi checked her watch. "Almost seven-thirty."

"Great. Look, can you just drop me off down the street from my house? I'll sneak back in through the window. I don't need any drama with my dad. My mom's probably on her way here and I have to get into O.S. and meet Tane. We have another job tonight."

"Are you sure you're up to it?" Emi asked.

"I need to stop at the Gas and Splash to get a caffeine fix. I'm running dangerously low on Mr. Pew."

"She's okay, Maxx."

"Yeah, I know."

CHAPTER 8

"I don't take kindly to strangers."

Behind the desk, a shadowed figure eased his muscled frame up from the chair, aiming his shotgun towards the entrance. His bald head glistened with sweat. He frowned, which pulled his mustache closer to his matching red goatee. Inching towards the door, his eyes were shielded behind a pair of highway patrol sunglasses.

"I was expecting somebody. You ain't him." He pumped the shotgun with one hand. The brisk slap of a round chambering pierced the otherwise quiet room. Drawing down on his target, he smirked. "Time to say goodbye, chimp."

Another door cracked open as someone crept inside the office, unnoticed by the armed man. Stealthily making his way across the floor, the second figure slid in behind the man, close enough to touch. Slowly drawing up beside him, the figure whispered in his ear.

"Boo."

Throwing his shotgun in the air, the man spun around and stumbled back, grabbing the arm of a nearby chair. The gun slapped against the floor, discharging on impact. The blast blew a hole in the back of the couch.

"Maxx! You suck! You scared the crap out of me." Tane bent down to retrieve his gun.

Wisps of smoke and the smell of gun powder filled the room from the newly ventilated furniture. Maxx poked a finger into the hole and pulled out some of the stuffing, tossing it casually into the air.

"Look, it's snowing. Let me guess, you watched a biker movie last night. That or you unscrambled the adult channels again. And it's chump not chimp." Maxx picked up Tane's sunglasses from the floor, handing them to him.

"What? You told me to get more creative with my look. How much more bad ass can I get?" Tane shrugged and set the shotgun on the desk. He pouted all the way to the chair as he plopped down and typed something into the keyboard. The shotgun disappeared.

"You're late, by the way," Tane added.

Maxx sat down on a bullet hole free chair, propping his feet on a small table.

"I was visiting my grandma. She had one of her episodes."

Tane's expression turned from contempt to concern. "Is she okay?"

"She wanted to get some rest. I felt so helpless. I don't know what to do for her, you know?"

"Yeah."

They sat in silence, both staring out the patio window. One of Tane's more endearing qualities had always been his ability to understand the situation and not invade it with a million questions. From that height, the city's lights and streaming message boards painted an infinite mesh of dots and symbols. The sky was shadowed in light sepia, Other Syde's version of night. Vehicles zigzagged across the patterns of streets below, powered by jet thrusters booming underneath and leaving faint vapor trails in their wake. Maxx thought of them as the stitching that held the virtual city together. It had taken Maxx and Tane most of their savings to rent that much office space in O.S. but it gave Maxx a feeling of entitlement inside the computer world.

"Do we need to go over the plan?" Maxx dropped his feet from the table and moved over to the window.

Cracking open the balcony door, Maxx held his breath, reflexively waiting for the rush of air to hit his face. He remembered that no breezes blew inside the virtual city, one of the few details he actually missed from the real world.

Maxx let out his breath. "Do you think this is what he had in mind?"

"Who? You mean Daniels?" Tane shrugged. "I don't know. Everything I've ever read about him said he wanted a place where people could come together and exchange ideas and experiments to make the real world a better place."

"And instead, we got virtual tattoo parlors," Maxx said.

Tane rubbed his hand over his chin, jerking it away when he reached his new facial hair. Maxx figured he forgot he had it.

Tane leaned against the door frame. "They say he's still out there, somewhere inside the city. There are a million rumors saying he has a place somewhere in-world."

Maxx pulled the door open wide. "Well I doubt if he's happy about how commercial everything got."

"You mean like a couple guys running a fake ghost hunting service?" Tane asked.

"Yeah. Yeah. Okay, Captain Integrity, let's do this. You can fade down to the street if you want. I'm going to take the express." Maxx stepped out on the balcony and climbed up the railing.

"Come on, Maxx, I hate when you do that. It's just weird." Tane followed him out to the patio.

Maxx casually waved to him. "It's a rush. Think of it like base jumping but no strings attached."

Maxx stepped off the top rail. He plunged down towards the street, yelling as he dropped. "See you at the bottom!"

Maxx felt the rush of velocity as he raced towards the sidewalk below. He twisted his body to see Tane's head sticking out over the balcony before spinning back towards the fast approaching pavement. Gravity in O.S. was nothing more than a part of the larger program. After spending enough time there and with some practice, someone could learn to defy those basic laws. When phasing inside O.S., the person, in effect, paused whatever was happening around them in the program. Re-emerging at another point in the city, the program rebooted itself to preset parameters for that person's avatar. Falling at certain death speeds was not one of the factors that carried over. Timed just right, someone could phase out close enough to ground level and then immediate phase back in. It proved to be a visually stunning spectacle to anyone passing by. Of course, timing it wrong disrupted the program completely and sent your virtual persona to one of three main intake centers located throughout O.S., a painful nuisance at best but one that marked you as a definite newbie. Maxx hadn't missed a mark in a long time. He enjoyed the simplicity of the fall, no complications, no parents, no past. That and, to be honest, it made him feel like a super hero. With the sidewalk fast approaching, Maxx focused on his timing.

"five, four, three, two….."

Maxx faded from view and instantly re-appeared a couple feet lower. He dropped the remaining two feet to the sidewalk below, picking the toes of his sneakers up from the pavement and confidently tapping them back down.

"Dude, that was awesome. You gotta teach me how to do that."

A guy in eighteenth century formal garb complete with top hat and cane stopped dead beside Maxx. His arm was wrapped around a young girl in brown baggy pants and an old World War II bomber's jacket. A worn leather helmet with goggles covered most of her short pink hair that outlined her freckled cheeks. Pulling his rounded sunglasses down on his nose, the man gawked at Maxx.

"You are the frickin' man."

Maxx adjusted his jersey, pulling it down at the waist. The looks on the couples' faces were trophy enough. He did his best to conceal a smirk. This world was his, even defying gravity. If only the real world was that easy.

"Sorry. It's not a skill that's easily picked up," Maxx said.

The air next to Maxx bulged and warped. Tane phased in next to his friend and noticed the couple standing near them. He was still in his biker/hit man guise.

"You need directions or something, pal?" Tane growled.

The young man moved his hand from the girl's shoulder to under her arm and pulled her down the sidewalk behind him. "No problems here, mate. We're just heading off to the club."

Maxx waited until they were out of ear shot.

"You're such a goof."

Tane beamed at having successfully intimidated the young Steampunk couple.

"You were right, Maxx. I did really need to get more creative with my look. I'm a mad bother."

"You're a bad something but how about changing up from the Carrot Top meets Terminator look. We want to make a good impression on our clients."

Tane shifted looks as they walked, transforming into a one piece black jumpsuit and losing the facial hair.

"Better?" Tane asked.

"Much." Maxx paused in front of a giant monitor attached to a nearby building. He touched the display screen and typed in an address. A gridded map of the city popped up showing Maxx and Tane's current position with a pulsing dot and a trail of green arrows leading them to their destination. Maxx traced the path with his finger before he moved on.

They stopped at the next intersection. A young man with a blue hair rode through on a hover bike, the thrusters rumbling across the street. He nodded his head at Maxx as he passed. Even though there were literally hundreds of ways to get around the city, most virtual residents preferred some type of vehicle. It was a status thing. Maxx had surfed the hover bike listings a time or two himself but the thought of Tane riding in a side car with him sort of ruined it. And after everything that happened with Jason, Maxx preferred the feel of his feet on the pavement. Other than O.S.'s security dogs, there was no real traffic enforcement on the virtual streets and Maxx read Other Syde traffic made Thailand look tame.

They made it about three blocks from their office when Tane tapped him on the shoulder and pointed up to the sky. A half-dozen dots soared against the purple horizon above them, silhouetted by the digital moon overhead. The lights flashed and changed trajectory like wayward shooting stars, pivoting in the night.

Maxx recognized the pattern. "Oh, crap."

By the time Maxx finished his comment, the incoming figures changed trajectory one last time, setting a course directly for them. Maxx grabbed Tane by the arm and herded him towards a large mass of people that just exited a movie theater. They made it halfway to the crowd before being cut off by the group of flying men. Landing with a muffled thud on the sidewalk, the pavement bent slightly under the added pressure before the programming corrected itself. Six men encased in red and blue armor fanned out around Maxx and Tane. The armor conformed to their bodies with meshed material around the waist, joints, and neck. The armored suits stopped just below their chins and they all wore thick plastic visors streaming computer code along the outside of the lenses. The armored man closest to Maxx spoke first.

"Maxx Fragg, Virtual Paranormal Investigator, purveyor of bullshit and conman extraordinaire. Where are you and the over-stuffed teddy bear off to tonight?

Maxx stepped forward and met the approaching agent. "Agent Ketchup, O.S. Security Agent of the year. Were we jaywalking or something? Kind of overkill with the response, don't you think?"

Maxx felt Tane retreat a couple steps back. The last thing Maxx needed was the extra aggravation of a confrontation with Ketchall. He and his band of merry security agents were the equivalent of hall monitors on the ultimate power trip inside the virtual world. Maxx enjoyed Other Syde for its general lack of rules. He could have lived without being hounded by a group of high tech mall guards. Getting under the agent's skin, which was far too easy, was the only bright point in their exchanges.

"That's Agent *Ketchall*, Fragg. You should have that memorized by now after seeing it on all the violation notices I send you. You wouldn't be heading out to scam any of our residents out of their well-earned credits, would you?"

Maxx tried moving around him but Ketchall side-stepped to match him. As much as he savored stroking the agent, after the episode with the grandma earlier, his heart wasn't in it.

"Look, Ketchup, we aren't bothering anyone. We're just two virtual residents, same as everyone else, trying to walk down the street. Why don't you go find someone behind on their maintenance dues and shake them down or something? I'm sure you and your cronies would enjoy that. Come on, Tane."

Maxx faked to the right but countered left and made it around the agent. He waved for Tane to follow and saw two of the agents had sandwiched him between them. Pushing away, Tane hurried after Maxx.

"When you and the Lollipop Boys have an actual reason to harass us, you know where we are. We're late for a date, something you probably know nothing about." Maxx waved, adding a sarcastic smile.

Ketchall motioned for his group to fall in behind him.

"We've shut down every bogus business you've tried to start up in here, Fragnelli. We'll figure this one out too and then we'll have enough to get you kicked out of here permanently. It's just a matter of time. You're too stupid to stop."

Ketchall activated his back and boot thrusters and hovered above the street. "Let's fly." His fellow agents followed suit and they fell into a flight formation as they blasted into the city's skyline, disappearing around a nearby skyscraper.

Maxx deepened his voice to mock Ketchall's. "Let's fly." He slapped Tane's shoulder. "The day that wad catches me, I hang up my syn-skin."

"You have to admit, those are some mool cods."

Maxx shot him a quizzical look. He could usually decipher his friend's speech quirks but every once in a while, even Maxx got hung up on them.

Tane drew in a deep breath and closed his eyes. "Cool mods."

"Forget them. O.S. Corp gives those posers all kinds of special abilities in-world and they act like a bunch of jerks. Let's get moving before our clients change their minds."

"Why do you hate Agent Ketchall so bad?" Tane hurried to catch up with Maxx.

"I don't need anyone telling me how to live my life."

"But he's not really-"

"Whatever. Let's just concentrate on getting our game faces on. The Steadready's aren't going to know what hit them."

CHAPTER 9

"It's almost eight-thirty. You said eight."

The man at the door crossed his arms, glaring at Maxx and Tane. In his twenties, he bore touches of gray on the sides, a typical sign in O.S. of someone much older than the image they crafted for themselves but self-consciousness enough to leave a reminder of their true age. He wore a pair of black cotton pajama bottoms with matching t-shirt and slippers.

The man called over his shoulder. "Honey, your weirdoes are here."

Maxx stepped inside the apartment. He'd morphed into his older, more muscular version in the hall and modified his uniform to include having his forearms encased in high tech armor that stretched from his shoulders to his hands, leaving the fingertips exposed. An array of gadgets, most of them for show, was fastened neatly around his belt. Maxx believed in first impressions and after Tane told him about Mr. Steadready's skepticism, he wanted to pull out all the stops to convince them their operation was legit.

Removing his sunglasses, Maxx held out his hand. "Sorry, sir, we were held up on our last job. We had a pair of ghouls cornered that didn't want to go down. My partner and I had to break out the heavy-"

"Yeah, yeah, look you two, I think you're both full of crap. The only reason you made it through my front door is because my girl freaked out over hearing a couple moans at night and she found a broken picture frame. Put on your dog and pony show, gather up your credits and get out. Fair enough?" Mr. Steadready walked back into the living room without shaking Maxx's hand.

Maxx ran into non-believers on jobs before but that was the first time someone called his bluff from the get go. It was like trying to hypnotize someone who didn't want to be at the show. The job had to go down mistake free and that meant Tane being totally on his game. His partner filtered in behind him. Maxx looked around the apartment, searching for something he could use.

"Is that yours?" Maxx asked.

He pointed at a canvass set up on a nearby easel. Dark green swirls encircled the painting with a set of misshapen yellow eyes in the center.

"Me? Not hardly. My wife thought if she painted the ghost, she could rationalize her fear or something like that. All that junk cost me five hundred credits."

Maxx jockeyed to recover. "It's really good."

Mr. Steadready turned to the canvass and squinted.

"It looks like a six year old on a sugar rush finger painted it."

Standing silent in the door, Tane brushed some imaginary lint off his sleeve. He fumbled with some of the devices on his belt. "How about those Circuit Breakers? Do you think they'll make it to the Cyber Bowl this year?"

"You guys suck." Mr. Steadready plopped down on the couch.

The room fell silent. Maxx waited near the edge of the living room and Tane shifted his weight back and forth on his heels.

A woman appeared at the top of a spiral staircase. "Oh, thank goodness, you're here!"

Gliding down the metal steps, a flowing white nightgown dancing gracefully around her legs, she twirled her ebony hair over her shoulder, dashing across the living room. She looked like something out of an old movie, her hair and makeup perfect as she moved with a grace Maxx thought only reserved for super models. Grabbing Tane around the neck, she buried her head in his chest.

"My saviors," she cried.

Tane's eyes widen and he blushed, a gesture in total contrast to his current image. He pushed the over affectionate woman back. "It's okay, ma'am. We'll take it home free."

She politely smiled but looked at Maxx, waiting for an explanation. Maxx led her away from his friend. There was nothing that threw Tane off the mark more than physical contact with the opposite sex.

"He means, you're perfectly safe now, ma'am. We'll have your home ghost free in no time," Maxx said.

Her look of elation returned and she hugged Maxx. "That's all I needed to hear. Did you hear that, Geoff?"

"Oh, I heard it, honeysuckle. Feel better already." Mr. Steadready cracked open a beer on the couch.

Oblivious to his sarcasm, she beamed at Maxx. "You know, I've dealt with so many spirits back in the real world. It's exhausting. The medications help but the presence I feel here is different. It's palpable. He wants to hurt us." She motioned to Geoff, who raised his can in reply.

Pulling Maxx across the room, she stopped in front of the easel. "I tried to capture the presence in oils. I don't think I've done it justice but Geoff says it's deeply moving."

Maxx squirmed and freed his hand. He could feel Mr. Steadready giving him the stink eye from across the room.

"He was just telling us about it." Maxx guided her away from the art. "It's Evelyn, right? Just try to relax. Why don't you both have a seat on the couch while we set up the lures and traps? You can watch the whole thing from there." Follow the steps, Maxx thought. Get the introductions over with, move them into position, and then scare the hell out of them.

Following Maxx's instructions, Mrs. Steadready sat down beside her husband. She pulled him in close. "Hold me, my cyber-sweetums."

Maxx read the brief Tane prepared on the couple. Their profile bios were started on the same date, meaning they met one another in the outside world. They rented the apartment the same day they entered the system, which meant they were using Other Syde as their own private hideaway. Who needed to rent a cheesy hotel room like Maxx saw in the movies when you could hook up the in the privacy of your own place.

What sealed the deal for Maxx was the virtual marriage certificate they applied for a month after they got there. No real married couple cared about getting a phony certificate in-world. Either he was a cheating spouse or her, maybe both. It really didn't matter to Maxx. As long as their credit was good, they could play house all they wanted.

Evelyn pulled Geoff's arm across her shoulders, watching as Maxx started the preparations.

"And you're sure we'll be safe here?" she asked.

"Absolutely." Maxx adjusted a dial on a tripod. Famous last words. Just ask Travis and Debbie he thought. "All of the ghost's attention will be focused on me and my partner and we have the equipment to handle anything it throws at us. Think of this as Sea World but with ghosts instead of whales."

"Oh, Geoff, remember the penguin encounter? That was your favorite." Mrs. Steadready practically leapt off the couch.

"I'll be surprised if you two dorks catch a cold before you're done. Hang on a minute. I want to make a bag of popcorn before the show starts." Mr. Steadready got up and headed for the kitchen.

Evelyn grabbed his wrist, yanking him back down. "You promised me that you'd take this serious."

Geoff sighed and sat back down. "Yeah, Evelyn, but I didn't think you'd take it this far. This is a virtual world, honey. It's impossible for ghosts to be in here. I told you that I can handle this. We don't need *professionals*."

Maxx pretended to calibrate a box near the window. He motioned to Tane and whispered, "Can you adjust the program for big green and ugly to try and eat Geoff the loud mouth over there?"

Tane peeked over Maxx's shoulder. "I can't change it now. I can tweak the volume some."

"Good enough. Let's at least give him a migraine by the time we're done." Maxx turned back to the couple. "Sir, you're Louisville special beside the couch isn't going to do much against one of these nasties."

On cue, Geoff gripped the bat and held it across his chest. "Maybe the bat's for you two, not the ghost."

Tane finished setting up the equipment. He peered through a scope on the tripod and adjusted a dial. "We'll all set."

Maxx nodded. Maybe old Geoff would knock himself out swinging that bat. He didn't know what bothered him the most, that Geoff wasn't buying into their scheme or how cocky he was about it. Either way, he'd show his true colors when the ghost program kicked in.

"Okay, let's do this," Maxx said. "Remember, no sudden movements and if the apparition sees you, stay very still. They watch for sudden movements, like sharks."

"Is that another Sea World reference? Really?" Geoff jumped up and formed his arms into two imaginary jaws, aimed at Mrs. Steadready. "Land shark!"

She gut-punched him for his attempt at humor.

Tane giggled, a disturbing sight for a leather clad maniac biker. "That was pretty good."

"Whatever. Let's get this over." Eager to quiet the conversation and Geoff's jokes, Maxx flipped the switch to the bait cube at his feet.

A green dot rotated in small circles on the floor. It accelerated and blurred, shaping into a small circle that rose up from the carpet. A green inverted cyclone formed, emanating a high pitched whine

Maxx gave commentary to his temporary employers. "That's a ghost call. If there's a spirit anywhere around, it'll brings him right to us."

Mrs. Steadready tilted her head and paused before shouting back to Maxx, "How did you know the ghost is a male? I never said that."

Maxx gazed into the twirling cyclone. He knew that if he lost her confidence too, the whole night would be a wash.

"Spectral pheromones. The place reeks of them," Maxx answered. "It's an acquired smell." It was the best he could come up with on short notice.

Geoff pounced on the opportunity. "Something stinks alright."

Tane pointed at the floor. "Look. There's something coming through."

Pulling out a pair of over-sized work gloves, Tane adjusted each one around his wrists. He plugged a cord from his belt into a small port, causing them to hum.

Maxx removed a length of rope from his own belt pouch and flung it toward the ceiling. Two glowing orbs ignited on each end. Pinching the center of the chord, he twirled the globes at his side.

"My partner is wearing ectoplasmic containment mitts. I'm wielding a spectral snare." Maxx realized he really did sound like a carnival performer. "Any moment now, we should see your unwanted spirit."

The practiced rhythm of the scenario returned and Maxx regained some confidence. All eyes fixed on the spinning pyramid, expanding out with each rotation. A green fog seeped from inside its core. The haze spiraled across the room and a shape formed above the twirling mists.

Maxx whipped the energy bolas faster at his side and checked with his partner.

"Give it an extra boost of power. He's coming through."

"Gotcha, boss." Tane thumbed a dial on his belt and the outline of the figure focused.

The couple cupped their hands over their ears. Maxx and Tane took up positions around the materializing specter. Tane adjusted one of his earplugs.

"I guess you couldn't have brought us some ear plugs too?" Mr. Steadready asked.

Maxx flanked to the right of the growing ghost. "Sorry, we don't bring spare equipment. Just use a pillow." Stuff it up your nose for all Maxx cared. It was time to assert himself and turn Mr. Steadready into a sniveling mass.

The spirit appeared in full form. Ragged green hair flowed like tendrils around its face, searching the corners and crevices of the room. Two black and hollowed eye sockets scanned its new surroundings. A misshapen nose jutted out beyond a row of rotten teeth, allowing generous amounts of green drool to drip down to a ragged night shirt and ending in a vaporous tail. The ghost spun towards the virtual couple.

"Who has called me here from my slumber? Do you fools realize what torture you've brought upon yourselves?" it hissed.

Mrs. Steadready shrieked and buried her head behind Mr. Steadready's back. He pointed the end of his bat at the hovering creature.

She screamed from the safety of his shoulder blades. "Do something!"

Maxx let a smile slip and advanced on the ethereal intruder. "Not to worry, ma'am. Everything is under control."

Maxx hurled the bolas at the floating monstrosity. The glowing line expanded and the orbs wrapped around their intended target's chest and arms. He hated to rush through a performance but he had a bad feeling from the start with this one.

"Mortal fools, I'll have your souls!" The creature struggled as its skin bubbled underneath the energy strands.

Maxx called to Tane, "Ok, it's secured. Use the gloves to get it into the spectral safe box."

Tane struck his palms together. The gloves sparked and bright yellow strands of energy arched between them, flowing like captured lightning. Tane eased toward their captive spirit.

"Easy there, big guy. This won't hurt."

Mr. Steadready still pointed his bat at their uninvited guest, hands trembling on the handle. Maxx enjoyed the look of terror in his eyes and the impromptu conductor routine he carried out with the bat.

Tane stopped short of his target. "Uh, Maxx?"

"What is it?" Maxx turned towards his friend.

A blue hand erupted from their generated ghost's chest. The claw ripped up along the creature's torso, tearing through the energy bands and effectively parting the ghost's head into four pieces. The apparition fell to the carpet, blinking in and out before finally fading away. The energy bolas sizzled into the carpet.

"You and me have unfinished business, boy," a grizzled said.

Where the green phantom had faded, a new terror took its place. Radiating with a dull blue glow, the incorporeal intruder's hair wisped in thin strands around its narrow face and nose. Two pins holes of intense blue light burned within otherwise empty eye sockets and intensified as they focused on Maxx.

"Time to die."

CHAPTER 10

Maxx eased across the room. His back found the safety of a nearby wall. He expected some small glitches in the programming, it happened on their last job. Still, a new ghost appearing and killing off the old one was definitely unexpected and something he wasn't ready for. Having the ghoul directly threaten him was way off the charts. Maxx tried to re-assert his authority over the situation.

"The only business you'll be getting is the business-end of our spectral atomizer."

It was bragging at best but also all Maxx had. None of their gadgets actually did anything except make pretty lights and loud noises. Maxx noticed Tane motionless near the window. His partner's eyes glossed over with fright. Whatever this thing was, Tane didn't add it into the scenario. Someone else was behind this and trying to set him up.

"Who are you?" Maxx asked. He needed some time to come up with a plan.

The wraith answered with a smile, running translucent fingers through its mass of unkempt hair. The glowing follicles slicked back for a second before returning to their naturally unruly form.

"Oh, you and I got history, boy. I'm hurt that you don't remember me. Things didn't go too well with your job the other day, huh? Someone threw a couple snags into your well-oiled plan? You do nothing in this world that I don't know about." The grinning ghost slithered closer to him.

"Just tell me what your angle is." Maxx touched the wall behind him with his hand.

"You think everything is always a scam. Don't you, boy? That maybe someone's running competition in your neck of the woods. This is *old* business. You owe me and I've waited a long time to collect."

The wraith raised a translucent claw above its head. Maxx processed the scene unfolding in front of him but the danger didn't register. His head churned with a hundred questions and he had trouble focusing. Who was after him and had the tech to pull this off? Trevor from back at the Wash? No way. Maybe Geoff? It was his apartment. He'd have the time and opportunity to set up an ambush.

"Maxx!" Tane charged across the room, his arms rotating in large circles against his sides, coming in full windmill attack.

The cybergeist casually backhanded Tane, sending him soaring across the room and toppling over the couch.

Mr. Steadready shielded his wife as Tane rolled over top of them. "It doesn't look like you have this under control," he said. "Maybe I should call O.S. Security?"

"NO!" Tane and Maxx screamed in unison from opposite sides of the room.

The specter grunted as a blue haze oozed from its nostrils. The fumes bellowed around Maxx's face. It grabbed him and pulled him in tight.

"You're right, boy. We don't need any more intrusions. What we got between us is personal." Its breath smelled like a combination of a dead cat and puke. Licking a putrid tongue over decayed lips, it hissed. "Are you ready to die?"

The creature swung at Maxx's neck. Dropping to his knees, the talons brushed through Maxx's hair. Scrambling to the couch, Maxx frantically searched for some type of weapon. He needed some time to think and that blue bastard wasn't about to give him any. His hands wrapped around the thicker end of Geoff's bat. It took a couple tugs to free it from Geoff's grasp but Maxx finally pried it away. Spinning around, he swung wildly into the air. The wooden shaft passed through the ghost's chest.

"Nice try, boy. You can't touch me but, oh, can I touch you." The ghost raked a claw across Maxx's chest.

Maxx felt a warm ooze rush over his torso. Looking down, he saw the fresh tear, at least a half inch deep, seeping blood over his body armor. He instinctively covered the wound with his hand to control the bleeding. It made no sense. No one bled in Other Syde. It wasn't in the program. Maxx felt the sting from the cut. He didn't care about saving the job any longer. He just needed out of that apartment.

"That was just to get your attention. This one will keep it." Rearing back again, the ghost aimed for Maxx's head as its fingers warped into one long blue spike. Its face contorted into a mix of rage and anticipation.

Maxx's legs wobbled. Turning away, he waited for the hand-spear to connect.

A burst of light caught them both by surprise and Maxx spun towards it.

Hands shaking, Tane aimed a giant flashlight in the ghoul's face. "Get away from him."

"You little puke. You get in my way once, I may let you live. You come between me and revenge twice, you die!" The ghost dropped Maxx, who crumpled to the floor.

Maxx watched as the blue ghoul lunged at Tane. His friend reflexively shielded himself with the flashlight. The blade pierced the light's outer lense. Sparks exploded across the room, showering down on the carpet. The phantom reeled away in pain. It faded and blurred, becoming almost transparent.

"Impossible. Nothing can hurt me here."

Dropping the shattered light, Tane ran over to Maxx, grabbing him under the shoulder and pulling him towards the door.

"Time to go," Tane said.

Mrs. Steadready jumped up on the couch. "You can't leave with that monster still in my living room."

Maxx saw the panic in her eyes as his friend dragged him across the floor. He looked over at the ghost, which had regained its form.

It locked eyes with him. "You got some space between us. That's a good idea but you'll be back. You're too stupid to stay out of here and I'll be waiting. We ain't done yet, boy. You owe me too much."

Still clutching his bloodied chest, Maxx screamed back across the living room. "Who are you? I don't owe you anything!"

The ghoul slicked back its hair again and pretended to straighten out its shirt, finally noticing the frightened couple on the couch. "Nice place you got here. You should be more careful who you invite in."

Mr. Steadready pulled his virtual wife behind him. "Do what you want with those two. Just leave us alone."

"Oh, I've got big plans for that one." The ghoul pointed directly to Maxx. "He owes me a special debt, one that can only be paid back in blood." Shaking its finger at Maxx, it said, "I'll be seeing you soon."

The creature faded, leaving behind small wisps of blue vapor.

Maxx felt Tane's arms tighten under his shoulders. The room faded and blurred around him.

He heard Tane's voice. "See, the ghost is gone. Another couple of satisfied customers."

Maxx wondered who turned on the switch that sent the whole room spinning like a carnival ride. He wondered if you could puke in O.S.

Geoff jumped off the couch and grabbed the bat Maxx dropped during the fight.

"I can't believe this. You two didn't trap it. You just made it mad. What if it comes back?"

Tane whispered in Maxx's ear. "Hey buddy, why don't you go ahead and fix the damage to your chest there. It looks pretty gross. This isn't a part of the plan that you didn't let me in on, is it?"

Maxx tried to raise his head but couldn't. "I already tried to fix it, Tane. It's not working. I can't heal. We need get out of here and reboot." He raised a quivering hand in the direction of the frightened couple. "You'll be refunded your whole advance. I doubt if you'll have any more ghost problems here."

It was all Maxx could do to get the words out. He knew Geoff wasn't buying it but in another couple minutes, Maxx would be useless.

He braced against Tane's shoulder and pulled himself up from the floor. "Get over to the house as soon as we fade out so we can figure out what happened. We're done here."

Tane waved to their clients. "Don't worry about the online survey."

Maxx waited until Tane started fading and then they both disappeared.

CHAPTER 11

"Ow."

Maxx leaned forward in the chair. Covered in sweat, he peeled the syn-skin connection from his neck. Resting his head against the cushion, he took a deep breath and held it, trying to slow down his racing heart. He could still feel the cybergeist's claws slashing across his chest.

"That sucked."

Limping over to his dresser, Maxx saw his reflection. His face was pale. The trauma from his attack certainly carried back to the real world. His pupils were wide from the adrenaline rush and his hands shook.

"How did that thing know we'd be there? Who's gunning for me?"

Some color returned to his cheeks as he glanced down at his chest. A dark red line crossed the middle of his t-shirt.

"No way."

Raising his shirt, he stared at the gouge above his stomach. Blood seeped from the cut and streamed down towards his waist. He touched the open cut and immediately regretted it. He hissed from the pain, raising blood-soaked fingers up to his face.

"That's impossible."

Knees buckling, he fell on the corner of his bed. Grabbing a towel from a nearby pile of dirty clothes, he pressed it against his chest and laid back. It really cut him. That maniac tried to kill him. If he hadn't ducked, that thing would have speared him and his mother would have found him sitting in his chair with a sword hole punched through his head. He'd be known as the kid who was killed by the internet. Rumors would start circulating and before it was done, he'd have committed Hari-kari performing some perverted sex act he found on-line and become the butt of the joke for millions worldwide. Don't be such a Fragnelli, they'd say.

Wiping away as much blood as he could, Maxx looked at the cut again. It wasn't as deep as he thought, less than a quarter of an inch, but enough to create some serious blood loss. He crept out into the hall and opened the closet, still holding the towel to his chest. Rummaging through the shelves, he found a small plastic tackle box.

His mother called from downstairs. "Maxx? Why are you in the closet? "

Crap. What in the world was she still doing up? There was no way she would understand what happened. He still wasn't sure he did. If anything, it would give his parents the reason they were looking for to ban him from Other Syde.

"Nothing, Mom," he said. "I need the *boo boo box*. I cut my...finger. I'm fine."

Maxx wedged the makeshift medical kit under his arm and hurried back to the safety of his room.

"Are you sure you're okay? You don't sound right. I'm coming up," she said.

He heard her footsteps as she climbed the first couple stairs and he slammed his bedroom door shut. If she saw any blood on the carpet in the hall, he'd never talk her out of coming into his room.

"I'm fine, Mom. It's nothing. I've got the kit. I just needed a band aid or two."

"If it's deep, use the antibiotic. You know how easily you get infections. Remember when you got that cut right under your butt and we had to-"

"It's just a paper cut. I've got it under control."

Leaning against his door, he waited until he heard her walk back downstairs. Moving over to the dresser, the bloody towel fell to the floor. He wiped the fresh blood away using a medical swab. The bleeding had slowed down and it actually stayed clean for a minute. The antibiotic gel stung and his chest felt like it caught on fire. He smeared the medicine all over. Thankfully, his mother meticulously stocked the family medicine box. Maxx cringed as his finger dipped too deep into the cut. The bleeding had almost stopped. He opened several square bandages, securing them with some tape on his chest, and examined his handy work.

"Well, it's not pretty but it'll do."

He picked up the bloody towel from the floor. Opening his closet door, he pulled out an old gym bag and stuffed the towel under several layers of unwashed clothes and threw it in the back of the closet. Satisfied that all the evidence was disposed of, he collapsed on his bed and pulled out his cell phone. He texted Tane, hoping they could make sense out of it all.

"*U need 2 b ovr here…now*"

Tossing his phone down, Maxx stared at his computer. Gingerly, he sat at his desk and slid out a wireless keyboard. Typing the words *ghosts in O.S.*, he watched the responses pop up. The first entry advertised Club Undead, a popular night spot within Other Syde. It featured different post-mortem themes nightly. That night was Zombie Living and offered drink specials until midnight.

Maxx hit his share of clubs after discovering Other Syde but his interest faded pretty quickly. To simulate the consumption of alcoholic beverages in O.S., attendees allowed the club owners limited access to their syn-selves, who then gauged the amount of virtual drinks the patrons consumed into an equation that compelled their clients to do things they normally wouldn't. The program also altered their reaction and agility levels to provide Syders with the whole intoxicated feel. Maxx never bought into that social scene and didn't enjoy the company of most people his own age. He definitely wasn't letting anyone play around with his avatar's settings.

More results flashed on screen and he scanned the headers, looking for a more appropriate hit. He made it half way down the page before focusing on one in particular.

"*Ghost Sightings on the Rise in O.S.*"

Clicking on it, the link directed him to the premier underground website for all of O.S. It was operated by an unidentified group from a boasted untraceable location where they published a weekly newsletter relative to the virtual society. Completely un-authorized, the corporate big wigs at O.S. didn't seem to appreciate these vigilante newsmen's rights to free speech. O.S. tried their best to filter what news streamed out about their cyber world with carefully crafted news releases and press conferences, especially with the pending litigation from the accidental deaths associated with their patents. The folks at the Black Hat News Network proved too tech savvy for them and made good use of available proxy servers and open sourcing to keep its authors anonymous.

The screen blinked as the next page loaded with the O.S. corporate logo and a crude animated pile of excrement, complete with smelly haze. The top line caught his attention.

"Paranormal Activity Growing in O.S." by Promo.

The article detailed at least two dozen reports with what residents termed some type of bio-technical apparitions. Eight alleged injuries occurred with one possible death. No explanation was provided to the ghost's origins and no rogue programmer claimed responsibility for what many believed to be a new hack. No one had identified matching code associated with the attacks. Some religious zealots claimed that God did not approve of all the pretend musings and a virtual Armageddon lay on the horizon.

"But this weirdo said he knew me? It still doesn't make sense."

This was exactly the kind of news O.S. Corporation would never allow into public forums and Maxx felt sure their corporate office had taken measures to keep the term *Virtual Armageddon* under wraps. He checked to make sure the bleeding had still stopped and closed his eyes to process the day's events. No one had that serious of a grudge against him. Sure he scammed a few credits here and there but his customers were satisfied at the end of a job. Ever since he graduated high school and Jason died, his personal life was non-existent outside of Tane and Emi. Who'd have the technology necessary to find him inside O.S. and disrupt his own programming, let alone hack the system and find a way to actually hurt him? That still didn't explain his injuries carrying back to the real world. Sure the brain was powerful and Maxx understood the principles of mind over body but not at this level. He had plenty of questions but no answers. His chest throbbed, they lost the money from the Steadready gig, and some blue demon wanted him dead. What else could go wrong in one night?

The door to Maxx's room burst open. Maxx jumped up and the room immediately started spinning. He grabbed for the desk and missed, tumbling face first to the floor. Twisting around, his nose pressed against the toe of a dirty army boot. He looked up at the figure looming over him.

"Holy crap bat! What happened back there?" Tane hoisted Maxx off the floor, like a small boy picking up his favorite action figure.

Tane's strength was a gift bestowed upon him naturally. While not chiseled like a body builder, spending hours a day in a gym, Tane could out bench most of them right after finishing off a twenty inch Hoaginator from the Wash. He casually plopped Maxx down on the bed.

"I got here as quick as I could. What were you doing on the floor? That was some crazy chiz. What did you do to your chest?" Tane rambled, even faster than normal, and bent in to take a closer look at Maxx's chest. "That looks like the same place where that thing sliced you...no way. It is the same place, isn't it?"

"Can I talk now, motor mouth?" Maxx asked.

"Does it hurt?" Tane poked one of the adhesive squares with his finger.

"Of course it hurts! That thing cut into my freakin' chest, you nub. How did it do that?"

Tane pulled his hand back. "Sorry, Maxx, I didn't know. It's *not* possible."

"Yeah, tell that to my bleeding gut." Maxx spun around. "How'd you get in here anyhow?"

"Your mom let me in. She was glad I came over to check on you."

"Well check this out. I've been researching some other stuff on the web and it looks like paranormal activity is going through the virtual roof inside O.S."

Maxx leaned away to let Tane see the monitor. Clicking another link, a story popped up about a female claiming her boyfriend was attacked by what she referred to as a blurry blue woman with a remarkable resemblance to his dead wife. The article went on to say the enraged spectral ex-spouse savagely attacked them while in the privacy of their shared O.S. apartment. The ghost pulled out large portions of the girl's hair and left a deep gouge very high on the guy's inner thigh. The unidentified girlfriend reported that when they faded back out of the program, they both suffered the exact same injuries back in the real world.

Maxx looked over his shoulder. "Sound familiar?"

Tane re-read the screen. "We're in tig brouble."

"Yeah I'd say it's big trouble." Maxx let Tane take his place at the desk and moved over to the bed. He instantly regretting not being more careful on the way down as pain shot across his chest. Tane worked the keyboard with a speed that seemed impossible for his large fingers. The screen shifted as he navigated through the web pages.

"So I did some research of my own on the way over and came up with some interesting stuff too," Tane said.

"How did you do any research from the time you left your house until getting here? It's only been like fifteen minutes and you were on your bike."

Tane pulled his phone from the front pocket of his jeans and shook it at Maxx.

"Mobile browser, my friend. You can keep your fancy touch screen keyboards. I'm a nine keyer for life, allows for smooth one handed operation on the go."

"And other one handed pursuits." Maxx grinned at the ceiling. "You still into vampire burlesque?"

"That was one time. Okay? And I hit the site by accident and just watched for a couple minutes. Har har har, welcome to the open chest wound comedy hour. Seriously, listen to some of this. I cross referenced Other Syde with the occult and got some interesting results."

Tane read out loud.

"The man responsible for the creation of this generation's most popular social networking site has also been associated with some of the earliest dabbling of the occult and cyber space. Nathaniel Daniels, the man who changed the face of the virtual world, is also credited with being a pioneer in using the internet as a conduit to attempt to contact the dead. Daniels' motivation for contacting the original other side began with the death of his beloved wife, Clarissa Daniels, in a fatal car accident while he was deep into development of his ground breaking virtual software."

"I didn't realize that Daniels was into the occult." Maxx propped a pillow under his head. His friend was entering the *info zone* and he knew he needed to keep up.

Tane continued, "Oh yeah, it says that he was a mess after losing his wife and quit development on the O.S. software for months and turned all his attention to trying to find a way to contact his dead spouse using the internet. The higher ups at O.S. Corporation were peeved about him up and quitting on the developmental end of the software, pretty much because they'd invested every company asset into the program. Got any brain food?"

Maxx pointed to a desk drawer. Tane pulled out a fluffy yellow cream filled pastry in plastic wrap, consuming the tasty treat in one mouth full.

"anks. Ath a wuz thaying."

"Mush mouth. Get a couple chews in first," Maxx said.

"Thorry." Tane chomped. "You got any Mr. Pew?"

"What am I, room service? Check under the desk."

Tane felt around under the work station and pulled out two green plastic bottles of soda.

"It's warm." Tane pulled one free from the plastic binding. He took a long drink, savoring the caffeinated delight. "Ahhh, nectar of the gods."

"I hope that's really soda. Sometimes when you're in the middle of a game and the bathroom seems so far away…" Maxx shrugged.

Tane side stared at Maxx, the bottle still up to his lips. "I think I know the difference between Mr. Pew and a bottle of whiz."

"And you know that how?"

"Shut up, Maxx." Tane held the bottle up to the light before he took another drink. "Anyway, while Daniels was trying to find his virtual bridge to the nether world, O.S. Stock took a nose dive. The company was about to go under, when all of a sudden the software debuts but Daniels is nowhere to be found. Questions abounded about where the man who changed the face of virtual software disappeared to but no answers followed. The O.S. suits said that he wanted to grieve over the loss of his wife in his own way and asked that the public respect his privacy. A lot of people weren't buying it but without Daniels around it was the only story out there. No one has heard from him since but with syn-skin and O.S. Software taking over the world and making them a tech giant, their public relations department has done a pretty good job of glossing it all over."

Maxx sat up in bed. "Take a breath and toss me a Zinkle."

Tane grabbed another package from the same drawer and tossed it over his shoulder with practiced precision to his waiting friend. Maxx tore open the plastic wrap and mimicked his friend's eating habit by stuffing the whole thing in his mouth.

Tane clicked the mouse and the screen changed. "Okay, now get this. I looked further into Daniel's work in reaching out to the dead. There's a whole subculture movement based on the principles he started, Cyber Necromancy. There's several chapters right in O.S. It seems to be growing in popularity with the celebrity circuits. Someone got a hold of some of Daniels notes on the project and they've formed an online manual outlining the basic principles. There aren't supposed to be any printed copies in existence. It's like their badge of honor. Knowledge and fulfillment found only on the internet. I skimmed a couple chapters, kind of hokey but whatever gets you through the day. I couldn't find any real success stories with it though, more superficial than anything."

"All that in fifteen minutes?" Maxx finished off a second Zinkle.

"You know I read quick," Tane said.

Maxx threw the empty wrappers in the trash. He leaned next to his friend and stared at the monitor. "Well, so now we know the guy who created O.S. was heavy into ghosts and was looking for a way to write code to bring those two worlds together. Maybe he was more successful than anyone thought and he found a way to do it. That's why no one has heard from him. If we could find and talk to Daniels, maybe he could shed some light on this."

Tane spun around to face Maxx. "I'm working on that. I think I might have a lead but I need to do some more research. Of course, it will probably involve us going back into O.S. and I'm not sure that's such a good idea."

"What choice do we have? Stay out of O.S. permanently? Watch our business go under? I can't do that, Tane. I didn't let those O.S. bozos keep me out and I'm not going to let Jasper the Unfriendly Ghost do it either. Besides, we have another job lined up for later tonight. They already paid and for a double extraction. We just lost the money from the Steadreadys. I'm not refunding another."

Grabbing a clean t-shirt, Maxx pulled it over his head, wincing from the pain. Tane needed a little more convincing.

"That doesn't mean we're not going to take some extra precautions before we go back in," Maxx said. "Do you have your toolkit on your thumb drive?"

Tane pulled a chain necklace out from his shirt. A black plastic rectangle dangled from the end. "Never leave home without it."

"Good. We just need to make some mods to give us a faster reaction time to get out if we need to. Do you have anything in there to help with that?"

Tane plugged the drive into Maxx's computer and started searching files. Maxx's cell phone lit up and he tapped the screen.

"Crap! I forgot about Emi. She's waiting outside in her van. We had a date tonight. She'll kill me if I blow it off."

Maxx smiled empathetically at Tane. His friend was accustomed to doing most of the programming and technical work but Maxx still felt guilty for bailing when they had stuff to do for a job.

"Yeah, yeah, go have fun. I'll hang back here and take care of the tech. I think I have something that'll work for us. I'll meet up with you back at the office. Just don't be late. I'm not going back in there alone." Tane turned and focused on the screen.

Maxx figured he'd buy him some expanded memory after they figured this whole mess out.

"Thanks, Dad. I promise to be home by midnight. And don't worry, I have protection."

Tane shook his head. "If Emi heard you say that, she'd kill you. There really is something wrong with you."

Maxx rubbed Tane's head before he climbed out the window and watched as Tane started hammering away at the keyboard.

CHAPTER 12

Maxx's stomach sank. He stopped cold, standing on the sidewalk in front of his house. He expected to see Emi's van waiting outside but it was nowhere in sight. Messing this up would cost him major points with her.

"I'm not that late. There's no way she left me."

He walked to the street, looking for the van's headlights. A car horn blared behind him and Maxx jumped. Spinning, he saw headlights blinking on and off, parked several houses down.

Maxx jogged up to the door and could see Emi covering her mouth inside.

"Very funny," Maxx said.

Emi pulled her hand away. "Sorry, I didn't think you were going to freak. You almost jumped into that tree. A little extra edgy tonight, are we?"

"It's been a weird night. I'll tell you about it when we get to the Wash."

Maxx walked around the front of the van.

"Maxx, hold on." Emi jumped out and motioned for him to follow her around back. "I was thinking we'd try something a little different."

She opened the rear van doors. A small wooden table with lace tablecloth sat in the cargo area. On top were two paper plates and plastic cups. A single candle burned in the center. Green milk crates were positioned on opposite sides of the table and an MP3 player was hooked up to two small speakers placed on the inside fender wells. A flowered bed sheet separated the cargo area from the driver's compartment.

Maxx stood speechless. It was a night full of surprises.

"Wow, I should have worn a better shirt," he said.

"Shut up and get in." Emi waved her arm towards the door.

Maxx picked a crate to sit on. He hoped Emi had feelings for him beyond friendship and this confirmed it. If only he could find a way not to run his mouth and mess it all up. He knew he walked a fine line at times between sarcasm and charm.

"Do we wait for the waiter or is it a buffet?" Maxx asked.

"Don't be an ass. I just thought it would be a nice change of pace from eating at the Wash. It's always crowded and filled with…distractions. If you want, we can climb in front and drive there. This is kind of lame, huh?"

Smooth move, Fragnelli. Thirty seconds into their first real date and he was screwing it up. Emi started towards the front of the van.

Maxx stopped her. "No, this is awesome. Really. It'll be fun. I just wasn't expecting this is all. Come on, you went to a lot of trouble. Let's just stay here."

"Are you sure?"

"Yeah, I mean people pay good money for this kind of ambiance. What's on the menu?"

Smiling, she returned to her seat. Reaching under the table cloth, she produced a pizza box.

"Tadaa! You didn't think you were getting all this and home cooking too, did you?"

"Ha. Well played, Ms. Briggs. Sausage and mushrooms?"

"Yep, I even asked for extra mushrooms on half for you."

Emi placed the steaming box on the floor and served a slice on each plate. She pulled out a bottle of green soda pop, holding it like a champagne bottle.

"Mr. Pew! You're really pulling out all the stops," Maxx said.

Emi unscrewed the cap and foam rushed out of the top of the bottle.

"Guess it was a little warm in here. They told me it was a good year at the Suds Mart."

Maxx swished it around in his mouth.

"Good carbonation, tangy citrus, I'll take the whole bottle."

Emi refilled his cup.

"I've always been impressed by a big spender."

Maxx finished off his slice before realizing how hungry he was. He hadn't eaten anything since yesterday. He self-served a second piece and shrugged.

"Hey, you can't expect looks and manners."

"Trust me. I've learned to lower my expectations." Emi shot back.

Maxx laughed out loud. Sitting on a milk crate in the back of a candle lit cargo van and Maxx felt comfortable. It was a feeling he lost six months ago along with his brother. He kept the world at arm's length but Emi found a way to sneak in and he was becoming increasingly grateful for that.

"This is nice. Thanks, Emi." He flashed a genuine smile.

His parents wanted to help and Tane was a good friend but Emi offered something different. She knew something tragic happened but never cornered him for the details. Everyone else judged him based on what they knew about the accident and Jason's death. With her, he was still plain old Maxx, like before his life was torn apart.

"You're welcome. So how's the ghost hunting thing going?" she asked.

Maxx reflexively touched his chest. She'd freak out if he told her what happened and would try to keep him from going back in. He had to get to the bottom of his mystery attacker and the less she knew about it, the better.

"Nothing too exciting, me and Tane are going back in tonight. We have a double dipper set up for midnight."

"Don't you ever feel bad taking their money?"

"They want to believe in something. I give it to them. It's no more of a scam than going to the movies and getting lost in some schlocky fantasy film. At least I give them real drama, kinda."

Emi wiped her mouth with a paper towel.

"Ok, but why ghosts? I mean, people really believe in that, Maxx. It's not like you're tricking them out of money with a shell and cup game. Why do you have such a bad attitude about people believing in the afterlife? Is it because…because of your brother?"

It was a fair enough question but Maxx could see she felt guilty asking it. She broke away from his stare and focused on the floor.

"Sorry," she said. "I'm not trying to pry but it seems to really bother you. I didn't mean to bring it up."

"It's okay, Emi."

She still didn't look up at him. "I mean, who am I to talk? It's not like I have it all together. I never expected to be stuck between my parents. My mom wants me to come to the city and live with her. My dad expects me to stay with him and work part time at the agency while going to Union City Community College for pre-law. I so don't want to go there."

"Emi," Maxx said, trying to break in.

"Why should I have to choose between the two of them? Their stupid divorce already ruined my senior year of high school and now they want to suck the life out of my college years. They should be the best years of my life, right? Instead I'm spending quality time with Dad and feeling like a total dweeb going on a date with my mom and her new boyfriend. Sorry, I'm babbling."

Maxx poured another glass of soda. Taking a long drink, he rested the cup on the table. Emi had no problem pouring her soul out to him. How could he expect their relationship to go anywhere if he wasn't willing to do the same?

"Jason was about as opposite from me as you could get. Every day for him was another chance to meet someone new. Those people who walk into a room and change the mood just being there? That was him. He was good at school and sports. He volunteered at shelters, with the boy scouts, picking up garbage along the road. You name it, he did it. My parents loved him. They couldn't have been prouder of him and, seriously, who could blame them?"

"Maxx, I didn't mean to pry. You don't have to talk-"

"I know. It's okay. Did I ever show you a picture?"

Maxx took his phone out, tapped on the screen, and handed it to Emi.

She smirked. "I see who got the looks between you. Were you trying to grow a mustache?"

He snatched the phone from her. "We were down at the airport. They had open drag racing on Sundays. Jason had a 65 and a half Mustang with a 289 V-8 engine. He loved that car, restored it from the ground up. We went there every weekend. My dad came down sometimes too."

Maxx rubbed his forehead with his thumb. Every time he talked about it, the memories rushed back like a tidal wave. He felt Emi slide her hand into his.

"He sounded like a really special person," she said.

Maxx closed his eyes and opened his memories. "Jason and I were coming home from a race. I was going for my driver's permit in like two weeks. Dad refused to take me practicing anymore and said I gave him gray hair. Jason already had his license but I wasn't in a big hurry to get mine. It was like no big deal to me but Jason convinced me it was time and let me get behind the wheel. I was the only person he'd let drive his car. We were almost home. It'd been a good day and the 'stang blew everyone else away. We had the top down, tunes cranked high and the sun shining down."

Maxx opened his eyes. Emi stared at him but said nothing. She didn't have to. Her eyes told him what he needed. He focused on their intertwined hands.

"I came up to the intersection and stopped. There was no one else there. I checked. I always checked. I pulled out into the intersection and...wham! Some guy in an old beater station wagon crushed into Jason's side of the car. I got thrown out and ended up on someone's front lawn. Jason was pinned under the car when it caught fire. There was a ton of confusion. Fire trucks and cops rushed in, sirens blaring, blurs of people and legs running around me. They put out the flames and rushed us both to the hospital. They couldn't say if he died from the impact or in the fire."

Emi squeezed his hand. "Maxx, I didn't know. I'm so sorry."

"And the kicker is…the guy who creamed into us? Drunk. He took off on foot but of course the cops knew who he was because of his license plate. He lived like three blocks away."

"So they got him?" Emi asked.

"Yeah, they got him in his house. His wife let the police in and they found him in the garage downing a bottle of vodka to try and beat the drunken driving charge. They busted him for involuntary manslaughter and leaving the scene of an accident. He took a plea deal and got three to six years but ended up hanging himself in jail a couple weeks into his sentence. I know it's wrong but I'm glad he's dead. That asshole took my brother from me."

"Why didn't you ever tell me this?" Tears rolled down Emi's cheeks. "Maxx, you said you checked the intersection. How could you have known?"

He let go of her hand and sat up on his crate.

"Yeah, that's what everyone says. You know, I don't remember a lot but I swear I could hear Jason yelling for help underneath his car. He gave and gave without a thought and the one time he needed help? No one. Not even his own brother."

Maxx noticed the time on his phone.

"This was great, Emi. Thanks for doing all of this but Tane and I have that other job lined up back in O.S. and I really need to prep for it. I need to scam the scammers while I still can, right?"

He didn't expect to tell her that much but once he started, he couldn't stop. It felt good to talk about the accident but he wondered if it changed how she looked at him. He was afraid of the answer.

"Maxx." Emi moved toward him.

"Serious. I hate to eat and run but I promised Tane I'd meet him at the office and it's not safe…I mean he doesn't want to be there alone."

Opening the back door of the van, he paused. He was being a jerk and knew it but he felt the tears welling up in his eyes, not a part of him he wanted Emi to see. He felt her hand on his shoulder and he stopped.

Without turning, Maxx asked, "Are you going to be around tomorrow?"

"Yeah, I'll be here."

He reached up and touched her hand. "I'll see you tomorrow then. How about we meet around four down at the Wash?"

"It's a date."

"Good night, Emi."

"Nite, Maxx."

Closing the van door, he left his hand on the lever. He saw the hint of candle light go dark through the window. All he had to do was open the door and she would still be there for him, just twist the handle and she'd be waiting with a smile and open heart. He could text Tane and blow off the next gig and spend the night talking to someone who'd listen. Forget the whole ghost hunting scam and let the world back in.

Wiping the tears away with his sleeve, he walked back towards his house.

CHAPTER 13

"Why can't you get a passport through the embassy again?"

"I told you, Taney, my uncle locked down every border crossing. He's trying to gain access to the millions in gold bars that make up the bulk of our family fortune. He's thrown us out of our home and no one can exchange the gold that we took with us. We need cash to bribe the crossing guards. Don't you want us to be together?"

Tane turned off the lamp on his desk and looked around the office before he typed his response.

"You know I do, Ariana. The last couple weeks have been incredible. I keep the picture you emailed with me at all times. I'd really be stretching myself with the five hundred dollars though, on top of the thousand that I already sent you."

Opening another window on the screen, Tane scrolled down through his Other Syde bank account listing. The balance read five hundred and forty two dollars.

"This is the last time, I promise. The money will help cover the costs to arrange transportation, buy my fake passport, bribe the border patrol, and get an international flight to Mexico and then cross into Texas. You can pick me up from there."

Tane rubbed the top of his head, staring at a small photo taped to the top corner of the monitor. Ariana's piercing blue eyes stared back at him. He stroked his finger along her smooth black hair and olive cheeks.

"And then we'll be together? I mean together together?"

"Yes, my love. Then we can arrange to get my parents out of the country and we'll have access to the family fortune and you and I can start a new life."

Tane tapped his finger against the screen over his account balance. *"Do you want me to wire the money to the same account as last time?"*

"I'll be right here waiting for it. Give my picture a kiss good night."

"Good night, my princess," Tane typed.

The chat window closed, leaving only the box with his bank account. Maxx repeatedly warned him about wiring money overseas but Ariana needed help. He knew there was a chance that it was all a hoax but maybe, just possibly, there was someone out there who accepted him, freckles, speech impediment and all. Besides, he never felt comfortable with all the money Maxx and him made from their ghost hunting business. If he didn't have it then he didn't need to feel guilty about it. Tane clicked on the money transfer option and typed in an account number. His finger hovered over the enter key.

"She sent a picture. She has to be real." Tane self-asserted aloud.

He felt the enter key under his finger.

"Tane!"

Tane jumped up from his chair. The voice came from just outside his door. He noticed the time on his screen.

"Crap. I didn't think it was that late."

Maxx yelled again.

"Come on, Tane. Whatever you're doing in there, I'm sure I'm just saving you money. We've got work to do."

"Hold on a minute. I'm almost done. I'm just going over some numbers for the business."

Tane glanced down at the enter key and the blinking cursor. Maxx had a knack for always knowing what he was doing, especially when Tane didn't want him to.

Maxx pounded on the office door like he played bass drums for the school marching band. "Tell the princess, who's probably some forty year old overweight dude sitting in an internet café that I said to get a life."

Tane slid open a desk drawer and placed the photo inside. He couldn't concentrate with Maxx breathing down his neck. He'd complete the transfer later, after they got back to the office. Maxx never stuck around for the cleanup anyway. Tane always took care of making sure the credits transferred and removing the ghost-bot from their client's settings. He didn't want to let his friend down but they seriously needed to have a talk about getting out of the virtual ghost hunting business. His conscience couldn't take much more.

"I have a picture," Tane said.

"Yeah, it's probably out of a Nigerian underwear catalog. Would you please get out here?" Maxx banged louder on the door.

Tane shouted back. "I'm coming."

Tane snuck across the office and paused at the door. He put his ear up to the wood and waited. He hated when Maxx bossed him around, which was most of the time, and figured he'd leave him waiting another minute.

Maxx pounded on the door again, in the exact spot Tane's ear was pressed against.

"Ow. How did you know?" Tane asked.

"Tane, if you wiki'd the word predictable – your profile page would come up."

Tane opened the door. Maxx had already retreated to one of the office's couches.

Pointing at him, Tane said, "Better to have loved and lost than lever had noved at all."

Maxx threw out his hands, steadying himself against the cushions. His face contorted.

"Did you just feel that?" Maxx asked.

"What?" Tane spun around, looking around the room. His nerves were extra thin since starting up their new venture, let alone the recent ghost attacks.

"I think I just felt Shakespeare turn over in his grave." Maxx bounced up from the couch. "Booya, I just dissed you old school."

Tane replied with a sarcastic grin and sat down behind the reception desk. He never could match wits with Maxx but knew one thing he could counter attack with.

"So how was your date with Emi? Did you man up and tell her how you feel?"

It was a cheap shot and he knew it but Maxx *did* attack Lady Ariana. Tane felt a small pinch of guilt nonetheless.

"I know. I know. It's complicated." Maxx joined his friend at the desk. "What if I tell her that I have feelings for her and she laughs in my face?"

That was the one thing his friend wasn't any good at, taking chances. Tane watched Maxx stand with his back to him. Even though Maxx was comprised of mostly false bravado and fast talking, there was a side to him that most people never knew. Even in grade school, Maxx kept the other kids at a safe distance. He was afraid someone would see through his carefully constructed walls of tall tales and twisted truths. Maxx would never admit it but he needed a friend like Tane as much as Tane was thankful to have him.

"That's what life is, taking chances," Tane said.

"Yeah, well, chance hasn't done real well by me so far. I prefer calculated risks. Are we ready for Ms. Fiona and our habitual party crashing blue friend? "

Tane's fingers glided across the keyboard. Typical Maxx move to change the subject.

"Yep, I'm finishing an upload for our suits. I added a jump button in the center of the chest. All we do is hit it and we're back at the office immediately. I found a couple small security flaws in the system and was able to cut the transfer time in less than half, so there's almost no fading, more of a pop. I also added a distortion trailer, so if the ghost would try to follow us, it'll take him somewhere we're not. We should be okay. Dueling husband and wife ghosts are set to go all domestic violence like for Ms. Fiona at midnight."

"You are a tech wizard. Can you set the program to drop us right outside of her dating service? Does that even make any sense? Virtual dating? Give me a break. And they call us scammers," Maxx said.

Maxx transformed into the newest version of their work suits. Inserted across the front chest and torso were two overlapping leather straps embedded into the material and a bright red circle where the bands joined.

Maxx nodded in approval. "Subtle. What's the name of this place again?"

Tane thought the new suits looked pretty cool. He spent an hour designing them.

"Virtually Yours."

"And you wonder why people call us."

"Everyone gets lonely, Maxx."

Tane performed his own costume transformation. Tane was an only child. He referred to himself as a *single* until he was ten. He envied Maxx's relationship with Jason. As close as Tane and Maxx were, the bond between Maxx and his brother was special. They fought and argued as much as they laughed and were as opposite as two people could be at times. Still, they were family and could count on the other when they needed them most. When Maxx lost Jason, his support system crumbled and Maxx shut his door to the world. He needed space and time to heal and Tane accepted that. He missed his friend for the months that followed and was glad to have him back in his life, which was a big part in him agreeing to join in on the whole ghost hunting gig.

Tane patted Maxx on the back. "No one said love is easy."

"You're a member, aren't you?"

"What? No." Tane looked down at the carpet.

"Tane?" Maxx nudged his shoulder.

"Just because you've decided to live out your life as a lonely hermit doesn't mean the rest of us have to. There are a lot of nice people on that site."

Tane lacked Maxx's skills at deception. Socializing on the internet gave him time to think and prepare. He didn't have to worry about jumbling words. The backspace key was a trusted friend.

"And what's your screen name?" Maxx asked.

"Hotred25"

Maxx exploded into laughter.

Tane's face reddened. "All right, lone wolf, shut up already. Let's go."

"Whatever you say, hot sauce."

Tane took a swing at Maxx but he popped out of the room before Tane could connect.

"I should let that blue guy eat him."

Tane wasn't sure how he felt about being back inside O.S. with this thing chasing after them. He would have been just as content letting the job go until they figured out who was gunning for Maxx. There was no talking him out of it though and it wasn't like he could let his friend come back here by his self. Maxx was his best friend. After this job, he'd convince Maxx to lay off until they had more time to put it all together. Tane hit the button on his chest and was gone.

CHAPTER 14

"Now that is instant gratification," Maxx said. They faded into the front of an alley between two buildings. The dating service sign shined above them. "Right on the mark, Big Red."

"You promised you'd stop calling me that," Tane said.

"I like the hair, very post-apocalyptic," Maxx added.

Tane touched one of the several orange spikes sprouting from his head. "Thanks."

Maxx scanned a list of names under the glass panel at the front of the building. When someone purchased space inside of O.S., it truly became their property. No one could fade there uninvited. Your location was blocked to unwanted visitors, except for O.S. Corp of course. Another reason Maxx couldn't account for the unexplained ghost back at the Steadready's. Maxx found the listing for Virtually Yours, showing it on the third floor.

"Here we go." Maxx pressed the button and waited.

"She knew we were coming, right?" Maxx rang the buzzer again.

"Yeah, I messaged Ms. Fiona this afternoon. She was excited we were coming."

Maxx pressed the intercom button. "Everything look normal with our ghost-bot?"

The red light beside the name placard remained solid.

"Yeah, he's been active for the last couple weeks, knocking over things, making flash appearances, disrupting some programming. She thinks he's the ghost of her ex-husband, trying to keep her from finding love."

"Finding love?"

Tane paused. "She not only the owner…she's a client."

"Give me a break," Maxx said.

"Be nice when we get up there." Tane took a turn at pressing the panel. "Oh, come on"

The light changed from red to green and the lock mechanism clicked. Maxx pulled the door open just in time.

He held it open for Tane. "Do we need to go over any lines?"

Tane threw a shoulder into Maxx as he passed. "I got. I got it. You just need to worry about yourself."

Maxx shoved him from behind. "Okay, Mr. Stross-the-creams. You're the one who made it sound like a soda flavor."

The lobby had a small sitting room and fireplace burning in the corner. Several bookcases furnished the walls. An open book rested on a coffee table. The floors were covered in plush brown carpet. Maxx tapped the up arrow at the elevator and they waited.

Once inside, Tane tapped his foot in rhythm with the music.

Maxx asked, "Don't you have this downloaded on your top ten?"

Tane caught himself and stopped. "I grew up on eighties pop. That's all my mom played in the car. That and reggae."

The doors opened and they headed down the hall.

"I never figured you for a Rastafarian."

"Hey, now, 'mon. Pite the flower."

"I doubt we'll ever see that on a t-shirt. Get your game face on, Marley. We're here."

A black placard titled *Virtually Yours* was centered on the door. Maxx knocked.

For a business, they didn't seem very open to new clients. He waited another minute before trying the buzzer. Finally, he tried the knob and the door swung open. Shrugging at Tane, they walked inside a small waiting room, reminding Maxx of a doctor's office. Metal chairs lined two opposing walls and a small table covered in brochures sat in the middle. Maxx picked up one of the pamphlets. There was a picture of two clutched hands over a computer keyboard.

"This is definitely the place." The only other door was on the far wall. Crossing the waiting area, Maxx gently tried the knob.

Maxx called into the next room. "Hello? Maxx Fragg, Virtual Paranormal Investigative Services. We have an appointment." He whispered over his shoulder to Tane. "The lights are off."

Maxx felt along the wall and found the switch. The room was easily ten times larger than the waiting area, portioned into smaller sections with office cubicles. Each section had a chair and a computer.

"Hey, are you coming or not?" Maxx motioned for his friend. He took a few tentative steps into the room.

Tane stayed in the doorway and asked, "Is there anyone in there?"

Maxx pointed to a female sitting in a cubicle on the other side of the room. Blond hair flowed over the back of the chair and images of various men and women flashed across the screen in front of her.

Tane started towards her. "She must be wearing headphones. Hello? Ms. Fiona?"

"Hold on." Maxx grabbed his shoulder. "If she turns around and sees you, she'll probably freak out, Mad Tane. I'll handle the introductions." Maxx pointed at Tane's hairdo. He crossed the room. The pictures flashed across her monitor in dizzying succession. Maxx wondered how she even knew what she was looking at. He reached down and touched her shoulder.

"Ma'am, we're here to help with your ghost problem."

The chair spun around as a gnarled blue hand grabbed Maxx by the wrist. He tried to jump back but the grip was too strong. Maxx looked up at her face and met the crazed eyes of their ghost stalker glaring back at him, his maddened stare enhanced under the tangled blond wig.

"Hello, Maxx, did you miss me?"

Maxx was held fast as the ghoul sprung up, allowing the white robe and wig to fall to the floor. He pulled Maxx in close.

"I've learned a few new tricks too, boy. Let's finish this."

Inches away from the creature's fractured features, Maxx shouted, "Jump, Tane! Get out of here!"

Frantically grabbing for his chest, the cybergeist clenched Maxx's free hand and yanked it down to his waist. Impossible. How could he have known they'd be there? Kicking the chair out of the way, the blue-skinned abomination forced Maxx across the floor, pinning him against the wall. Maxx struck his head, embedding it into the virtual plaster. Dazed and covered in white powder, he searched the room for Tane. No trace of him. At least it looked like he got out of there.

Turning back, he locked both hands around the creature's wrist, which had moved to Maxx's throat. The ghost frothed at the mouth, enjoying every second of attacking Maxx.

"What the hell are you?" Maxx asked.

Maxx's head pounded as he fought to free himself. Kicking at its groin, Maxx's foot passed straight through it. He lost his balance and toppled down the wall, face planting into the carpet. He felt the ghost's foot press down against his neck. Maxx felt sorry for dragging his friend into all of this and angry at the same time that he left him there to die. He never told Emi how he felt about her and her last memory of Maxx would be him leaving her alone in the back of the van. Maybe this was payback from God for killing his brother. Retribution had come for him in the form of this blue abomination.

"Don't you just love it? I can touch you but you can't lay a finger on me. I love this place," the ghost snarled.

Hoisting Maxx back up to eye level, the cybergeist wrapped a claw around Maxx's hands, pinning them over his head. Drawing back its other arm, the digits morphed into individual finger blades.

"Let's get rid of all this false bravado first." A blue pulse erupted from the ghost.

Maxx's armored hunting suit disappeared, replaced with a plain t-shirt and boxer shorts. His muscles reverted to their real world form.

"There, that's better. It's more how I remember you. Let me hear you cry for your mommy. Come on, like back at the intersection."

Those last words struck a chord in Maxx and fear was replaced with anger.

"Get bent," Maxx snarled.

The ghoul's smile widened as it reared back its blades.

"Get dead!"

Maxx turned away. He wasn't going to give this thing the satisfaction of seeing the fear in his eyes in his last moments of life.

An orange flash rocketed across the room. The grip on Maxx's hands released and he fell to the floor. The walls of the surrounding cubicles exploded as the two forms tore through the office and scorched to a stop along the carpet. Maxx morphed back to his virtual armor and placed a hand on the suit's jump button. This was his chance to get out. He might not get another. His hand hesitated over the control. The two blurs of light battled in the corner of the room. The one figure, cast in an orange glow, was pinned to the floor by the blue ghoul.

"Maxx, get out of here!"

Maxx's first thought was that Tane came back to help. How he pulled off the orange sunburst thing, he didn't know. He'd have to ask him when they made it back. Maxx pressed his hand against his chest, still watching the fight unfold. The figure in orange lifted the blue ghost off the ground and slammed it into the ceiling. Maxx made eye contact with his rescuer just as he faded out of the office.

Throwing out his hand, Maxx lunged towards them. "Jason!"

CHAPTER 15

Maxx hit the ground running, slamming into the front of a desk.

"Jason!"

Realizing he was back at their office inside O.S., Maxx punched the jump button on his chest.

"Come on! Work!"

"Maxx," Tane said.

Maxx felt his friend's hand on his shoulder and he pulled away. He steadied himself against a chair. "It was Jason. I saw him, Tane. That blue bastard was going to rip me open and Jason saved me."

Tane stood next to him, sucking in gasps of air. He had his hands on his knees. Even as freaked out as Maxx was, he could tell Tane was in the throes of full-fledged hyperventilation.

"I thought you were going to hit the jump button, like I did," Tane said. "I was freaking out. I tried to get back but forgot I installed the delay. I'm sorry, Maxx. I heft you langing."

Maxx patted his friend's shoulder. He was still trying to process the last couple minutes himself. He helped Tane over to a chair.

"Tane, it's okay. I'm fine. Look at me, buddy. Breath," Maxx said.

It took two huge breathes but Tane calmed down enough to say, "I'm better, thanks. You saw Jason? He was there?"

Maxx pushed the jump button on his suit but remained in the room.

"No doubt about it. He saved me. He tackled the blue bomber and told me to get out of there. How long of a delay is there until the jump kicks back in?"

"Like a minute. It should be reset by now. Let me-" Tane looked at his watch and Maxx disappeared.

Maxx popped out of their office, leaving Tane in mid-sentence. He looked around and realized he was back in the Virtually Yours building lobby. He sprinted up the stairwell to the third floor. The door was still open. He ran across the waiting room and stopped. Cautiously, he rested his hand on the doorknob, fingering the escape button with his other hand.

"Let's hope it's been a minute." Maxx pushed it open.

He noticed the fallen chair from the fake Fiona but the room was quiet. The white robe and blond wig were strewn across the floor. There was a hole in the wall where the ghost rammed Maxx's head. He followed the trail of damaged cubicles to the spot he last saw his brother fighting. The ceiling tiles above him were broken and blue ooze dripped down on his arm. The gelatinous trail led across the carpet to an exterior office wall, a large splotch of orange slime splattered across it. It looked like someone shot an enormous paintball against a plaster canvass. Maxx brushed his fingers across the thick orange gel.

"Jason?" he called out into the empty room.

Someone pushed Maxx in the back and he fell to the floor.

"Just exactly how stupid are you?" Tane asked.

"Ow." Maxx rubbed his shoulder.

Tane reached down. "You couldn't say, hey, I'm jumping back over. Come with me, Tane. No, the great lone wolf just disappears and runs off on his own. We're supposed to be teammates. "

There were very few times Maxx remembered seeing Tane truly angry, that was one of them and his size became all the more intimidating.

Maxx raised his finger to his lips. "Shhh."

"Don't shhh me..." Tane said as he realized where they were. He whispered, "So, did you find anything? Is Jason here?"

Maxx took his friend's hand and pulled himself up.

"No, but it was him. I know it."

"Wow, Mr. Skeptical showing a little blind faith."

"Yeah, I know. But he's gone now. It looks like him and the blue booger had a pretty good fight. Jason was covered in some kind of orange glow and there's a lot of orange goo on the wall. I hope he's okay."

Tane stood quiet.

Maxx shrugged. "I know. How okay can he be? You know what I mean."

Questions filled Maxx's head. This was his chance. The one he hoped for ever since the accident. One he figured would never happen. Jason was somewhere inside the program. Maxx wouldn't stop until he found him.

"You hear that?" Tane asked.

"No. What?" Maxx twisted around, ready for another attack.

Tane walked over to a nearby door.

"It's like something scratching," Tane said. "I think it's coming from in here."

"Hold on. Maybe it's another set up." Maxx stopped at the door, hugging the wall with his back. He motioned to Tane with three fingers held up and counted backwards. On one, Tane yanked the door open. A body toppled out of the closet. It was a female with long blond hair. She hit the floor with a thud, covered in hundreds of small cuts.

"Sholey hit!" Tane screamed.

Maxx rolled her on her back. The woman's bloodied blond hair tangled across her face. Her only clothing was a red bra and panties. Brushing the hair from her face, he saw dozens of slashes across her cheeks, neck and chest. The carpet underneath her was already damp with blood. Maxx curved his hand under her neck and pulled her closer.

"Ms. Fiona?" Maxx asked.

He listened for signs of breathing and feared the worst. The whole game had just become much more serious.

"Where?" Her voice was barely audible.

Maxx let out a sigh of relief. "She's alive."

Her eyes opened, focusing on Maxx. She thrashed and pounded at his chest but she was too weak to actually hurt him.

"No! Get away from me!" She struggled to pull free.

Maxx shook her by the shoulders. "Ms. Fiona? It's okay. You're safe. He's gone."

Realizing her situation had changed, she stopped fighting. She noticed the blood oozing from her arms and chest.

"Am I going to die?" she asked.

Maxx remembered what he could from a CPR class he took with his brother years ago. He did a quick visual examination, scouting for any life threatening injuries. Satisfied with his on scene evaluation, he tried to comfort her.

"I think you're going to be okay. The cuts aren't deep, just a lot of bleeding. You need to try to relax."

He gingerly rested her head against the floor. Crying, she wiped her hand across her face, leaving red streaks down both cheeks.

"It came out of nowhere, some blue hideous monster," she said. "It attacked me without saying a word. It just kept slashing and cutting."

Tane knelt down beside her and wrapped one of the deeper cuts with a small cloth he pulled from a pouch on his belt. He dabbed at some of the cuts on her face. He attended the same CPR class as Maxx and Jason, but as usual, he paid attention.

He nodded at Maxx. "She's okay. They look pretty superficial."

She touched Tane's hand and smiled. "Thank you. You're very kind." Looking around the office, she asked, "Is the ghost gone? Did you get rid of that wretched thing?"

Maxx shrugged. "Not exactly. It attacked us too but it got away. Sorry."

Ms. Fiona shuddered, fresh tears forming in her eyes. "Do you think it will come back?"

Maxx sat next to her on the floor.

"I doubt if he'll be back. I don't think it's you that he's after." What the hell. She deserved a little truth after everything that happened to her. Maybe he needed some too.

"Well then, who is it after?" Ms. Fiona asked.

Maxx never expected anyone to get hurt in all of this. Ms. Fiona seemed innocent enough, a little overly dramatic but nice. The longer he stuck around, the more risk he put her in.

"I think it's after us." Maxx glanced at Tane. "Well, actually just me."

Ms. Fiona wiped the tears from her cheek with one of Tane's bandages. "But why you? You're the ghost hunter."

Maxx lifted his shirt to reveal the slash on his chest.

"I think it's personal." He patted her on the shoulder. "Look, let's just say that there's no reason for him to come back and as for the other ghosts…" He paused. "We can pretty much guarantee they're gone too. You don't need to worry about paying. We'll make sure you're credited everything back. There's one more thing."

"What?" she asked.

"Did you try to fade back yet?"

She nodded. "I tried the whole time that thing attacked me but I couldn't leave the program."

"There shouldn't be a problem with that now. Just remember that when you fade back to the real world, you're going to have the same injuries there," Maxx said.

Ms. Fiona gasped. "But how?"

"I don't know but that's how it works. I just wanted you to be ready for it," Maxx said.

"Can I ever come back to O.S.?"

Maxx's hand paused at his chest.

"I don't know. I'm sorry. I just don't know."

CHAPTER 16

"This sucks." Tane face planted into the couch back at their office.

Maxx worked at one of the computers. "That's an understatement. I don't know how or why, but it was Jason back at Ms. Fiona's. I've got to find him again, even if it means running into big blue and ghostly."

Tane covered his face with a pillow.

"I feel you, Maxx, I really do, but if that thing is a real ghost and that was really Jason, then what exactly does it all mean? I mean, should we even still be in here? If it found us at Virtually Yours, then why couldn't it track us back here?"

"I already told you to get out of here. I just wanted to check a few things out first. You have this place shielded like Fort Knox anyhow," Maxx said.

"Before tonight, I thought so too. But now…do you think Daniels actually found a way to cross over to heaven?" Tane pulled the pillow away, looking Maxx in the eye. "And maybe hell?"

Tane threw the cushion in the air and let it smack him in his face. He moved over to the balcony.

Maxx stopped typing. "When's the next job set up for?"

"It's tomorrow night at eight," Tane answered. "You're not actually coming back in here? Come on, Maxx, haven't you been attacked enough in one week? I don't think my nerves can take another round with that thing."

"I have to, Tane," Maxx said. "If that ghost knows when all of our gigs are then maybe Jason does too. What choice do I have?"

Tane tapped his forehead against the glass doors.

"But you're not going," Maxx said.

Tane stopped his self-induced pain therapy.

"What do you mean, I'm not going? Of course I'm going. There's no way I'm letting you fly solo on something like this. Look at your chest. Look at what happened to Ms. Fiona. No way, dude. I'm with you."

Maxx knew the only way he could convince his friend to stay out of O.S. was to use logic on him. "I need you at the controls. You could be my wing-man to keep me anchored in the real world in case I need to bail." It was a lie but the best one Maxx could come up with. He was the one who dreamed up the ghost hunting scam and Tane only followed out of friendship. He couldn't handle someone else close to him getting hurt because of one of his ideas.

"This conversation is closed, Maxx. If you go, I go." Tane folded his arms. "I was thinking though, what if Ms. Fiona had been hurt worse? If he killed her, would she stay stuck in here? I mean, what would happen to her soul? It makes you wonder if those other deaths are tied into this. We could have been accessories to murder. Man, that's too much to process."

Maxx joined his friend at the window. He put his hand on Tane's shoulder.

"Yeah, seriously, bud, you're on the verge of blowing a fuse, but you make a good point about the other people getting hurt. We need a plan for tomorrow night and a good one. I think I know what to do, just let me work out a couple details."

"I bot your gack."

"You always do."

Tane moved away from the doors and Maxx gazed up at the stars. He thought about a digital heaven and avatar angels. Focusing on one of the stars, Maxx swore the light grew brighter and bigger. Two other lights appeared on either side of it, each growing brighter. The cluster grew to five and plummeted toward the ground. Maxx heard of falling stars but five at a time might be a glitch in the program. He followed the glowing masses down to the city's nightline where they pivoted a full ninety degrees, careening toward him on a collision course with the building.

"Uh, Tane?" Maxx turned to find his friend.

"What?" Tane stood by the couch.

Maxx sprinted past him and dove for the desk, meeting Tane's confused stare in mid-lunge.

"Get down!" Maxx shouted.

The windows exploded. Glass showered the inside of the office as Maxx ducked under the desk. Shards of metal and glass embedded into the walls. The paintings fell and shattered on the floor. Maxx covered his head, waiting for the debris to settle.

A synthetic voice barked, "Come out and play, Fragg!"

Maxx's ears still rang from the explosion. His hands crunched on the broken glass surrounding him. He leveraged his foot against one of the desk legs. He'd had enough of being a victim. Grabbing the first thing his hand could find, he charged the window.

"You ugly blue piece of crap! Let's do this!" Maxx skidded to a stop. "What are *you* doing here?"

The group of O.S. Security Agents from earlier had scattered out across the room. Agent Ketchall stood in the middle.

"Knock. Knock. Fragg. What are you planning to do with that? Staple us into submission?"

Maxx looked down at the stapler he was holding and let it fall to the floor. He stormed toward the grinning agent.

"You can't bust into our office, Ketchup. Get out of here."

Ketchall's smile broadened.

"Funny, that's what I was going to tell you." He met Maxx in the middle of the room, leaning down to get face to face. "You're out of here, con man. You can consider your virtual license in O.S. officially revoked."

He didn't like the agents catching him by surprise and especially how comfortable Ketchall seemed. Something was definitely up.

"Tane, you got any idea what this walking can opener is talking about?"

Tane jutted out his chest as he came up beside Maxx.

"I have no idea. We are paid lifetime members in O.S., which Agent Ketchall should already know."

Ketchall signaled for two agents to post by one of the doors. He leaned against the desk and flipped a switch on his belt. His visor slid up, exposing the rest of his face.

"I don't care how paid up you two are and don't worry, we know everything about you both. Your files takes up more memory than a hundred other clients put together. Guess who we got a call from tonight?"

Maxx shot back, "Your shrink? He said that your Oedipus complex is really getting out of control."

"You ain't getting under my skin tonight, smart mouth. Mr. Steadready filed a complaint against you. It looks like you two ass-clowns were there for one of your smoke and mirror exorcisms. He said the two of you did some heavy damage to his place and left in a flash without refunding his credits. Does any of this ring a bell?"

Tane stepped forward. "He'll get all his money back and we offered to pay for any damages."

Ketchall waved off Tane's answer. "It doesn't matter. That complaint officially took you over the limit of acceptable nuisances. That means I have the grounds to give you the virtual boot. It's over. I got you, Fragg."

Maxx's mind raced. He needed some time to think. "But...you can't...we're paying customers, the same as everyone else. What we do is no different than a hundred other businesses here. We don't force anyone to contact us. I want to talk to someone in management. We have rights."

Ketchall took in all of Maxx's frustration with noticeable enjoyment and stood up from the desk.

"You have the right to shut up and get out. I'm the final say for you. This isn't just business, punk, it's personal too."

"What did I ever do to you?" Maxx asked.

Ketchall poked an armored finger into Maxx's chest.

"Nothing, but I hate your type. You think the world owes you something and it doesn't. All you care about is finding the path of least resistance and the easy buck. No one handed me anything growing up and I didn't ask. See, I don't just despise you but everything there is about you. You got no idea what it's like to grow up without..."

Ketchall stopped and composed himself. He cleared his throat before continuing.

"This is your formal notice that your accounts with the Other Side Corporation have been null and voided due to excessive nuisance complaints by other O.S. cliental. Your accounts have been expunged and the costs of your memberships have been refunded. Any remaining credits in your financial holdings here in O.S. have been forfeited to O.S. Corporation. This ruling is irreversible and permanent. If you attempt to re-establish an account using your own or any falsified and/or fictitious information, you will be immediately dispatched from these virtual properties and both criminal and civil charges will be filed against responsible parties. The appropriate authorities have already been given notice of our internal investigation and both of your identities provided."

Ketchall motioned for to his other agents.

"Any last words?" Ketchall entered a code into a keypad on his forearm.

Maxx sneered at him. "Yeah, go to ..."

Ketchall pressed a final stroke in mid-sentence and Maxx and Tane disappeared.

Moving over to the broken windows, the agent powered up his suit's thrusters and blasted out into the city.

"Sometimes, I love this job."

CHAPTER 17

Maxx was back in his bedroom. He ripped off his syn-skin and jumped to his feet. The whole room spun around him. He didn't give his body time to adjust to coming back from O.S..

He waited for the spinning to stop before texting Tane.

"U ok?"

Before he could put the phone down, Tane answered.

"K b rite ovr"

Maxx checked the time. It was just after two thirty in the morning. He dragged two large pieces of wood from under his bed. They were bracketed together in the middle. He opened the window and positioned the small platform outside, securing the boards with a couple latches. Satisfied with his handiwork, Maxx crept over and listened at his door. He snuck down the hall to the bathroom and splashed his face in the faucet. Dark circles formed under his eyes and his complexion looked even paler than usual.

"It looks like I went full on Goth."

Creeping back to his bedroom, he eased the door shut. He waited for his eyes to adjust to the dark. "Tane?"

No one answered. He didn't figure his friend could make it there that fast but he didn't want to chance Tane scaring the crap out of him. He didn't think he could take another shock. He sat down at his computer and grabbed a photo off the shelf, resting it on his chest. The waves splashed against his and Jason's feet. They stood knee deep in the middle of a lake. Maxx had his arm around Jason's neck, pretending to wrestle.

The monitor lit up and he brought up the HeadRoom website. He clicked a couple icons and Jason's profile page popped up.

Maxx scrolled through the entries. He'd left messages for Jason ever since he died. After the accident, he went there to delete the account but just couldn't do it. Instead, he changed the settings to private. A few days after that, he started posting messages. Maxx added daily recaps of what happened, a birthday note for his brother, maybe upload some holiday photos from his phone. It was Maxx's way to keep his brother in his life. Not even Tane knew the profile was still active.

Jason's photo popped up in the corner of the screen. He read his last post. "*Hey bro, Emi and I went to see G-Ma today. She was good. She told us the story about you building a set of wings out of newspaper and drinking straws and launching yourself off her porch roof. Two broken arms later and you were still smiling about it and how you said it would have worked if you used staples and not glue. Miss you, bro. Later.*"

Maxx typed in a new post.

"*Hey bro, it's been extra crazy around here. Me and Tane just got booted out of O.S. tonight. I almost got killed by some crazy blue ghost who's got it out for me and as crazy as it sounds, I could swear I saw you in there. I know, it sounds crazy. You always hated me wasting time online but it was you. I know it. You saved my skin, again. Thanks. I just hope you got out ok.*"

Maxx hit the enter key and leaned back as the words changed color from red to blue to signal it posted. He checked the window for any signs of Tane. A new message appeared below his.

"*Be careful, Maxx! He's after you and he's strong. Don't come back in here. Someone's got to shut it down. The door needs to be closed. Stay out of O.S.! Jason.*"

Maxx rubbed his eyes. He re-read the message and clicked on the account link to make sure he didn't accidentally change the privacy setting. He flipped back to the main message board and typed a response.

"*Jason? Is this really you? What's going on? Who is this guy?*"

Maxx hit enter and waited. He stared at the screen, refusing to look away. A bulge formed in his throat and his heart raced. He typed another message.

"*Jason, its Maxx. Where are you? Why is that blue guy after me? I need your help. Please.*"

He yelled at the screen.

"Come on. Send something back."

A post popped up.

"*The accident, Maxx. Remember the accident.*"

Maxx typed back, almost in reflex.

"*What about the accident?*"

He waited but nothing appeared. Frustrated, he typed the same message.

"*What about the accident?*"

No reply.

"*Jason?*"

Maxx pushed away from the monitor.

"Shit."

Closing his eyes, he took a couple deep breaths. He pulled up the Morning Herald Newspaper site and clicked on the archives. He entered the name Jason Fragnelli and waited. Twelve headlines hit on his brother's name. The first half dozen dealt with sports awards and community related stories for Jason. He found a headline titled, "*Local teen killed by drunk driver*".

Maxx brought up the story, complete with a photo of the accident scene. He scanned the article and found the name of the other driver, Warren Talbot. Talbot was a local school teacher with a history of alcohol related incidents prior to the accident, including two former D.U.I. charges. After fleeing the scene, the police picked him up at his house and transformed him into an unwitting media darling. Maxx linked on Talbot's name and other related stories appeared, "*Man involved in death of local teen*"; "*Trial set for local teacher*"; "*Teacher convicted of Involuntary Manslaughter*"; "*Talbot receives three to six year sentence.*" Maxx saw Talbot's mug shot on one of the related hits. His eyes were drawn to the picture.

"No way."

Maxx enlarged the image.

"It's those same creepy eyes."

He copied the picture and pasted it into a photo viewer and edited it with a blue overcast.

"I should have seen it before. What an idiot! But why does he want to kill me?"

Maxx sat in silence, still staring at Talbot's picture. A silhouette reflected across the screen and Maxx jumped.

"Wow, and you tell me I have a nervous condition." Tane stuffed a Zinkle in his mouth and he sat down on the bed. "Thanks for helping me get in the window. I almost broke my neck dropping down from the roof."

Maxx took a deep breath. "Maybe if you lay off the Zinkles, Commander Lightfoot, it wouldn't be such an event. I knew it was you anyway."

He was right. Maxx wasn't usually this jumpy.

Tane looked over Maxx's shoulder at the monitor.

"I was quiet enough to sneak up on you. Hey, where'd you get the picture of big blue and belligerent?"

"It's him, Tane, the guy driving the car that hit me and Jason. I pulled up a photo of him. I don't know why, but it's him."

"So, he's always been blue?" Tane moved closer to the screen.

Maxx clicked the mouse and the photo reverted back to the original.

"No doofus, I edited that in."

"But what does he want with you? I thought he hung himself?"

"He did. He committed suicide in jail," Maxx said. "I don't know what his problem is but I don't think he's done with me."

Maxx traced his finger around one of the keys. "There's something else. It's Jason. Right before you got here, he sent me a message and told me to stay out of O.S."

"Jason e-mailed you? Come on, Maxx. This is someone messing with you. You've made enough enemies with all your scams in O.S. that I think somebody's trying to get to you."

"I don't think so. It wasn't an e-mail. It was on his HeadRoom page. Look." Maxx pulled up his brother's profile and scrolled to the newest messages.

Tane read the posts. "Anyone could have posted that. I didn't know you kept Jason's page up."

"Yeah, well, no one knew. It was just something I did. I'm the only one that can get on. No one else could have posted on here."

Tane sat down on the bed. "Okay, let's say I believe you. I mean after everything else that's happened in the last couple nights, I'd believe pretty much anything. What are we going to do about getting kicked out of O.S.?"

Maxx spun around. "Same thing we always do. We figure out a way around it. I have to find Jason and that means we need to go back in."

"We can't keep popping in there and getting attacked by your personal poltergeist. We've gotten lucky so far. Next time, we might not and if that thing can really hurt us in there then we need to quit taking chances."

"So we just give up? We let the business go and I forget about ever seeing my brother again?" Maxx's face reddened.

"No, but...okay, I think I can get us back in. I'm working on something that should do the trick but I need a little more time." Tane rested his hand on Maxx's shoulder. "We need to slow down and come up with a plan. I mean, how are we even going to find Jason? All our appointments have been wiped clean. If we show up in there, you know Ketchup will be waiting."

"I've been thinking about that and you're right, we need to quit going in blind. I have an idea where we can get some answers and maybe the upper hand. I think we've both had enough for one night. Let's get some sleep and meet up at the Wash. Emi's supposed to meet us there. We'll get her input on this mess."

Tane sighed and fell back in the bed. "I can't believe they wiped our accounts clean. How am I going to get Ariana her money? She was counting on me."

"We'll figure it out, buddy. I promise. I need you to focus on getting us back into O.S. Can you do that for me, big guy?"

"I'll take care of it. It'll have to wait until tomorrow though. I need to crash for a while." Tane twisted off the bed and moved over to the window.

He squeezed through the window to the home-made wooden landing. Crouching on his feet, he looked back in at Maxx. "You sure you're okay?"

Maxx took Tane's place on the bed. "Not even close. Grab some sleep. We'll meet up tomorrow. Don't be late."

Gripping the handles, Tane hoisted himself up to the roof. "Yeah, right, just get there before I get jumped this time, okay?"

Tane's legs dangled outside the window and then vanished. Maxx adjusted his pillow and stared at the ceiling. Sleep wasn't coming any time soon.

CHAPTER 18

"Wake up." The voice sounded both distant and close.

Maxx flipped over on his stomach and pulled the blanket over his head.

"Come on, Maxx. It's me."

Someone shook Maxx's shoulder. Grunting, Maxx cinched the covers tighter around him.

"It's Jason," the voice whispered.

Maxx's eyes shot open. Throwing his blanket off, Maxx bolted up in the bed. His brother sat next to him.

"Jason?" Maxx tried to focus but his eyes refused to cooperate.

Stretching across the mattress, he flipped on a small lamp, never taking his eyes off the figure next to him.

"It's really you. I can't believe this. How? Are you a ghost? Can you stay? We've got to get Mom and Dad up." Maxx tossed the blankets off the bed.

Jason laughed.

"Easy, little bro, take it slow. I'm not going anywhere. I can't explain it but I'm back. We'll wake Mom and Dad up in a minute. I want to talk to you first."

"You're really here." Maxx touched his brother's face. It felt warm. He looked over to his computer to make sure he wasn't somehow hooked up to his syn-skin. It dangled from the desktop.

Maxx hugged him tight, never looking to let go. Jason gently pushed away.

"I know, Maxx, I know. I missed you too." Jason got up and crossed the room, pulling back the curtains. He looked outside. "Where's my mustang? I didn't see it in the driveway."

Still dumfounded by the sight of his brother, the question took a minute to register.

"Uh, they towed it here after the..." Maxx searched for the word.

"Crash," Jason finished.

"Yeah, Dad let them haul it to Jenkin's junkyard and they crushed it. I thought about fixing it back up but, without you to help, I figured it wouldn't be the same. Sorry."

"Wow, my 'stang got junked? That reeks. Oh well, it was just a car. We'll find another one and fix it up. What do you say?"

"That would be awesome." Maxx glanced at the clock beside his bed. The numbers were a red blur. His cell phone was nowhere to be found. He swore he left it on the night stand. "How exactly do we explain that you're back from being, you know, dead?"

"Does it really matter? I'm back, Maxx. You don't have to be afraid anymore. It'll be just like before."

"Yeah, like before," Maxx said.

Jason moved over to the desk and stared at some of the photos taped on the wall. He noticed the syn-skin cord and picked it up, dangling the end of it near his nose like a pendulum.

"So what made you give up?" Jason asked.

"What do you mean? You were dead, Jason. What did you expect me to do?"

"Not on me, goofball, I'm talking about life. When did you give up on life?"

Maxx walked over and snatched the chord from him, letting it drop to the floor. "I didn't give up. People suck, Jason. They're mean. They don't give a crap about each other. It's a hard world. You have to get hard to survive."

Jason nodded in mock approval and picked up a photo. He turned the picture towards Maxx. It showed the boys and their parents next to a tent in the woods taken about five years ago.

"Remember Lake Pyhatooie? You sure don't sound like the boy in this photo."

The memories of that trip rushed back to Maxx. "Yeah, those days were great, Jason, but we were kids. Mom and Dad shielded us from all the outside garbage but it finds a way to seep in."

"What seeped in, Maxx?"

Maxx took the photo from Jason and held it against his chest, trying to protect those innocent days at the lake from hearing what followed. "Life, Jason. Life crept in. After the accident, we all changed. Mom got overly protective of me and Dad got quiet. And when he wasn't quiet, he was angry, like I was supposed to somehow make up for what we lost in you. His expectations for me were like double, so I just quit." Maxx felt a rush of nervousness sweep over him. He didn't like to feel that vulnerable.

Jason just smiled. "Quitting isn't the answer. If you ignore life long enough, it starts ignoring you back."

Maxx looked out the window. "That's easy for you to say. You weren't around for any of the dark stuff. You didn't have to deal with the pain. You still got to be perfect Jason. Hell, you were more perfect than ever. I was the one who made the mistake."

"What mistake?"

"I was driving." Maxx spun around. "Why doesn't anyone get that? It was my fault!"

"Maxx, you were stopped. He ran the intersection. Look, it doesn't matter." Jason stepped closer. "Look at me."

Maxx looked at everything in the room except his brother.

"Give life a second chance," Jason said.

Maxx shrugged. "Maybe. I'm just glad you're here. I missed you."

"I missed you too, little bro," Jason said. "Are you still hanging around with Tane?"

Maxx moved over to his computer and fiddled with the keyboard. "Yeah, we're as tight as ever. He's a good friend, probably better than I deserve."

"Yeah, I always liked him. What about on the female front? Did you ever get enough courage to ask that cheerleader out? Maggie?"

Searching his desk for a photo, Maxx found a picture of him and Emi sharing an ice cream at the Wash, blue cream smeared on their noses.

"No. We never really hit it off. This is Emi."

He handed the picture to Jason, who nodded in approval. "She's a looker. Your girlfriend?"

"Not exactly."

"Don't mess around and let her go. Second chances don't always come around."

"I know. It's complicated."

"Only because you make it that way," Jason said.

Maxx turned back to the computer. "What about the guy from the accident? Why is he trying to kill me?"

"Talbot? I don't know, but he's bad news, Maxx. Stay away from him."

"I get you but take a look at this." Maxx tapped one of the keys and the monitor to his computer lit up.

Jason lunged towards him. "Maxx! No!"

An arm erupted from the screen and gripped Maxx by the throat. He tried to break free.

He struggled to breathe and gurgled out his words. "Jason?"

Jason grabbed him around the waist and tried to pull him away from the computer. The arm pulled Maxx's face closer to the glass.

Laughter pierced the room. "I gotcha, boy."

Letting go of Max, the hand grabbed Jason by the arm. Gasping in deep breaths, Maxx fell to the floor.

Jason's arm disappeared into the monitor and he screamed, "Maxx! Help!"

"I've got you, Jason. Hold on." Maxx jumped up and latched onto Jason's waist.

Jason sunk farther into the rectangular abyss as his head and shoulder were pulled inside.

"Maxx! Don't let go! Help me."

Maxx clenched both hands into Jason's t-shirt and he threw his body back. He braced his legs against the desk and strained, his arms burning.

The shirt ripped as Jason screamed, "Don't let me go, Maxx! Don't…"

Maxx flew across the room, knocking over a chair and smashing into the wall. He looked at his hands, still clutching pieces of his brother's shirt.

"…let me go." Jason's voice faded and the monitor turned black.

"Jason!" Maxx ran over and pounded on the screen. Tears streamed down his face as he punched the glass. It exploded and the room filled with blistering light.

Maxx sat up in bed, his brother's name still ringing in his ears. His face and hair was drenched in sweat. He was breathing like he just ran a marathon. The room was dark. Tossing his covers off, he stumbled over to the desk. The chair was tucked neatly underneath. The screen was cold to his touch and he checked for damage to the wall. He sat on the edge of his bed until his breathing slowed.

"I let him go…again."

He checked his hands, half expecting to see traces of his brother's shirt still wrapped between his fingers. Someone pounded on the door.

"Maxx, are you okay in there? Your father and I thought we heard you scream."

"I'm okay, Mom. It was just a nightmare. Sorry I woke you up."

"Are you sure? Do you want to talk?"

"I'm fine. Go back to bed, Mom."

He waited until he heard footsteps moving down the hall before he crawled back under the covers and stared at the ceiling. It wasn't the first time he dreamed about Jason since the accident but they'd never seemed so real before. He glanced at the computer monitor, making sure it was still off. He grabbed his MP3 player, hoping to drown out his memories with music.

CHAPTER 19

Torture was the only possible answer. Maxx had no doubt someone had captured and was slowly performing brain numbing acts of cruelty to the Klingensmith's dog next door. It was the only explanation why an animal would make so much noise. He considered calling the humane society on his neighbors. He fumbled for his phone - three o'clock. His room was dark. Between the blinds and the heavy curtains Maxx installed, very little natural light found its way into his room.

"What could that mutt be barking about at three in the morning?"

Pulling back the curtain, a blast of daylight cut into the room. Maxx shielded his eyes. He thought it was still night. Remembering the dream with Jason, he turned towards his computer. His reflection stared back at him.

"What the heck, Jason? It seemed so real."

Walking out into the hall, he stumbled over a laundry basket near his door.

"So much for stealth mode." Maxx put the basket in his room and made his way downstairs.

His mom was in the kitchen. "Maxx, don't tell me you just got up. Have you eaten anything today?"

"I've been in my room, working on some school stuff. I had some leftover pizza." Maxx sat down at the table.

"Let me fix you something. It's the only time I get to see you anymore," she said.

His mom grabbed a loaf of bread and some loose meat from the refrigerator and made him a sandwich.

Maxx got a half empty bottle of soda from the fridge.

"Thanks, Mom. Where's Dad? Isn't this his early day?"

She poured some potato chips into a bowl.

"Sorry, hon. I never know when you're going to make an appearance so it's a fast meal. Your dad's still at work. They're merging with another company and he's trying to keep from getting laid off. He's going through a pretty tough time. A little extra help around here would mean a lot to him."

Maxx chomped into his sandwich. It wasn't that he was lazy. He avoided alone time with either of his parents because he knew where it led. She was right though, she usually was.

"I know, Mom. It's just that I got some stuff…what needs done?"

He stuffed some chips in his mouth.

His mom moved on to washing dishes. "Grass, garbage, hedges, garage cleaned. It's still filled with a lot of your brother's stuff. I was thinking you and your dad could tackle that together. Maybe this weekend?"

Maxx devoured his sandwich.

"I thought Dad did that a couple months ago?"

"Well, he wanted to, but he didn't," she said. "I think you both should do it, for me."

Maxx swallowed a huge drink to clear his throat. "Okay, Mom, I'll be around this weekend. I promise."

Satisfied, she returned to her chores. "Thank you, Maxx." She wiped the same spot on the dish in her hand. "I still miss him too."

Maxx crammed in a couple more chips and got up. Even though he felt the urge to head straight for the door, he resisted. "I'm meeting Tane and Emi down at the Wash in a little bit. I need to get moving. The sandwich was good. Thanks."

He kissed her cheek and glanced back as he shut the door. She stood at the sink, staring at the dishes.

Maxx jogged out to the street. A light rain misted down and he felt the dampness on his skin. He pulled his hoodie up. The overcast sky was covered in an army of grey clouds.

He texted Emi. *"Where r u?"*

There was no sign of her van anywhere.

His phone vibrated with an incoming message. *"Heading to Wash. U?"*

Maxx forgot she wasn't picking him up.

He messaged back. *"B there in 10"*

Maxx checked the time. He figured he could walk and the rain helped him relax. He knew his mom was trying to find a way to get him and his dad talking but he dreaded the idea of going through Jason's stuff. He never realized how much the little stuff meant until it was all he had left. Wandering down the sidewalk, he crossed a couple intersections. Growing up in Maxx's hometown was quiet and that equated to boring as a kid. To make it worse, he only lived two hours from Newton City, what many called the center of the modern world. His parents took him and his brother into the city at least once a month before Jason died. They loved visiting the shops, going to the theater, riding the subway, and just watching all the people. It was sacred family time that they all looked forward to. They hadn't been back since the accident.

Maxx paused at the next intersection, *the* intersection. For months after the accident, the skid marks remained infused into the asphalt. He refused to travel anywhere near there and went blocks out of his way if he needed to go to that side of town. He remembered driving passed with his mom and dad and feeling the car involuntarily slow down and the uncomfortable pause at the stop sign. The conversation would automatically stop as they retreated into their respective memories.

A car horn blared, snapping Maxx back to the present. He twisted around to see a blue sedan's headlights glimmering back at him through the rain. Someone yelled something. He couldn't make out actual words over the rain falling but the tone was angry. Maxx froze, unsure of his next move. He felt like an animal caught crossing the highway.

A car window slid down and the driver stuck his head out. "Are you crossing or what?"

Maxx's brain tried to process the question. "What?"

The driver said it louder and less polite. "Hey buddy, go be crazy somewhere else, huh? I'm running late here!"

Maxx looked down and realized he was standing in the middle of the road.

He raised his hand towards the driver. "Yeah, yeah, I'm going. You'll still make happy hour."

He stepped up on the sidewalk, turning to watch the car pass. A small girl in a lace dancing costume stared at him from the back seat. He was probably the first crazy person she'd ever seen. This would probably be the highlight of lunchroom conversation for her tomorrow.

Maxx stopped in front of the barber shop. He stared into the giant glass window with Harry's Two Bits Plus painted on the glass. His hair hung down in his eyes. He pulled his hoodie tight around his face. His wet clothes clung to his skin. No wonder the little girl stared. His mental status definitely looked questionable.

Maxx kept moving until the sign for The Wash flashed up ahead. The bike rack out front was empty, so Tane wasn't there yet. He looked for Emi's van in the lot. A full sized white cargo van stuck out pretty easy from all the rice burners and wannabe street racers that usually littered the lot. His brother had instilled an admiration for American made automobiles in him. The purr of a V-8 engine made his skin tingle. He crossed the lot and figured he'd wait inside, hoping Emi would have a new perspective to add to all this. She always had a knack of putting things into perspective.

CHAPTER 20

"You haven't got a brain between the two of you!" Emi slammed her milkshake on the counter.

"Aww, don't say that, Emi." Tane worked on a mouth full of pretzels, sitting next to Maxx at the Wash's soda bar.

Ignoring him, she looked directly at Maxx. "From what you just told me, you both could've been killed. Demons, O.S. Force Agents-"

"O.S. Corp," Maxx corrected her.

"I don't care if they're the Peace Corps!" Emi shouted back.

Tane raised his hand to interrupt.

"Don't even go there, Tane." Emi glared at him and he put his hand back on the counter. "Look you two, it's obvious you're not thinking straight. It's over. Your money is gone. You just need to deal with it. There are a lot more important things in life than that." She took a breath and softened her tone. "I know that seeing something in there that looked like Jason freaked you out. Who wouldn't? Somebody is just trying to play some sick kind of practical joke on you and it's not funny."

Not exactly the response he was expecting but Maxx could hardly blame her. "I know this all seems impossible but then explain how I got this cut in my chest. You saw it. That isn't make believe or someone pulling a sick stunt."

Emi looked down at Maxx's shirt. "Sometimes the mind can do unbelievable things to the body, some kind of post-traumatic stress. I'm sure someone has done a study on that. I bet you didn't look anything like that up on the internet, did you?"

"No, but, this wasn't like that," Maxx said.

"Exactly, you looked for the answers you wanted. All the messing around you two do in that computer world, hooking gizmos into your nervous system. It's no wonder your body doesn't know what to believe is real. You've seen the articles about people dying from being in that program. Maybe this is just some new type of symptom. It's your body's way of telling you to stop what you're doing and I think it may be right," Emi pleaded.

"Then explain the HeadRoom page?" Maxx asked. "I wasn't in O.S. when that happened. I was sitting in my room, Emi. It was real."

Emi wove her fingers together. "I don't know, Maxx. I'm not like you. I'm not a computer geek to the nth level with macro this and leet that. Maybe someone is after you. Maybe you ticked off one too many people with all this scamming. I'm just glad you got thrown out and you're safe."

Maxx saw the concern in her eyes, which made his next statement all the more difficult. "That's exactly why we're going back in."

"What?" Emi jumped up.

He felt the eyes of the other patrons drawn away from their own conversations and focus on them.

Motioning for Emi to sit back down, Maxx waved to the room. "There's nothing to see here. Go back to your meals." He checked to make sure Emi was back in her seat. "Now hold on. I know what you're thinking."

"That you're an ass." Emi smirked.

"Well, I thought I knew what you were thinking. Look, Emi, we have to get back in there. Maybe getting hurt was some kind of weird mind over body thing and maybe someone is just messing with me with this Jason thing but I have to know. You weren't there. You didn't see him. The motions he made, the way he looked at me. Those aren't things anyone else knows."

Emi didn't seem convinced. "But you just said that Jason came to you in a dream. Are you saying that was real too? You weren't hooked up to that stupid machine then. What is real, Maxx?"

Maxx answered louder than he intended. "I don't know! Okay! I don't know!" He caught himself and clenched his fists. His arms trembled and he forced a deep breath. "I know this is crazy. I don't expect you to believe me but I need to find out if that was Jason. Everything in me says that it was."

Tane patted his friend on the back. "It's okay, Maxx. I was there. That blue jerk attacked me too. I believe you. Try to calm down."

Emi pushed her drink away. "Maxx, it's not that I don't believe in you. You know I do. I just don't want to see you hurt. That's all. You…mean a lot to me."

"We're going back in. That's all there is to it. Tane and I have a plan. You know the guy that designed Other Syde? Nathaniel Daniels? Tane tracked him down to an address in Newton City. It's where he gets residuals from his work for O.S. Corp, so we figure it's good. I'm going there and confront him about all of this. Maybe he can tell me why ghosts are showing up in his program. Tane's figured out a way to get us back into O.S. without being detected too. Tell her, Tane."

Maxx knew his friend would jump at the chance to talk technology.

Tane put down his milkshake. "Well, back in the day, everyone that got on line could be tracked using the IP address they used to log onto their internet with from their base computer. It was kind of the standard that everyone used. It didn't take long for net savvy people to realize there was a whole bunch of ways to get around that. They started using proxy servers, IP sharing groups, stuff like that."

"What's IP mean? Don't look at me like that, Maxx." Emi pointed a finger in Maxx's direction without even looking his way.

"Sorry, Emi, it stands for Internet Protocol. Now a days I can get on my system at home and make it look like I'm logging in from anywhere in the world. The folks at O.S. didn't want people hacking into their system for free, setting up bogus accounts, counterfeit credit card information, the whole bit, right? So they came up with a new kind of tracking software, they call it bio imprint. By cataloging someone's imprint when they start up an account, it lets the powers that be at O.S.

Corp keep track of who's coming and going into their program and makes it real tough to mess with them."

Tane took another drink and checked to make sure he kept everyone's attention.

Maxx's hand swooped down along the counter, making it his pretend landing strip. "Okay, I wanted the crib notes not the whole half an hour infomercial. Let's bring this plane in for a landing."

Tane nodded. "Once you log in with that certain bio imprint, well, that's you. Forever. If you start an account using a stolen credit card, than you're stuck with it. They'll give you the boot and never let you back in. No multiple accounts, aliases, nothing. Total suckage. Anyway, me and a couple net buds have been working on a program to blur your bio imprints inside O.S. It doesn't change your profile but they can't accurately read it either and the program treats you as an anomaly and you don't register. We call it ghosting. You know, you're there but really not. Guess it's kind of ironic with everything going on."

Maxx placed a finger over Tane's mouth. "Okay. Shhh, little tech geek, she's got it. I'd like to get moving on it sometime this week."

Tane looked like a puppy slapped with a wet newspaper. "You're the one who asked me to tell her."

"It was a very good explanation," Emi said. "I'm impressed."

"Thanks, Emi."

Maxx threw a couple dollars on the table. "So that's it. I'm heading to Newton City first thing in the morning to locate Daniels and see what information I can get out of him. I'm hoping he tells me if O.S. is involved in paranormal research. Tane's going to finish up what he needs to do here to get us back into the program. We'll be invisible to them and everyone else in there, so we won't have to worry about getting attacked again. You're sure you can have the programming ready by tomorrow?"

Tane nodded.

Maxx got up to leave before Emi stopped him. "There's only one hiccup in your master plan."

Maxx paused. "And what would that be?"

"I'm coming with you." She kissed his cheek and headed towards the exit. Halfway to the door, she said over her shoulder. "I'll pick you up at six and we'll take the van down to the train station. I hate driving in the city. No offense, but grab a shower and change of clothes before we go, you're looking kind of grubby."

She waved to Tane as she walked towards the door.

Maxx waited until she was outside before asking his friend, "Did she just call me grubby?"

"Yep, it's a nice way of saying you stink." Tane wiped a stain from his own shirt.

CHAPTER 21

"Dibs on the window seat." Maxx edged passed as Emi drew in her knees.

"My knight in shining armor." She sat down near the aisle.

"Chivalry is a misunderstood and outdated concept." Maxx slid across the row and plopped down next to the window. "Besides, I get motion sick."

Emi stuffed her bag under the seat. She leaned forward and stared out the window at the graffiti filled train station wall.

"My, what a lovely view we have. Did you get any sleep last night?" she asked.

Maxx bent forward to take in the concrete scenery. "No one told you to come along you know."

He checked his phone, expecting a text from Tane. The light in the corner of the phone was dark and he slid it back in his pocket.

Maxx leaned his head against the back rest. "Tane must be slipping. I thought he'd have the program up and running by now. I might've got an hour of sleep. I spent most of the night surfing the internet and looking for stuff."

"Like Jason?" Emi asked.

"Yeah, but I didn't get anything back. So, how'd you get out of work today?" Maxx raised his eyebrows.

"I ditched." Emi couldn't look him in the eye.

"You criminal. I really am a bad influence on you. Next thing you know you'll be shoplifting, then petty theft, and finally grand larceny. It's a slippery slope, young lady." Maxx shook his finger in mock judgment.

"What are you? My parole agent?" Emi asked.

"Parole comes after you're released from jail. Probation is more likely for you."

"And how do you know that...never mind." Emi pulled a magazine from the pocket of the seat in front of her. She flipped it around.

"Hmmmm. Train Talk. That sounds interesting," she said. "Maybe Tane actually had to get some sleep, you know. Just because you're a creature of the night doesn't mean he is too. We won't be back until late afternoon. You should give him a break."

A voice crackled over the train compartment's speaker.

"Welcome aboard Coach 223. Estimated arrival time into Newton City is two hours and eight minutes. We'll be making two stops at Grantville and Denningtown along the way. Enjoy your ride."

"How can anyone enjoy the ride on these seats? I thought a train ride was supposed to be more comfortable than the bus. This bites." Maxx pulled one leg up and tucked it under the other. "Where's the attendant? I need a Mr. Pew."

"That's only on airplanes, brainiac. I thought you said your family took the train into the city all the time." Emi returned the magazine to the sleeve in the chair.

"We did but we always drove. It's been years since we took the train. I remember it better than this." Maxx watched out the window as the train exited the station.

The concrete barriers were replaced by the rural wood line outside. The train picked up speed and the branches meshed together into a blur.

He looked at Emi. "I should have brought my laptop."

"I'm surprised you actually got up before dawn. I figured I'd be waiting in the van until at least noon."

Emi pulled out her cell phone and flicked it open. She ran her fingers over the keys before flipping it closed.

"Are you expecting a call?" Maxx asked.

Emi stared at her phone. "Just thinking I should probably call my mom and let her know I'll be in town. She'd freak if she knew I was that close and didn't stop."

"We really don't have time for that, Emi. Daniels' address is nowhere near your mom's place. I want to get what we can from him and get home. I need to get back into O.S."

She nodded and put her phone away.

Maxx nudged her shoulder. "But, I mean, I guess we could stop by real quick to say hi."

She gave him a shoulder bump of her own. "No, it's okay. You're right. I don't need any drama with the new boyfriend. You're supplying more than enough of that in my life right now."

"Thanks. What's his problem anyway?"

"He thinks he can step right into my life. He wants me to call him Dad. Can you believe that? They've been dating for like three months."

"I've never been able to figure out the older generation," Maxx said.

"So...how's your grandmother? Is she feeling any better?"

Maxx traced a smiley face on the window with his finger and watched it fade. "I haven't been back to see her since the day you and I were there. She's okay. She's tougher than you and I put together."

"You need to spend some more time with her, you know. She lights up as soon as you walk in the room. It's good for her. It's good for both of you."

Maxx re-drew the face on his improvised canvass but changed the mouth to a frown. "Yeah, I know. There just always seems to be stuff going on."

"True, but nothing's more important than family. I lost my grandma when I was only eight. I still remember the smell of fresh baked bread when we'd visit her house on Sundays during the summer. The butter would just melt into the dough. I can't remember anything tasting better."

Emi smiled, slipping into her memories.

She caught herself and continued. "After that, we'd go blackberry picking in the afternoon. The woods were full of bushes and we'd take wicker baskets and fill them to the brim and have half of the berries eaten before we got back to her house. She loved the sun. She almost seemed a force of nature. Your grandma won't be around forever, Maxx. Take all the time with her that you can get."

Emi glanced over. "Maxx?"

His head was propped against the window and he was snoring lightly. His breath fogged the glass with each exhalation, bringing back small traces of his finger drawn creation. Emi shrugged and reached in front of her.

"Train Talk it is."

***

Maxx made his way down the sidewalk, the sun warming his face with each step. Along the walk were rows of blackberry bushes. He stopped and picked one. The berry's juices exploded in his mouth. He never tasted anything so sweet. He turned and walked through the front gate. It squeaked as Maxx crossed through the small white wooden fence. He made his way across the yard, stopping to look at a garden planted in corner. The sunflowers were in full bloom and stood at least six feet tall.

"I need to remember to oil that gate later," he said.

Maxx practically bounced up the steps to the porch of the house. Potted flowers adorned the porch and banisters. He plucked a daisy from one of the plants and tucked the flower into the front pocket of his suit.

He opened the front door and placed his briefcase down in the hall.

"Emi! Where are you, babe? Something smells great."

The living room was small but quaintly furnished. Photos hung in bulk on the walls, him and Emi at the lake, in-line skating at the park, a Christmas dinner with both sets of parents. Maxx wore a Santa cap and Emi accessorized with stuffed antlers on her head. There was a picture of Tane in an outlandishly loud patterned sweater and six kids hanging on him. Maxx stopped at their wedding photo. Emi stood at the church doors, her white gown flowing down the steps.

Emi was in the kitchen, cooking at the stove. The sunlight outlined her body in an ethereal radiance. He stopped in the door, transfixed by her beauty.

She glanced over her shoulder and smiled and the sunlight paled around her. "I just took a loaf of bread out of the oven. It's cooling on the table. How was your day?"

The slope of her bulging apron rested neatly under a bow tied in the center.

She followed Maxx's eyes and placed a hand on her belly. "He must have kicked at least ten times today. I think we're giving birth to a mixed martial arts fighter."

"We'll just call him Bruce," Maxx said, presenting Emi with the daisy he picked from the porch. "A flower for my flower."

Performing a small curtsey, she accepted the gift. "Why thank you."

She opened a cupboard and retrieved a drinking glass. Filling the cup with water, she gingerly placed the daisy inside it and placed both on the window sill.

"You know, I was saving those for my gardening club," Emi said.

Maxx shrugged apologetically and hungrily eyed the loaf of bread. He picked up a knife from the table.

"Sorry."

Emi kissed him on the forehead. "I'll forgive you just this once. Did you talk to Tane at the office today? Are he and Ariana still coming up to the cabin this weekend?"

"He said they couldn't wait." Maxx turned the bread to the side and held the knife like a surgeon preparing for the initial incision.

"Careful Maxx, it's still hot," Emi chided, turning back to the stove.

"That's when it's the best," Maxx said as he plunged the knife into the bread.

Carving it down the center, he grabbed an end with each hand and breathed in the moist warm dough as he tore it in half.

A blue claw burst out from the bread, wrapping around his face. Maxx tried to warn Emi but could only gurgle. The claws dug into his skin, drawing blood. He jerked away from the table but the arm stretched with him, extending into a shoulder and then a head appearing out of the baked good. A tangled mass of hair flowed around the man's face as a second arm emerged and braced against the table. Maxx thrust

137

both legs against the floor and fell over a chair, toppling to the kitchen floor. He tried to pull free. Blood oozed down his neck, causing the hand to slip. Maxx broke free.

He shouted to Emi, "Look out! The…the bread. It's in the bread!"

Emi spun around, her face twisted with concern and confusion. She saw the blue abomination freeing itself from the bread. It was almost completely free.

Kneeling on top of the table, it sneered. "Maxx! Emi! What a surprise. You haven't forgotten about me now, have you? You can't have a life without dealing with me first. You and your idiot brother stripped everything good in my life away from me. It's time I returned the favor."

The creature sprang off the table and landed on the floor.

She screamed, "Maxx! Help us!"

Gripping Emi's throat, it pinned her against the refrigerator. An assortment of magnets crashed to the floor.

Turning back to Maxx, it growled, "Yeah, Maxx, why don't you do something?"

"Let her go, Talbot!" Maxx tried to run to her but he couldn't move. It felt like someone had glued his hands to the floor. He yanked at his arms, trying to pull free from the kitchen tiles.

The mangled apparition dragged her away from the refrigerator and bounced her off a cabinet. Holding her in place, it laughed. "This is my world, boy. Not yours. We play by my rules. You got nothing on me here. Now sit still and watch me kill someone else you love." He dropped his hand down to Emi's stomach. His smile broadened. "Oh, a two for one deal. Even better."

The color faded from Emi's face. She pounded against Talbot's chest, trying to break free. Tears rolled down her cheeks as she met Maxx's eyes.

"Maxx, I'm sorry. I'll always love you," she sobbed.

Maxx tore his hands free from the floor, tiny bits of ceramic coming with them. He lunged for her. His vision blurred as he watched Talbot drag his claw down Emi's cheek.

Her scream pierced the room. Talbot yanked the fridge door open at the last second. Maxx's head crashed into the panel and everything went black.

***

"Fragnelli! I'm still waiting for my order. Let's move it."

Slowly shaking his head, Maxx looked around. Emi was nowhere in sight.

Instead, Maxx stared down into a vat of grease with a metal basket submerged in it. He was standing in the cooking area of a restaurant. A large greasy haired man wearing a red western print shirt and black bow tie shouted at him through a small window separating the kitchen from the front counter.

"C'mon, numb nuts. They call it fast food for a reason."

"Where's Emi?" Maxx was wearing the same outfit as the man.

"Who? Are you back on drugs, Fragnelli?" the man asked. "Just give me an order of doughy balls. It ain't rocket science." He spun around and spoke to customer waiting on the other side of the counter. "Sorry, sir, guy's been here almost two years and still can't get it right. What can you do?"

The customer nodded. "That's what's wrong with this generation. They don't know how to earn a dollar anymore. They want everything handed to them."

Maxx grabbed his name tag shaped like a sheriff's badge. His name was hand written under the catch phrase *Howdy Pardner*. He looked out the small window into the dining room. The shades were drawn on all of the windows.

"Fragnelli! The doughy balls! Now!" His boss spun around and shouted the order again.

Maxx got a good look at the guy's face. Somewhere in his mid-30's, he towered over the counter. His red hair receded into a horseshoe pattern across his scalp, a bushy matching colored mustache hung above his lip.

"Tane? Is that you?" Maxx blinked, still trying to figure out what was happening. He was just with Emi, in their house. She was pregnant, wasn't she? And then something happened with the bread.

"You don't get to call me that, Fragnelli. You lost that privilege a long time ago. It's boss now, or sir." Tane pointed a finger through the order window. "Get to work, slacker. I need those doughy balls."

Maxx half-heartedly nodded and looked at the grease fryer below him. He grabbed the metal handle jutting out from the basket and tried pulling the mesh box free. It was stuck in the oil. He yanked again but it didn't budge.

"You got two seconds and then you are so fired. Got it?"

Maxx yelled back at his fast food cowboy friend. "There's something holding the tray down. Hold on. I'm going to take a look."

Maxx leaned closer into the bubbling grease. He could make out the outline of something wedged inside the basket. He felt the heat on his face and splashes of hot grease stung his cheek. Maxx found a set of metal tongs and plunged them down into the fryer. It gripped whatever was holding the basket and he yanked again.

A hand erupted from the grease and clenched the bolo necktie around Maxx's neck. The dark blue skin ignited into flames and its flesh boiled. Maxx pulled away and grabbed both sides of the fryer to keep from being pulled in. Its grip was like a vice. His face inched closer to the fiery pit.

"Doughy balls! Where are my doughy balls?" Tane screamed from the front counter.

Maxx tried to scream but his rope tie strangled him. His hand slipped in the grease and his face plunged into the boiling oil.

Maxx screamed.

***

"Doughy balls!" Maxx's voice echoed off the metal walls of the train's compartment.

Someone was shaking him by the shoulders as his eyes snapped open. An open copy of Train Talk was on the floor at his feet.

"Oh my God, Maxx. Are you okay?" Emi's lips pressed against his ear. "You're freaking everyone out."

Maxx jolted forward in his seat. He twisted toward the window and smacked his face on the glass.

"Ow."

Emi hissed in empathy and noticed the other passengers staring at them.

"He just had a bad dream. He's okay. Thanks for rushing over to help. Not." She touched his cheek with the palm of her hand. "Wow. That must have been some nightmare. You sure you're okay?"

Maxx blinked a few times before smiling to reassure her he was all right. She didn't need to know how freaked out he actually was. Sweat dripped into his eyes and his arms felt cold.

"Yeah, I'm good. It was just a crazy dream. Man, it seemed so real though. How long was I out?" He rubbed his arms to help get the feeling back.

"You've been out for almost two hours. We should be pulling into Newton City in a few minutes. I've read every possible piece of literature here while you were snoring away. Do you want to know the evacuation procedure in case we're de-railed?"

Maxx laughed. "No, can't say that I do. That was one strange dream and let me tell you that I've had some pretty good ones lately."

"So you've told me. What was this one about?"

Maxx rubbed the bump forming on his forehead. He didn't want her to worry about him and wasn't sure how she'd react to him dreaming they were married, let alone her being pregnant. Whether his future held, domestic bliss for him and Emi, or a personal hell of making minimum wage and serving doughy balls in a cowboy costume, one thing seemed for certain, a confrontation with the ghost of Warren Talbot was coming.

"Let's just say it wasn't a happy ending," he said. "Is that fair enough?"

"I'll let you get away with that for now. You better get yourself together. We pull into Newton Station in like four minutes." Emi glimpsed at a passing mile marker. "Make that three minutes."

Maxx pulled himself up in the chair. "Wow, you memorized the train schedule too?"

"In its boring entirety." Emi held up a pamphlet to prove her point.

Maxx picked up the magazine from the floor, handing it back to her. "Were we talking about fresh bread before I fell asleep?"

Chapter 22

Newton Square Train Station reminded Maxx of a public swimming pool, just without the water, and the pool. The place bustled with activity. Maxx watched the throngs of people herding through the gates and turn stills. He slipped his bag over his shoulder, looking for an exit. He felt his neck and shoulders starting to tighten.

"Over here, country mouse." Emi stood next to one of the gates.

She seemed oblivious to the hundreds of people scurrying around her. Maxx was glad she insisted on coming. His nerves were on edge from the attacks and dreams, coupled with the prospect of meeting one of his personal heroes before the day was through. She always brought out the best in him and he needed to be extra sharp.

Emi waved for him. "We don't have time for sightseeing."

"I know. It's been a while since I've been here. I forgot what it's like, takes a minute to get used to it."

They merged into the human stream as it flowed up to the street. Maxx switched his bag over his head so that it crossed his chest.

"So, city mouse, you're saying I shouldn't wear my camera around my neck and ask for a lot of directions," he joked.

"I'll let you buy a T-shirt before we leave," Emi said.

Maxx craned his neck to take in the surrounding skyscrapers. As a child, his father told him they touched the clouds and you could see heaven from the top floors. Maxx imagined someone waving to a passing angel on their lunch break. He dreamed of living in a penthouse someday and taking in a real sunset from his balcony. He wondered if Emi would be beside him if that happened.

She grabbed his wrist and yanked him along behind her. "Do you have Tane's directions?"

Maxx jiggled his phone in front of him. "Yeah, I got them. Tane forwarded the address and the best walking, cab, biking, and public transportation route. He's like a second mother sometimes. I think we're okay with just walking. It's only like a dozen blocks. I don't trust cabbies and I don't think my butt can take another uncomfortable seat."

Emi's hand slipped from his wrist to his hand and she tangled her fingers in his.

"Well, for your butt's sake, we'll do our part for the environment," she said.

They waited at the cross walk. Maxx checked Tane's directions again before he pocketed his phone.

He pointed down the street. "It looks like we get to cut across Newton Park. And you say I'm not a romantic."

"Come on, Romeo," Emi said.

They walked a few more blocks before coming to an iron gate. Forged into the top of the gate were the words *Newton Park.* The buildings and streets were replaced by trees and grass. Emi stopped at a group of orange Star Gazers planted near one of the park benches. She pulled one of the flowers to her face.

Emi savored the lingering aroma. "They've always been my favorite. My mom used to plant them in the spring and we'd bring them to the park and help her garden club plant them all over."

"Stay there a second." Maxx took a picture of Emi next to the flowers with his phone.

She brushed a finger across the petals as she walked away. "Taking photos of flowers? I didn't know you had an artistic side. If you start bird watching, there may be a problem."

"Sorry, I left my net and binoculars at home. But look, there's some more random beauty up ahead." Maxx pointed at a park bench.

A mass of rags lay strewn across the wooden planks. A tangle of black hair rested on one side and two mismatched boots marked the opposite end. Maxx guided Emi to the edge of the sidewalk.

He leaned into her. "And now I remember some of the things I didn't like about the city."

Emi let go of Maxx's hand and walked up to the bench. "Everyone needs help sometimes, Maxx. If not for the grace of God, you know."

She pulled a five dollar bill out of her pocket.

Maxx reached for the money. "A five? Are you kidding me? He's just going down to the closest drug store to buy a bottle of their finest mouthwash for the alcohol content. He may be drunk but he's got the freshest breath in town."

Emi blocked Maxx's hand. "Sir?"

The pile of rags stirred and shifted like it was transforming into something all its own.

"I ain't doin' nuthin'. Why don't you cops go catch a crook or sumpin'?"

"I'm not a cop. I wanted to give you this," Emi said.

The rag man turned over and eyed the money. He grunted and slowly sat up on the bench.

"Much obliged. Thanks." The vagrant eased his hand inches from Emi's and snatched the bill away.

He grabbed her wrist with his other hand. The motion caught her by surprise as he pulled her in close.

"Wanna see some magic?" he whispered.

Balling the money in his hand, he clenched his fist. Emi swooned, getting a full blast of his breath.

"Let her go, whackadoo!" Maxx stepped towards them.

Maxx grabbed the guy's coat. He growled at Maxx and stared with pale blue eyes. His thick dirty hair hid most of his face. He held his arm out in front of them.

"Now you see it." His eyes were wild with anticipation. Unclenching his fist, the hand was empty. The vagrant blew a gust of alcohol infused breath through his fingers to emphasize his point. "And then it's all gone."

He let go of Emi. She stumbled back but Maxx caught her.

Smiling with his remaining teeth, the bum laughed. "Ha! You get it? S'all you really need to know. You'll see. You'll all see. That one's free of charge, darlin'. But thanks for the tip."

Maxx rushed Emi down the sidewalk, away from the man.

"It's all in the timing, boy. Don't let it pass you by," the man shouted as they hurried away.

Maxx waved after they put some distance between them. "Okay, thanks there Hobo Houdini. That was a great trick. I'm sure they love you at children's parties."

When Maxx felt they were far enough away, he slapped Emi's shoulder. "Smooth move, city mouse. I think you completely turned his life around." He noticed Emi rubbing her wrist. "Are you okay?"

"Yeah, I can say that was definitely a first for me, philosophy from a vagrant. At least we have a story to tell Tane."

Maxx looked back one more time. "I could have took him. If it went any farther, I mean. I was ready to, you know, get ready to rumble."

"Now that would definitely have been worth the five bucks to see." Emi grinned.

"Gee. Thanks," Maxx said.

Maxx wasn't the violent type. Between doing tech favors for the other kids and using Tane's size for a tactical advantage, he survived the threat of schoolyard beatings better than most. Jason taught him some simple self-defense moves a couple years ago but Maxx quit when he found out they wouldn't be smashing cinder blocks with their bare hands.

Maxx noticed a jogger coming towards them. He scrolled through his phone and pulled up an app. As the man passed, he pressed the screen.

"*Brraapp.*"

The runner turned around and shot a disgusted look at Maxx who pointed at Emi and waved his hand in front of his face.

Emi tried resisting the urge but laughed anyway. "I almost get mugged and you pull a fart prank."

Accomplishing his task of making her smile, Maxx pointed towards another gate. "There really is an app for everything. Let's go before the other bums form a chorus line."

Exiting the park, they were surrounded by car horns and market fronts again. The smell of pizza filtered into the street and Maxx eyed the family pizzeria on the corner. A young girl was wiping down the tables out front, getting ready for the lunch rush. Beside that was bakery and Maxx's stomach growled.

"Stop for a bite?" Emi asked.

"No," Maxx said, even though it was tempting. "We're too close. Maybe afterwards."

Emi pressed the pedestrian button at the next intersection and crossed the street.

"What's the name of this place again?" she asked.

"Crossroads Rehabilitation and Better Living Center, it's only one more block up." Maxx pointed down the street.

"Sounds like a nice enough place," she said.

CHAPTER 23

"You've got to be kidding me." Emi stood on the sidewalk staring at the dilapidated brick building in front of them.

A faded wooden sign hung from a post in the yard. Two worn plastic chairs sat on the small porch. A planting pot rested between the chairs, devoid of any growing vegetation but filled with cigarette butts. Maxx handed her his phone.

"Yep, this is it," she said. I can't believe the guy who created your super geek world stays here. Tane's got to have the wrong Nathaniel Daniels."

Maxx shrugged and walked up to the porch. Something cried wrong about the whole thing but they were too far to stop. Maybe this was a front for Daniels to stay hidden from prying eyes.

"I guess we'll find out soon enough. And it's not a geek world," Maxx said.

"Oh, don't be such a baby. I was kidding."

He pushed the doorbell and noticed there was no screen on the outer door. He traced a set of wires up to a small speaker duct taped against the wall.

A voice called out from the tiny box overhead. "What?"

Maxx leaned closer to the speaker. "Uh, is this CrossCreek Rehab?"

"That's what the sign says, ain't it?"

"Well, mostly," Maxx said. "Sir, we're here to see Nathaniel Daniels. He's a patient here."

"Mr. Daniels doesn't take visitors."

"Sir, it's an emergency. Please, we only need a couple minutes," Maxx pleaded.

"You're not going away until I let you in to see him, are you?"

"No, sir." Maxx replied.

A buzzer sounded and the locking mechanism released. Emi pulled the door open.

"That was easier than I thought," she said.

"He's not in front of us yet," Maxx said.

An old wooden desk sat in the center of the lobby. Western print wallpaper hung on the walls. Maxx watched the same cowboy chasing the same bull around the width of the room. A black rotary phone rested on the desk beside several piles of sloppily stacked papers. A woman in her mid-sixties and dressed in a white nurse's uniform manned the desk. Her hat was secured with bobby pins into short salt and peppered hair.

She waved them over. "Are you some of Mr. Daniels' family?"

Maxx stepped in front of Emi. "No, ma'am, we're more friends of the family." Maxx flashed a smile and noticed the tag on her uniform. "It's really urgent that we speak with Mr. Daniels, Bonnie. I know you're a busy lady but we only need a couple minutes. The gentlemen on the intercom told us to come right in."

Maxx screwed up with the friends of the family line but tried to make up for it by playing it off that they were expected. Besides, he always did better with charming the ladies.

"That was me, smart ass. Why haven't I seen you here before if you know Mr. Daniels' family so well?" Nurse Bonnie asked.

Another swing and a miss on his part, Maxx needed to turn up the charm factor.

"We're new in town?" Emi chimed in, saying it as much as a question as an answer.

Maxx appreciated the help but they were barely treading water with Nurse Bonnie and Emi may have caused them strike three. The nurse grunted and braced her hands against the desk as she got up. She shuffled to the back of the room and opened a door.

"You two have a nice day. Mr. Daniels is not allowed visitors," she said. "I've smelled enough of it to know when crap comes through the door."

She disappeared, leaving Maxx and Emi alone at the desk. Emi picked Maxx's backpack up from the floor and slung it over her shoulder.

"Well, that was a waste of a trip," she said. "For a professional con man, you really need to work on your people skills."

"Hold on, Ms. New-In-Town, we're already inside the electronic door. I'm not giving up that easily. What are they going to do, kick us out? Then we're right back where we started anyway."

Tugging Emi along behind him, Maxx headed for the same door Nurse Bonnie just exited. She planted her feet and jerked Maxx to a stop.

"No, Maxx, they call the police and we get thrown in jail for trespassing. I don't think so. This isn't a small town sheriff's department jail. This is thrown in a cell with the drug dealer and rapist's jail."

"Come on. They're old," Maxx said. "We can out run them if we need to. Any trouble and we bolt. I promise."

He gave her arm an extra pull and she fell off balance.

"Okay. Just remember how we got in here so we don't get lost."

"My mind is a steel trap." Maxx winked and gently turned the latch, cracking the door open. He peeked into the next room and whispered, "Okay, it looks clear, just a big empty hall. I would never have guessed you for a jail bird."

Emi pushed in behind him. "Be quiet. You suck at being a criminal, so someone has to step up."

Maxx led them down the hall, rows of doors on each side. He guessed there were twenty rooms. A couple of the ceiling tiles were broken. His sneakers squeaked with each step.

"Are you kidding me?" Emi asked. "Can't you walk more quietly?"

"Is it my fault the janitor uses too much wax?"

Emi read the name placards as they went. "They look like patient rooms. You didn't say he was in a nursing home."

"I didn't know it was. This doesn't make any sense. Why would Daniels be here? I wonder how big this place is. This could take a while."

Emi found a cleaning cart halfway down the hall. A clipboard was hooked to the side.

She flipped through the pages. "It's a patient roster."

"Great. Which room is his?" Maxx read over her shoulder.

Emi scanned the pages and stopped on the second sheet. "Here he is. He's in room 312. It's marked private. I guess we need to go up." She returned the clipboard. "Look, there's a sign for the stairwell."

Stenciled on the wall was the word *stairs* in black paint.

Maxx gently opened the door, holding his breath. "At least there isn't a fire alarm."

Emi covered her nose as they started up. "What do they use to clean around here? It smells like industrial strength bleach."

The yellow paint on the walls peeled away in large sections and the only light came from one long incandescent bulb above the door at each platform. Maxx grabbed the metal railing as they climbed. He immediately realized his mistake.

"I wonder if they have one of those hand sanitizer stations nearby," Maxx asked.

"Judging by what we've seen so far, I wouldn't count on it. Are you sure this is the right place?"

Stopping at the next landing, Maxx peered through a small glass window on the door. "Tane's never wrong about stuff like this. But something is definitely screwy here."

Maxx checked the hall. He waved for Emi and they snuck down to the closest door.

Maxx read the placard. "It should be the next one down."

The stairwell door closed and Emi jumped. "Sorry, I thought I heard someone. You know, not that I'm complaining, but you'd think there would be more people moving around here."

Maxx was already at the next room. "This is it. It's his room. I can't believe I'm actually about to meet the guy who invented the Other Syde." He straightened out his shirt and ran his fingers through his hair.

"Do I look okay?" he asked.

"Would you just get in there before someone sees us?" Emi pushed him from behind.

Maxx pushed open the door.

Emi hurried in behind him. "Why are there no lights on in here?"

"I don't know. Maybe he's asleep. Try to find a switch," Maxx whispered as the door closed behind them, the last bit of light fading from the hall.

Emi flipped the switch and the overhead light came on. The middle of room was cordoned off by a large hospital curtain attached to a ceiling mounted railing. The drapes were drawn on the room's only window.

Maxx called out softly, "Mr. Daniels?"

Emi walked to the middle of the room and grabbed a handful of fabric. She whipped the curtain to the side. The hinges hissed against the metal rail.

"Oh my God!" Emi gasped.

The man in the bed weighed at most eighty pounds. The hospital gown loosely covered his chest and groin. His complexion matched the pale hospital room tile. Tubes protruded from his arms and chest, leading into an array of machinery aligned on the side of the bed. Gray patches of hair sprouted sporadically near his temples. The same signs of aging found their way into a straggly beard flowing down his neck.

Emi placed her hand on the bed rail. "This is Nathaniel Daniels?"

Maxx stumbled back. He'd envisioned meeting the inventor of Other Syde, someone who realized the benefits of escaping their own world to a place where they controlled their own destiny. Daniels would be impressed with Maxx's quick wits and budding entrepreneurship and offer him a high level position right out of school. They'd negotiate his six figure salary and move him into the Other Syde Corporate Offices. His father would be speechless.

He stared at the corpse-like man in front of him before noticing his neck. "Look. He's wearing syn-skin."

A wire ran from Daniel's shoulders, slumping down across the mattress and onto the floor. Maxx traced the cord to a computer in the corner.

Kneeling down, he read the machine's specifications on the tower. "This thing is a dinosaur. There's no way Daniels would be running O.S.-ware on this brick."

"What do you two think you are doing?"

Maxx and Emi froze. They slowly turned around to find a young woman standing at the door. Her red hair curled past the shoulders of her green scrubs, touching the edge of a white name tag pinned over her pocket. The name Holly was printed in black marker with a smiley face added inside the letter o. An orange box was in her hand containing a variety of tubes and syringes.

Answering her own question, she casually entered the room. "You're trying to get some tips about that game, aren't you?"

Maxx searched for an escape route, which appeared to involve pushing past the red haired nurse. He gripped Emi's hand in case she didn't follow his lead but wanted to at least test the path of least resistance.

"Not exactly, we need some information from Mr. Daniels about his program but it's no game. You're not going to bust us, are you?" Maxx asked.

Holly seemed to enjoy the power play she stumbled into and frowned at them. Giving it an uncomfortable moment, she broke into a smile and laughed. "I'm not going to tell."

She bounced passed them and stopped at Daniels' bedside. "I make like seven bucks an hour here as an aide. I'm just here to push the meds, not security."

Maxx felt his confidence coming back. He joined the nurse at bedside while she placed a hand on Daniels' forehead.

Maxx asked, "So *this* is really Nathaniel Daniels? The guy who invented the Other Syde software and is supposed to be like a millionaire fifty times over?"

"The one and only." Holly dabbed Daniels' forehead with a moist sponge and replaced an intravenous bag from a pole. "He's our resident celebrity."

Since Holly didn't seem to mind, Maxx kept up the questions. "But how does someone with that much bank end up in a place like this? It doesn't make sense."

Holly pulled up Daniels' gown. "Hmmm. His feeding tube needs flushed." Maxx's question registered and she looked up. "I'd tell you but they'd fire me for sure."

Maxx looked away. He didn't want to know his programming idol that intimately.

"We wouldn't want to get you fired," Emi said. "It's just that we came a long way to see him and we weren't expecting to find him like this. Why doesn't his family throw a fit?"

Holly lowered his gown and checked the monitors. She removed a clipboard and jotted down a couple notes.

Satisfied with her charting, she answered. "He doesn't have any family. His wife died a while ago and it was just him. Everyone says that he lost his mind after that and ended up here." She replaced the board and checked her watch. "If you're not fans, then who are you two?"

Maxx edged Emi towards the door. "Uh, school newspaper. We wanted to do a story on him for our technology section and hoped to get an interview from him."

Holly rubbed cream around the patch on Daniels' neck. "Mr. Daniels hasn't spoken to anyone in a long time. His bills all get paid by that company he used to work for and their one stipulation is that he stays hooked into his computer program. It's in like a contract or something he has with them. We keep him alive with the feeding tubes and respirator and they pay his bills. That's all I really know. Sorry."

Emi watched a screen beside Daniels intermittently pulsing. "So he's basically brain dead?"

Holly's face lit up at that question. "Not at all. His brain functions are normal. Actually, they're above normal. Whatever he's doing in there, he's staying busy. Look, I have to check on my other patients. If they catch you two in here, they'll definitely call the cops. This is supposed to be pretty top secret and all. The other nurse on the floor is on break right now but if she sees you up here, you're toast. She's a real ball buster." Holly checked her watch. "You've got like five minutes."

"Thanks." Maxx waved as she closed the door.

Maxx bent over the bed rail and whispered, "Mr. Daniels?"

The only sound was the beeping monitors.

"I guess this is a dead end. How could O.S. Corporation just dump him here like this? They owe him everything," Maxx said.

"I don't know but we need to get out of here before that other nurse comes back." Emi reached for the light switch and motioned for Maxx.

"Clarissa!" Daniels' screamed. His hand locked onto Maxx's wrist and squeezed it so hard Maxx thought it was going to break.

Maxx pulled away and fell backwards.

"I think he's awake," Maxx said.

Emi rushed over but Daniels' eyes were closed and his breathing rhythmic.

She looked at Maxx. "I don't think so. He must've had a nightmare or something and it was an involuntary reflex. He's still out."

"Crap."

"Who's Clarissa?" Emi asked.

"I'm not sure. We'll have to ask Tane. He knows everything there is about Daniels."

"What now?" she asked.

Maxx started for the door. "I think we've done all we can here. Let's get home and see what Tane accomplished. Hopefully he did better than us."

Maxx stopped and snapped a picture of Daniels with his phone, casting a last look at his programming hero before shutting off the light.

"Did you two find what you're looking for?"

Smiling, Maxx turned toward the voice. "Yeah, Holly, we're done but do you have any idea who Clarissa is?"

Maxx met eyes with the glowering stare of Nurse Bonnie, the middle aged lady from the front desk. Instinctively, he pulled Emi behind him.

"Oh, Nurse Bonnie. We got lost trying to find our way out. How in the heck did we end up here?" Maxx looked over his shoulder at Emi. "I told you we didn't come up any stairs when we got here."

"I'm such a goof," Emi said.

"You two just stay put until the suits get here. I called them the minute I walked out of the lobby." She tapped her pen against a clipboard to accentuate the point.

Maxx backed Emi down the hall, moving away from the angry little woman.

Emi whispered in his ear, "What is she talking about? Suits?"

"I have no idea. Just keep moving until we hit the stairwell."

Nurse Bonnie pulled a small black device from her front pockets. She pressed a button on its side. "This whole building just went on lockdown. You two can run around all you want. You're stuck."

The door Maxx and Emi were inching towards swung open.

"There they are. Don't move."

Two men in dark suits came at them. They did not look friendly.

"Maxx?" The grip Emi had on his shoulder almost brought Maxx to his knees. "What are we going to do?"

"Stay calm…and run!" He grabbed Emi's hand and sprinted down the hall. Nurse Bonnie threw her clipboard at Maxx as they passed. He ducked as it struck the wall.

"Hey! That was *totally* uncalled for." Maxx sprinted towards the door at the opposite end of the hall. He hit the push bar and it swung open. They skidded to a stop at the landing. "Up or down?"

Emi almost pushed him over. "Are you kidding me? Down. Always go down."

They rounded the second floor landing.

"What's going on, Maxx?" she asked. "Since when does a nursing home rate security guards in suits?"

"I don't know. Let's get out of here first and figure it out later." Maxx was almost to the last step when he heard a door slam above them.

They ran out into the main hall and stopped. At the opposite end, he saw daylight streaming in from a crack in the fire exit door. Grabbing Emi's hand, he took off down the hall.

"Come on!"

The entire length of the corridor was probably about forty yards and Maxx was no football player but he figured they covered the distance in about four and a half seconds flat. He saw the wedge of wood bracing the door open and formed a ram with his arms in front of him. They hit the door on the fly.

Maxx wasn't sure what surprised him more, the blast of sunlight hitting him in the face, the sound of gunfire echoing behind them, or the look on Holly's face as she sat perched on a small cement bench taking a drag from her cigarette.

He hardly broke stride as they ran across the small courtyard and back out onto the main street in front of the rehab center. Crossing traffic, the two kept running for two blocks until Maxx felt safe no one was following them.

"Was someone shooting at us," Emi asked.

"Yeah, I'm pretty sure. Are you okay?" Maxx drew in a couple deep breaths.

"I'm fine. What have you gotten us into, Maxx?" Emi tried to laugh but he could hear her voice shaking. She pulled her inhaler from her pocket and took a couple breaths.

"I don't know but let's take a taxi back to the train station. I don't think we should be out on the streets." Maxx stood on the curb and waved down the nearest cab. "I think we've both had enough adventure for one day."

CHAPTER 24

"Tane, slow down." Maxx grabbed for his friend's shirt but missed.

Tane raced back and forth across Maxx's bedroom. He bumped into a chair and stumbled but kept moving.

Holding his hands up to his ears, Tane spoke almost as quickly as he walked. "This is unbelievable. It's unacceptable. That's what it is. It's like some kind of covernment gonspiracy. Like a virtual Area 51. This is the biggest internet related story since one of the guys who started HeadRoom got murdered. Eagger biven."

"It's not like Daniels is being held hostage by aliens," Maxx said.

Tane started another lap. "I thought you were just snowing me when you sent those texts. Ha. Ha. Play another trick on old Tane. Wo nay they would stick the guy who created the biggest virtual social network in the world in some grungy nursing ward."

Tane pit stopped and grabbed a Zinkle from an open box on Maxx's bed.

"Then you sent me that picture and told me about the goons with the guns. I figured, yeah, right, Maxx spinning another one of his tales but I ran a face recognition program on it and matched it up with other known photos of Daniels. It's him. Croley Hap. Somebody's got to put the word out on this. People need to know!" Tane accentuated his last statement by holding the Zinkle in the air.

Maxx shook his friend by the shoulders. "Tane!" He changed direction with his shaking. "You need to focus, buddy. We need your help here."

About the third or fourth shake, he started coming around. "But we have to tell everyone what they're doing," he said.

"We will but that'll have to wait." Maxx maneuvered him to the bed and forced him to sit on the mattress. "First, we need to get back into O.S. You were supposed to be working on a way for us to do that, remember?"

The door to Maxx's room opened and Emi walked in. He told her they'd meet up later after they got back from Newton City but he wasn't expecting her to just show up at his house, let alone his bedroom.

"You never told me how funny your dad was," she said.

Maxx twisted off the bed. "Oh yeah, he's...my dad? What?"

"He let me in. You didn't think I was going to crawl across your roof and scale in through your window, like you and bat boy." She stopped in front of Maxx's computer. "He was showing me some pictures of you when you were little. You actually smiled back then."

"Why were you talking to my Dad? Never mind. Can you help me get Tane focused?"

Emi looked Tane in the eye and rubbed her thumbs across his forehead. Almost immediately, the tension faded from his face.

"Tane? Look at me." She touched his cheek.

Tane closed his eyes and smiled.

"I'm okay, Emi. Thanks. Maxx told me what happened. Are you ok?"

"I'm fine. Maxx protected me." She patted him on the knee.

Glad to have his friend thinking straight again, Maxx asked, "What's in there?" He pointed to a black duffel bag on the floor.

Tane followed Maxx's finger. "Oh, yeah. I brought some extra gear to get us all back into O.S. and a portable hard drive big enough to run the ghosting program to keep us under the radar."

Maxx unzipped a compartment on the bag and poked around inside. "What do you mean all of us?"

Tane moved Maxx out of the way and removed two extra sets of syn-skin cables and threw them on the desk.

"You, me, and Emi. She texted and said she was coming along. She told me that you were okay with it," Tane said.

Maxx jumped up. "No way! It's way too dangerous. Talbot's after me but he'll hurt anyone that gets in his way. Emi, you are not going."

"Yes, I am." Emi casually leaned back and cupped her hands behind her head.

Her confidence stunned Maxx. "And what makes you so sure of that?"

She flung her legs off the bed and sat down in front of the computer.

She spun the chair in circles as she talked. "First off, you agreed to take me with you the next time you went into your computer world back at the Wash. Remember?"

"Yeah, I know I did but that was for a regular ghost hunting job before all this craziness-"

Emi cut him off during her next spin. "Second, if you don't agree, I go down stairs and tell your parents all about your internet adventures, the ghosts, Talbot, the nightmares and then we'll see how fast they pull the plug on you. Literally. Any questions?"

Maxx stood in awe. He'd definitely rubbed off on her. Emi gave a singular ha as she took one last victory lap in the chair.

"Maybe a career in law *is* a better choice for our ballet beauty?" Maxx asked.

Tane scattered the equipment on the floor and worked at installing it. Down on one knee, he plugged wires into Maxx's hard drive.

"You'd be good at most anything, Emi."

"Thank you, Tane." With her victory firmly in place, she sprung up and asked, "So, where is it exactly that we're going?"

"ZeeYoo PeeYoo," Tane said. "It's a cyber-club in the west district of O.S. As soon as I get everything booted, we can strap in and I'll put us right inside one of the service doors of the club."

Maxx threw a bean bag down near the desk. "And how's that supposed to get us to Daniels again?" He pointed to the corner of the room. "Emi, grab those pillows. We'll all need something to sit on before going in. There's nothing worse than coming back to a numb butt."

Emi tossed two oversized pillows at Maxx. He clumsily caught the first one but the second hit him square in the head.

Tane chuckled. "Nice shot, Emi. We're all set major dumb butt."

Maxx started to correct him. "That numb-"

"Yeah, I know. That one was on purpose. We're looking for the club owner, Ginger Tanner. She supposedly has a good location for Daniels inside O.S. At least that's what all my sources say."

Emi jumped into the center of the pillow stack. "Nice one, Tane. Dibs on the pillows."

Maxx dragged the bean bag over and settled into it. He plugged his syn-skin to his neck and helped put Emi's on.

"This is my first time, you know." She pulled her hair back.

Maxx smelled the traces of perfume on her neck. "Yeah, I kind of figured. Don't worry. No one will know who we are or that we were even there. Any problems and we just hit the jump switch and we're back in a flash."

Tane attached his own patch and fiddled with the portable hard drive cables. "Yeah…about that, the software that I modded for the ghosting program took a little more time than I was expecting. I didn't get to add in the jump program. We're stuck with the old fashioned fade." Tane looked everywhere in the room except at Maxx. "Sorry. It shouldn't be a problem though. We get the info we need and we get back out. I can add it into the programming before we go back again. The club closes down soon, so we need to get going."

Maxx trusted Tane when it came to technology and he wasn't willing to wait another day. The extra precautions would have been nice, especially with Emi tagging along, but he didn't expect any problems.

"Okay. We go in with what we got then. You ready, Emi?" Maxx waited for her to nod. "Good. Just close your eyes, try to relax, and count back from ten before you open them. You'll feel your neck tingling. It's just like Alice and rabbit hole."

"And which character does that make you?" Emi smiled.

"The Mad Hatter, of course." He pointed at Tane. "Okay, Dodo, take us in."

Tane pulled up the Other Syde homepage.

Maxx closed his eyes and listened to Tane's voice. "Okay, folks, please remember to keep your feet and arms inside of…"

CHAPTER 25

The entire room shook around her. The crowd noise and thumping house music drowned out whatever it was Tane was trying to say to her. Emi's senses were overwhelmed. She could smell the cigarette smoke and someone's citrus perfume. She opened her eyes and the flashing lights above her made her dizzy. She could feel the music's bass thumping in her chest. People, hundreds and hundreds of people, crowded the middle of a giant dance floor, bumping and grinding against each other. They were laughing and singing, bouncing in time to the rhythm.

"Tane? Maxx?" Emi felt her stomach do a somersault as she tried to adjust to the all the new sensations. They came at her likes waves in the ocean.

She stumbled, like a sailor on her first steps of shore leave. Completely out of rhythm with the pounding music, she looked up and shielded her eyes. The multi colored laser lights crisscrossed over her face.

Someone tapped her on the shoulder. "Shall we dance?"

"No thanks," she said.

Emi got stuck between a lean Goth boy with glowing red eyes and a large muscular man with a handlebar mustache in full body armor. They both danced around her like a carousel set on light speed. The club must have been the size of a football field but she felt the room closing in on her. She could pass out at any second.

"Come on, don't be such a newbie!" The man in the battle armor raised his shield above his head, letting out a war cry.

Emi tried getting away from the disco warrior and ran straight into the arms of the young vampire. His flowing white hair draped over his face.

Softly hissing, he bore his fangs. "Don't let that twelve sided fool bother you, pet. I'll keep you safe."

Emi screamed, "Maxx!"

Someone grabbed her by the arm and yanked her away from her pale protector. She slammed into their chest and looked up. It was Maxx. He looked a little older with more muscles and his hair was spiked even more than it usually was.

He looked her over and smiled. "Nice outfit, mistress of the night."

"Maxx? This is incredible. I didn't think it would be…like this. It's like I'm really here. I mean, *really* here. I can smell the smoke machines, hear the music, the lights, everything. It's hot in here. I think I'm sweating. Can I do that?" Emi asked.

She gawked at the mass of people throbbing around her, everyone in beat with the song blaring from giant ceiling mounted speakers. Every age and race, dressed in suits and robes, armor and costumes, danced and thrived to the music.

Emi stopped looking around long enough to notice her own outfit. "Tane! Where is he? I look like a hooker at a thrift sale!"

She twisted her foot inside the six inch red pump beneath her ripped black nylons. She brushed her hand across the red leather mini-skirt and matching top and pulled a strand of her new hair in front of her face.

"Platinum blond? Really?" Emi looked around for Tane while Maxx seemed to enjoy her frustration.

Tane appeared behind them. He kept his same boyish face and red hair, which stretched down past his shoulders and was pulled into a pony tail. He wore blue jeans, a white t-shirt, and black leather jacket.

Tane sheepishly smiled at her. "I'm sorry, Emi. We were going clubbing. I asked Ariana what to dress you in and she suggested that."

Maxx chimed in. "And what are you supposed to be, the illegitimate offspring of Richey Cunningham and the Fonz? Aaayyyyyyy!"

"Mite be, Maxx. I got us here, okay. The ghost program is working. We need to find the back office. That's where Ms. Tanner should be." Tane navigated through the crowd.

Maxx waved for Emi to follow, still criticizing his friend. "I'll put us right inside a service entrance, huh? We're lucky we didn't end up on the roof or in the women's bathroom."

"Let's just go, okay? Now you got me feeling self-conscious about what I'm wearing. I thought I looked tough." Tane's shoulders slumped.

Tane led the trio through the crowded floor of dancers, who quickly parted as someone Tane's size and looking ticked off came towards them.

Emi leaned closer to Maxx. "You really need to go easier on him. He's way too sensitive and believes too much of the crap you feed him."

Maxx sidestepped a green skinned female in a bikini as their moving mountain guide continued his pouting march through the crowd.

"He can't go through life as an overstuffed teddy bear or people will eat him alive."

At the edge of the dance floor, Emi pulled on Maxx's arm. She stared back at the mass of people gyrating behind her. She'd only been there for a few minutes and was still trying to get used to it all.

Emi bumped into Tane. "Sorry, this is all a bit much, guys."

Maxx held her hand as they crossed a section of tables and chairs. "You're right, Emi. You're getting the full effect all at once. You usually get dropped into a Newbie Center first and ease into it. It's like you jumped in the pool head first. Just try to stay close." He scooped a couple ice cubes from an empty glass and wrapped them in a napkin, handing them to her. "Here, it'll help."

Tane pointed to a padded door cut into material on the back wall. "My people said we had to go through the green door."

Maxx took the lead. "Through the green door? Are you sure you didn't fall asleep watching the no-no videos again?"

Emi pressed the napkin to her head and felt the cold against her skin. She focused directly in front of her, trying to drown out the rest of the crowd as water dripped down her cheek. They stopped in front of the wall. Maxx ran his hand across the material, looking for a knob or handle.

"Now what?" Maxx asked.

Tane did his own search for a way in. "I don't know. Nobody said there wouldn't be a door handle. We'll try knocking."

Tane pounded his fist against the door but even with his girth the knocking was muffled by the soft material.

"This probably isn't even the right door," Maxx said. "I think your buds on HeadRoom were messing with…"

A small portal opened and some guy looked out at them. White lightning bolts were dyed into his short black hair and he wore oversized round sunglasses outlined in diamonds.

"This is for VIP's only. You got a flash?" the boy asked.

Tane stepped up and gestured with his hands in the air. A blue trail followed his fingers and formed a glowing ankh.

The boy nodded. "Why didn't you just say so?"

The panel slid shut as a door opened out into the dance hall. Emi wondered how much about Tane she still didn't know. He continued to surprise her almost as much as Maxx.

Their impromptu doorman waived them through with a sweeping arm motion. "Beware all ye who enter."

They made their way down a small dark hall. Emi was glad to get away from the music. She enjoyed dancing as much as anyone but her senses needed a breather. At the end of the corridor, they made their way through another door and found themselves in a small lounge. Red shag carpet covered the floors and walls, giving background to multiple purple leather couches and overstuffed chaise loungers dispersed throughout the room. Plastic domes cast a dim yellow haze from the ceiling. A dozen patrons rested on the cushions of the surrounding furniture. All eyes shifted to the newest guests and remained there until the door closed. They returned to their private conversations. Emi had a sinking feeling in her gut.

"Okay, Tane, what now?" Maxx asked.

"We need to find Ginger. Just follow my lead," Tane said.

Tane headed toward a couple of guys and a girl talking in the corner. The girl's hair was pulled into thin spikes shooting out at all angles. Large areas of her scalp were exposed between the braids. Her dark skin canvassed the rainbow of colors painted under each eye. The neckline of her tight black jumpsuit dipped down to her navel and held the attention of both men sitting beside her. The guy to her right wore a white collared shirt underneath of a pullover sweater, completing the collegiate look with wire rim glasses casually hanging on the brim of his nose. The other guy's pale skin seemed out of place with his tie died knit cap and thick cornrows. Rows of gold chains hung from his neck, hanging out over his zippered down crushed velvet jacket and matching pants. None of them acknowledged Tane as he approached.

"Has anyone seen Ginger around?" Tane asked.

The exotic eyed girl finished her conversation with her scholarly suitor before looking in Tane's direction.

Tane repeated his question. "Ginger, is she around?"

Waving her suitors away, the spiky haired girl sipped a pink liquid from a martini glass, savoring her drink. "And who would I say is calling, love?"

Tane pulled at his jacket collar. "T Rad…and friends."

The girl raised her eyebrows, bringing each respective rainbow to an arch.

"T Rad, huh? I've heard of you." She took another drink.

Tane relaxed. "Really?"

"No." She motioned behind her.

Emi and Maxx spun around. Maxx smashed face first into a sea of chest hair. Dressed in a fitted black suit jacket with no shirt underneath, the gorilla man scowled beneath a well-trimmed red Mohawk. His bouncer twin, except for sporting his own neon green Mohawk, towered beside him. Emi wondered if they just stumbled in from the '80's.

Mohawk Red growled, "You need to leave. Now."

Maxx wiped his face and tried to compose himself. "Gentlemen, we're not looking for any problems, we're just trying to find-"

Mohawk Green cut him off. "Now you got a problem."

"Whoa!" Maxx threw his hands up in the air. "We just need to find Ginger. Give us a minute with her and we'll be out of here and you two can do some squat thrusts or something."

Mohawk Green grabbed Maxx's shoulder. Emi saw his knees buckle.

Mohawk Red grabbed Emi by her arm. "You're out of here too."

"Let me go you hairless ape!" Emi tried to pull away.

Mohawk Green wrenched Maxx into a headlock, forcing him towards the exit while his partner dragged Emi behind him.

"Maybe I should be asking for Chiyoko?" Tane shouted.

The lumbering doormen paid no attention and continued dragging Maxx and Emi towards the door. Tane cupped his hands around his mouth.

He shouted again. "I said, where's Chiyoko?"

A girl in the corner stood up. Blond hair pulled into pig tails touched her shoulders and her jean shorts were cut high enough that the front pockets were exposed. She had her red flannel shirt tied above her navel. The room stopped.

"Let them go." Her voice was casual and unassuming.

The Red and Green brothers abruptly released Maxx and Emi. Maxx tumbled to the floor but shot back up, straightening his shirt.

Emi punched her unwanted escort in the ribs. "Jerk."

The girl sauntered passed them, opening a door back out into the hallway. "Follow me."

Emi pulled up the rear as the group made their way back down the corridor.

Maxx leaned in towards his friends. "You want to fill me in on this? What happened back there?"

Tane whispered, "Chiyoko is her real name. She just goes by Ginger here. The girl that started this club is a fourteen year old Japanese native. She loves American culture and started the ZeeYoo PeeYoo Club six months ago. She doesn't want anyone to know who she really is and registered it under the name Ginger Tanner. I didn't want to embarrass her but didn't see that I had much of a choice."

Maxx grinned. "Nice work, Tane. Very smooth."

Tane let an involuntary smile slip. Chiyoko stopped near the end of the hall and waved her hand in front of the wall. A door appeared. Maxx and Tane followed her. Emi looked back down the hall before following them.

The small room was barely ten feet squared. A small wooden desk with a flat screen computer sat in the center. Chiyoko waited for them to wedge inside as the door disappeared behind them. She typed something onto the monitor. Emi watched the ambient light reflect on the young girl's face as the screen changed. Seemingly satisfied with her task, Chiyoko pushed her chair away from the desk.

"Did my parents send you?" she asked.

"Your parents didn't send us," Maxx said. "We're looking for information. If you give it to us, we're gone with nobody the wiser."

Chiyoko stretched her legs out. "What if I don't have this information you're looking for?"

Tane spoke up. "We know you have it. I…we confirmed it with independent sources and initial login documentation tracing your bio signature through genealogical records back to your home in Japan."

Maxx picked it up from there. "Look, we really need to speak with Nathaniel Daniels. We know he keeps a place in-world. If we don't, there's a good possibility that there won't be an Other Syde for any of us."

Chiyoko tapped her finger against the desk before pinching the screen with two fingers. The top layer of the monitor peeled away. She folded the translucent sheet into a square and flung it at Tane. He fumbled with it but eventually secured the map in his pocket.

Chiyoko crossed her legs. "That'll fade you directly in front of his house. We're settled up now, correct? Secret for secret?"

"What secret do you think we're hiding?" Maxx asked.

"People with no secrets don't run cloaking programs." Chiyoko smiled. "T Rad, huh?" Her eyes took an extra slow elevator ride up Tane. "Why don't you stay and have a drink? I'm sure your friends can find something to amuse their selves with."

Tane blushed. Emi figured it was a combination of being hit on in general and the fact she was a fourteen year old girl. He pushed Maxx and Emi towards the door.

"Maybe some other time. We really need to get moving," he said.

Tane herded them all the way back to the dance floor before Maxx planted his feet. "Easy, buddy, you're safe from the pubescent predator. Get the co-ordinates out so we can fade."

Maxx leaned against one of the lounge chairs as Tane retrieved the virtual directions.

"I got it." Tane turned to Emi. "You ready?"

Emi was looking at some beer nuts scattered on a nearby table. They danced across the glass top, popping intermittently into the air.

"Did you feel that?" she asked. "It feels like something trying to get into the…"

An explosion rocked the roof of the dance club. Debris rained down from a gaping hole in the ceiling. The virtual clubbers scattered, trying to avoid the falling pieces.

Emi grabbed Maxx's arm. "Maxx! What's going on?"

He pushed Emi and Tane away from the explosion and shouted, "I have no idea. Just keep moving."

Lights streamed down from the roof, cutting through the thick dust from the blast above.

A mechanized voice boomed, "Nobody move! This is a raid!"

The entrance doors surrounding the club were kicked in almost simultaneously as the room flooded with men dressed in brightly colored armor. Emi didn't need know who they were but it didn't take much to realize they were in trouble.

"O.S. Agents! Of all the lumb duck." Tane unfolded the digital map. "I got Emi, Maxx. Here's the address. We'll see you there."

He handed the digital sheet to Maxx while taking Emi's hand. Tane's brow wrinkled as he prepared to fade. Emi held Tane's hand and closed her eyes, counting back from ten like Maxx told her to back in his room.

"You're still here," Maxx said.

Emi opened her eyes. They were still inside of the club.

Tane looked at her. "I don't get it. I can't fade."

Maxx closed his eyes. His image blurred, becoming translucent for a moment but he couldn't leave either. She may not have known all the technical terms Maxx and Tane knew but it was pretty obvious things weren't going as planned.

The agents herded the party goers to the center of the room and called out commands through a megaphone. "Come on people, let's move it. We need everyone together for a bio scan so head to the middle of the floor."

Emi asked Maxx, "Well, what's the plan?

He exchanged glances with Tane and they came up with the same answer.

"Crap."

CHAPTER 26

"Don't look directly at the red light! Repeat! Red light is bad! Malo!" An O.S. Agent barked orders standing on a small stage in the club.

Maxx, Tane, and Emi were standing in the center of the dance floor along with several hundred other club patrons, crammed shoulder to shoulder. Maxx was used to thinking on his feet, that's where some of his best ideas came from, but between the crowd and the agents barking orders, it was all he could do to hold his own ground.

Maxx asked, "Why can't we fade out, Tane?" He shouldered a couple people away to gain some breathing room.

Even at Tane's size, people rammed against him. He raised his arms over his head. "I have no idea. I've never heard of any tech out there to keep people from exiting the program, let alone at this level. It's like when your blue nasty showed up and you couldn't fade."

Emi found a small safe spot wedged between her friends. She used Tane's shoulders to jump and look out into the crowd. "They have the whole place locked down. No one is moving and it looks like people are starting to panic."

Another O.S. Agent climbed up on a table and addressed the crowd. "This is a sanctioned O.S. Corporation raid due to the increased amount of non-paying users hacking their way into Other Syde. Prepare to submit to a mass bio-scan." He stepped off the table to a chair but then stepped back up. "Oh, yeah, thank you for your cooperation."

Maxx smacked Tane's arm. "I thought you said no one can hack into O.S.? Are you sure your ghost program will work?"

Tane shielded his eyes as a wave of red light flooded over the crowd. The beam crossed through the mass of party goers and small flashes of green sparked over certain people. The light flowed in their direction.

Tane watched the incoming beam. "I knew of a couple people who could but not this many. This is not good."

The amber ray washed over Maxx and his friends. They all blinked green. A group of agents pushed through the crowd and grabbed the three of them, none too gently. They were forced across the room to another section of the club, joining about two dozen other captive guests. The agent escorting Emi shoved her harder than he needed to. She fell to the floor.

Maxx rushed to her side. "Hey, tin soldier! You're probably a momma's boy living in her basement with an unhealthy obsession for kittens in the real world." Maxx helped her up. "Are you okay?"

The crowd around Maxx chuckled in response to him heckling the security agent.

Emi pushed her hair from her face. "I'm ok." She put up a brave smile.

Another flash of light rushed over Maxx and Emi, producing the same green flare effect. A foot crashed into Maxx's side, knocking him across the floor. He skidded to a stop on his stomach. Someone grabbed the back of his shirt and hoisted him off the ground. Dangling in the air, Maxx twisted around. He instantly recognized the guy holding him.

"Agent Ketchup, I should've guessed. You always seemed like a kick them from behind guy." Maxx struggled to break the agent's hold.

Ketchall's helmet visor was raised and he smiled. "What do you know? It looks like I get my Christmas early. I sign up for a little over time to round up hackers and end up with an O.S. top ten fugitive. The bounty on you and your tubby friend just became the down payment on my new boat." He dropped Maxx to the ground. "Are you finding it hard to fade out of here?"

Maxx rushed Ketchall, bumping chests with him. "You can't keep us here against our will. That has to be a crime. And I mean a real crime, not your cyber junk."

"You're trespassing on O.S. Property, Fragnelli," Agent Ketchall said. "We have every right to keep you, dough boy, and your trashy girlfriend here until we contact the outside authorities and they show up at your house and take you into custody. I'm sure they'll seize all your computer equipment while they're at it. You're toast, kid."

Ketchall hailed another agent and they led Maxx and his friends through the crowds of captive people and out of the club into a waiting transport outside. Shoving them into the back of the vehicle, Maxx watched as agents escorted more rogue gamers outside. Ketchall climbed into the driver's seat and looked over his shoulder.

"Buckle up for safety."

They sped away. Everything happened too fast. Maxx tried to focus but drew a blank for possible escape plans. Things were just starting to come together but fell apart in a blink. How could the night get any worse?

As a joke or by coincidence, they wedged Tane behind the driver's seat, leaving him the smallest amount of leg room. One knee was crammed between the door pillar and driver's seat and the other angled out into the seat.

"How did O.S. get the tech to keep people from fading back out of the program?" Tane asked. "I've never even heard a rumor of anything like that on the net."

Ketchall darted through an intersection with the lights and sirens activated. He looked over his shoulder and answered Tane's question. "It's a little something we've been working on, cotton ball. O.S. is tightening down on illegal activity here in-world. We've got some big things coming up and the higher ups don't want anyone thinking that we can't control our own little chunk of the cyber-verse. This time next year, O.S. Corporation will be the most powerful company the world has ever seen."

Emi sat sandwiched in the middle and Maxx saw the tears streaming down her cheeks. She hung her head down so it wasn't obvious but finally met Maxx's stare.

Sniffling, she said, "This is going to ruin everything. Nobody's going to give a scholarship to a felon. My mom and dad will win. I can kiss my dreams of dancing goodbye."

Ketchall adjusted the rear view mirror to get a better look at her. "Don't cry, little criminal. I'm sure Mommy and Daddy will understand, after you spend a couple years in jail. Maybe you can be a professional exotic dancer?"

"You are one low class piece of crap, Ketchup." Maxx fixed eyes with him in the mirror. "Do you really have such a fragile ego that you even get off on making girl's cry? Why don't you give me your real world name and address and you and I will settle up when this is done?"

Ketchall cut the wheel and darted down a side alley. "You still don't get, do you? This is it for you, Fragnelli. You're criminally trespassing on our site. You won't be bothering anyone until they release you from jail in five to ten years."

Maxx pulled Emi close and whispered, "Don't worry. We'll figure something out. They don't even know who you are. You never had an O.S. account. Don't tell them anything if they separate us. Got it?"

Emi nodded.

The transport pulled up to a glass and steel skyscraper. The letters O and S stood five stories tall and shined a yellow haze for half a block on either side. No front doors were visible and the vehicle drove passed the façade and turned into an adjacent alley. Ketchall navigated the car up to a cargo door as the gate opened. Pulling inside an interior parking garage, they stopped near a set of elevator doors.

Ketchall opened his door. "End of the road. All delinquents get out."

He pulled Maxx and his friends out of the back of the transport and escorted them to the elevator. Ketchall flashed a beam from his forearm and the doors opened.

Ketchall totally enjoyed the whole scenario. Maxx searched Ketchall's belt for some type of weapon.

The agent followed his eyes. "Don't even think about it, Fragnelli. You're in deep enough. Take it like a man and admit you're beat."

Exiting the elevator, the hall was lined with transparent cell doors on either side. Maxx stared into each room as they passed. Some were empty but most held other O.S. captives. Ketchall flashed the same signal from his arm and one of the doors slid open. He motioned like a bellhop as they trudged passed him into the cell.

"What? No tip?" Ketchall laughed as the door slammed shut. He strutted back down the hall. "I'll be back when the authorities get to your house so I can say goodbye, slacker."

Maxx watched him get back on the elevator. "Man, I hate that guy."

Maxx checked out his new surroundings. Metal benches were attached to the floor along two of the walls. A panel light was embedded into the ceiling. Other than that, the room was bare.

"Tane, any ideas?" Maxx asked.

Tane sprawled out on one of the benches. "There's a keypad behind you on the door. It won't help us much unless you happen to know the code." He thumped the back of his head against the seat and waited for Maxx to answer. "I didn't think so."

Maxx examined the electronic alpha-numeric pad. No screws or any type of mounting hardware was visible. He punched a couple of the keys at random and a light above the pad turned red and blinked.

Maxx asked, "What's the chance of cracking it?"

Tane pulled his legs up and settled into his metal perch. "It's a ten digit pad, both numbers and letters. Not likely."

Emi sat on the other bench and tucked her feet under her legs, sitting Indian style. She tapped her fingers rhythmically against the metal. "This isn't good, Maxx. I think they have us. The police are going to show up at your mom and dad's and find us all conveniently in your room hooked up to this stupid computer program and take us away and there's nothing we can do about it. I wish that Nathaniel Daniels guy would never have made this stupid place and we never went looking for him." Emi put her face in her hands.

Maxx hung his head and stared at the floor. He'd let down his friends and for the first time in their whole crazy adventure, he started to think they really were beaten. His brother, his brother's killer, Agent Ketchall, his mom and dad, Tane, Emi, and everything else weighed down on him. If only they could have spoken with Daniels, they may have gotten the upper hand. He still felt that Daniels was the key to it all.

Maxx's head snapped up. He pulled Emi's hands away from her face, and saw the tears in her eyes.

"Emi, you're our new resident genius," he said. "Tane, you're fired."

"What are you talking about?" Emi asked.

Maxx walked back to the keyboard and start pressing buttons. The red light blinked but Maxx kept entering codes. The light glowed red again and Maxx paused before entering something else.

The door slid open and he triumphantly faced his friends, raising both arms in the air. "Sometimes I even impress myself."

Tane peeked out between his tangled arms. "How?"

Maxx strode out into the hall and made the same sweeping motion that Ketchall performed moments before. "Clarissa. Daniels called out his wife's name when Emi and I were in his room. Every good programmer keeps a backdoor into his creations. A computer nerd friend of mine taught me that. I just had to figure out how Daniels spelled it."

Emi kissed Maxx on the cheek on the way out. "Not bad, Maxx Fragg."

They started for the elevator but Maxx stopped. Tane and Emi were ahead of him and they looked back when they reached the doors.

Tane whisper-yelled, "Come on, Maxx. Let's go."

"I have a better idea," he said.

CHAPTER 27

"I get the whole diversion thing but why are we headed the wrong way." Emi stumbled along after Maxx through the crowded hall of recent escapees.

Tane followed a couple steps behind. "Yeah, Maxx, this is our best chance out of here. We need to make a break for it."

Maxx ignored him and led Emi against the flow of people to an exit door at the end of the hall. He didn't have time to explain and they may not want to hear what he had to say. Entering the stairwell, Maxx pulled Emi up the steps. A red warning light flashed overhead.

She pleaded with him. "We need to get out, not go up. Remember the nursing home? Up bad! Unless you're packing some virtual parachutes, you're going to get us trapped."

Maxx came down a step and rested his hand on the railing.

He drew a deep breath. "Look, I know. You two heard Ketchall. The real world authorities are on their way to my house right now. If we don't find something to hold over these guys than what's it going to matter if we get out of this building or not. They're just going to have us arrested and then they win. I'm not willing to let it end that way, not after all we've been through. First the guy that killed my brother comes back from the dead and attacks me, then I actually see my brother, me and Emi find Daniels trapped in a coma in some ratty old age home, and now O.S. is trapping all these people inside their program at will.

Something is definitely not right with this place and I'm going to find out what it is. It's the only way for us to win."

"This isn't a game, Maxx," Emi said. "There's no winning or losing. Maybe we can tell the cops everything you just said. They'll investigate O.S. and let us go."

Tane touched Emi's shoulder. "He's right, Emi. The only way for us to get out of this is to find out what they're hiding. I want to run out of here as much as anyone but Maxx is right. We've got to do this."

Tane headed up toward the next landing, taking the steps two at a time.

Maxx reached out for Emi. "Trust me?" He knew it was a lot to ask but all they had at that point were each other.

She sighed and took his hand. "Do you even know where to look?" They hurried up the stairs after Tane.

"The same place every company keeps their dark secrets, the penthouse," Maxx said. He hoped he sounded more confident than he actually was. What they were doing was a gamble at best but he didn't see any other choice. He hoped Jason was somewhere out there watching out for them.

They jogged up another ten floors before Tane cracked open a door and poked his head into the hall.

"You see anything?" Maxx asked.

"It looks clear." Tane waved them in behind him.

Red lights revolved at intervals along the ceiling and they found another set of elevator doors. Tane punched in the lettered equivalent of *Clarissa* on the key pad and the doors opened. Maxx looked over a company directory inside the elevator.

"That's convenient." Maxx read the list of names and offices. "Research and Development – Alpha Authorization, that sounds promising to me." He pressed the button.

Emi caught her breath against the back wall and asked, "What happened to the penthouse?"

"You heard Ketchall, they're working on something world changing," Maxx said. "That's where we're going to find it."

"Let's just hope no one's around," Tane said.

The corridor was dark as the doors slid open. The same red warning lights revolved above them. The trio worked their way down the hall, reading the placards on the doors as they passed.

"Anything?" Maxx asked.

Tane stopped and read the sign above the door opposite Maxx. "I don't think the supply closet is going to help us."

A young man in a lab coat walked into the hall a couple doors down.

Noticing the group, he stopped. "Hey, who are you?"

Never breaking stride, Maxx walked towards him. Moving out of the shadows, he morphed his clothing from club attire into a conservative business suit and tie.

"I could ask you the same question. This whole area is supposed to be clear. Didn't you hear we had a security breach? We're on lockdown," Maxx said.

The man pulled his eyeglasses down from his forehead as Maxx got closer.

"What do you mean lockdown? They said it was just a bunch of club kids who got loose in the building. How'd you get up here?"

Maxx grabbed the man's name badge attached to his jacket.

"Stevens, Jacob, huh? We took the elevator, Mr. Stevens. How else do you suppose we got up here? We didn't fly. We're doing a security clearance on the priority levels. You shouldn't be here. It's dangerous."

Stevens stepped back, causing the string connecting his name tag to his jacket to pull away from Maxx's grip and snap against his chest.

"Ow. But this floor is restricted. What do you mean dangerous?"

Maxx invaded his personal space a little further and whispered in his ear. "Can I trust you, Stevens?"

"Of course, I've been with the company for ten years."

"They aren't just *club kids*," Maxx said, finger parenthesizing the last part. "Some of them are industrial spies from Zero Corp. They got wind our agents were hitting that particular club tonight and infiltrated to get access to our building. We're with Other Syde Internal Investigations trying to figure out where the leak came from. We figure some of the Zero Corp people will try to meet up with their snitch somewhere in the building to break into our defenses. That's why we're doing a sweep. What did you say you were doing up here by yourself again?"

Tane and Emi transformed their clothing to match Maxx's outfit and stepped out of the shadows.

Stevens cleared his throat. "I had to secure the project. That's all. It's what I do. I don't even know anyone over at Zero."

Maxx put a reassuring hand on his shoulder. "Okay, I believe you. Besides, we have your name. We'll be running some checks to verify your story. If you're telling us the truth then you have nothing to worry about. I need you to go down to street level with everyone else until we get all the sectors secure. It shouldn't be long."

Stevens nodded but he held his ground. "But we're never supposed to leave the project alone."

"Uh...that's why we're here, Mr. Stevens. We've got a half dozen O.S. Agents on the floor below us finishing up and then they'll be up here until we get everyone back inside." Maxx helped turn Stevens around and half-pushed him down the hall. "It'll be fine. We know how important the project is to this company. Nothing will go wrong."

Maxx pushed the stairwell door open and escorted Stevens down the first couple steps.

"But it's almost fifty floors down." Stevens protested but kept going.

"Sorry, it can't be helped. Elevators are compromised. Try to pace yourself."

Maxx allowed the last few words to echo behind him as the door shut. He dragged a giant potted plant from the corner and braced it against the door.

"Now, let's find out what the project is." Maxx reverted his clothing back to his work outfit.

Tane followed suit and looked over at Emi.

"I hope you don't mind that I helped you change." Tane stared at the floor. "Since you're so new, I kept some access to your avatar in case you needed a hand."

"I wondered how that happened. How do I do it myself?" Emi looked over her pants suit.

"It's easy," Tane said. "You just concentrate on the clothes you want and they appear."

Emi closed her eyes and her outfit transformed into a sleek black jumpsuit similar to the ones Maxx and Tane wore.

She admired her handiwork. "Not bad, even if I say so myself. Sorry, Tane, I needed to go back to my natural hair color. Cheap prostitute blond wasn't cutting it."

"I'd never call you cheap." Maxx grinned as he came back down the hall.

Emi laughed. "I can't believe people fall for your crap. Double agent industrial spy club kids?"

Maxx was glad to hear her laugh after the trip over in Ketchall's transport and watching her cry. "Emi, I'm sorry I got you into…"

Emi placed her finger on his lips. "Save the apology until you get us out of this mess. Then I'm thinking you owe me a lobster dinner."

"It's a deal."

Maxx pushed the glass doors open to the room Stevens walked out of. They stood on a narrow metal platform twenty feet above the floor. The room was immense and empty except for the cat walk. A set a metal stairs led down to the lower level at each end of the narrow bridge. Below the grating housed a network of wires and tubing that fed into a giant metal five pointed symbol standing fifteen feet tall on the floor below. The device's center billowed with green lights and flowing vapors. A dull vibrant humming seethed from the machine.

"Wow." Tane stopped a couple steps inside.

Maxx walked to the middle of the catwalk and leaned over the railing to get a closer look. "You said it, buddy. I'd say this is definitely the project but what is it? It looks like a big star. Do you think it's a worm hole or something to do with space?"

Emi stretched down beside Maxx. "It's a pentagram."

"You mean like the Jewish Star of David?" Maxx asked.

Tane came up behind them. "Not really. The pentagram, also known as the pentalpha or pentangle is associated with the Jewish faith but also has ties to Christianity, Freemasonry, Wiccans, Neo-pagan faiths, and links to ancient Greece and Babylonia. Look, there's some type of control column."

Maxx leaned back up. "How'd you know all that?"

"I spend hours on the web every night." Tane shrugged. "I'm a virtual encyclopedia of random knowledge. That and I dated a Wiccan from Canada a couple months back, so I figured I'd better check up on it." He stopped in front of the control pedestal, which consisted of a screen and keyboard. "The shape is facing upside down. That symbolizes the physical world holding dominance over the spiritual. Let's see what we have here."

Emi stood on the platform, transfixed by the glowing mists. "What happened to the girl?"

"The wiccan? She wanted me to be part of some type of ritual ceremony thing she was doing. It kind of freaked me out, so I cut it off," Tane answered.

"She wanted to sacrifice him," Maxx said.

"It wasn't a sacrifice. Admittedly, there was some bloodletting involved." Tane shuddered but continued working.

Emi turned to Maxx. "Do you think this has anything to do with the ghost that killed your brother and keeps attacking you?"

"I don't know but seems awful weird for a pentagram to be in the middle of the biggest cyber system in the world," Maxx said.

"Oh, it's no coincidence. Look here." Tane waved them over. "Thanks to Daniels password, I got full access to their files. It looks like Daniels was working on a way to open a gateway to the great beyond. He was mixing cyber and the arcane arts in some pretty cool ways. It's machinery being powered by magic. He was trying to find a way to contact his wife. He made some real breakthroughs but then his notes just stopped and a bunch of other O.S. scientists took over."

Maxx read over his friend's shoulder. "Isn't that about the time the papers say Daniels broke away from O.S. and disappeared?"

"More like they made him disappear." Emi leaned on Tane's other shoulder to see the screen.

Tane scrolled down. "Man, it looks like they've had some success with it. There are notes about bringing ghosts into the cyber world, like the barrier between there and here isn't as solid as the real world. There are over a hundred documented transfers. That's what they call them. This is unbelievable. It could change the world."

"So it really was Jason. He's here somewhere." Maxx stared at the glowing mass inside the pentagram. "Tane, do you have a way to download all that?"

Tane wrinkled his brow, noticeably insulted by the question.

Maxx nodded an apology. "Ok, download everything you can and send a back-up to your encrypted personal email. This is more than enough to get O.S. off our backs. They won't want anyone knowing about this before they're ready to tell. We arrange a sit down with them and negotiate. I get to see my brother, clear our files, and call off the authorities, all of it. Now *we* have the upper hand."

The door to the outer hall slid open. Two shadowed figured stepped inside.

"Oh, I wouldn't go that far, Mr. Fragg."

CHAPTER 28

"You will go nowhere until I have given you permission to do so."

A man stepped onto the crosswalk and casually slid his hand along the railing as he approached Maxx and his friends. Only the outline of his suit and reflection from his wire rim glasses were visible. An O.S. Security Agent followed him, his armor tinted grey and black. An energy arc sparked across the agent's chest.

They stopped in front of Maxx. "I suppose I should be honored to finally meet you, Mr. Fragnelli. You are something of an urban legend around the office coolers here. You're a regular cyber-Abernathy. Isn't that right, Mr. Case?"

The agent grinned, his eyes hidden under his visor. "He looks like another punk kid to me, sir."

The man scoffed, "I suppose he would, Mr. Case. Would that make me the special agent who catches you? It would appear so and I, like the FBI, always get my man."

"Does your wife know about that?" The guy exuded confidence, which made Maxx nervous. "I mean, I'm flattered but it's much too early in the season for me to make those kinds of decisions."

Maxx looked back at Emi and Tane. Tane pulled the portable drive from the control port and hid it in his fist.

"Maxx, we don't need to offend this guy. Sorry, sir, we don't want any trouble. We just want to fade back home."

The man extended his hand to Emi. She paused but tentatively accepted the gesture.

He kissed the back of her wrist. "My apologies, dear girl, I didn't intend to be rude. I am Johan Silver and I am the C.E.O. of O.S. Corporation. It is a pleasure."

He bowed and Emi returned a nervous smile.

"It's nice to meet you, Mr. Silver. I'm Danielle," she said.

Silver's grin lengthened. "I do not like to be lied to, Ms. Briggs, or more precisely, Emily SummerRose Briggs, daughter of Diana Briggs and Jonathan Russell Briggs III, nineteen years of age, born in Newton City, attended Wallace Elementary School and Franklin High School, currently employed with Briggs Insurance Agency with an application pending at New Brighton Fine Arts Academy."

Emi stepped back. "How did you know all that? This is my first time here."

Silver turned to his armored bodyguard. "Always the same, Mr. Case, all bark and no bite." Producing a white handkerchief from an inner pocket, he wiped his hands. "I see you do not share in the inherent ability to lie that your associate, Mr. Fragg, has instilled in him. You should choose better companionship if you are not willing to accept the consequences of their actions, Ms. Briggs."

Silver glanced down at Tane's hand.

"You can't keep us here, Silver," Maxx said. "We have the dirt on your secret project down there but I'm willing to negotiate our release in exchange for the information."

Silver tucked his hanky into his pocket and walked passed them to center of the catwalk.

He gazed at the metal pentagram below them. "I never said you weren't clever, boy, just naïve. Imagine the possibilities this technology will bring to humanity. Families will be reunited with their loved ones. The great secrets of history revealed from the very persons who lived it. The most influential artists and writers will again infuse our society with fresh ideas, men of influence, in politics, in business, science and military, all waiting to reach out to us. And our company will control the meeting room. Here inside of this program, it will be as if time itself has lost its hold on mankind. Death will be an adjustment, not an end. The ramifications are endless."

"Yeah, I can't wait to have the ghost of Hitler running around again." Tane's face reddened as he flushed with anger. "There's an equal amount of bad that comes with all the hype you're spewing."

Silver remained focused on the metal structure beneath him, hypnotized by the swirling mists and the possibilities they contained.

"There are certain setbacks, some stumbling blocks, that we've taken into consideration but we're taking the proper precautions for those eventualities, I assure you. We will be in complete control of the process."

Emi shook her head. "You're dealing with powers way beyond anyone's control, Mr. Silver. Who gave you that right?"

Silver chuckled. "The same powers that first gave man the knowledge to strike flame, to launch a craft into space, or even split the atom. It's evolution, dear girl. It's progress. Humanity is compelled to move forward and evolve. This is the next step."

"Well good luck with that, Dr. Cyberstein." Maxx herded his friends to the end of the platform. "My friends and I would just like to go home. How about we schedule an appointment for the morning and we can discuss our terms of confidentiality? I have a few stipulations I need to hash out."

"I'm afraid that is not going to happen, Mr. Fragg. No one is leaving here until I get the information your friend just downloaded. After that, we will wait for the real world authorities to contact us and take you all into custody. That is the only deal you'll be getting tonight."

Silver turned from the railing and motioned for Agent Case.

Maxx pointed at Silver. "This is kidnapping. You can't keep us here against our will."

Case's hand crushed against the back of Maxx's neck. "Just relax, hack-boy. Don't make this more difficult than it has to be. I have no problem hurting you."

Silver pulled a device from his pocket and read something on the screen. "Oh, I can keep the three of you here as long as I want, just like I could keep this whole city trapped here if I chose to. Once you're inside of these virtual walls, you belong to the O.S. Corporation, which means me."

Emi backed along the platform beside Tane. "Maxx? Tell me you two have a backup plan?"

Tane tried to shield her behind him. "It's okay, Emi. Maxx will think of something."

Maxx's eyes met Tane's. He knew the blank expression on his face told Tane everything he needed to know. He had nothing. Agent Gorilla-grip had him practically pinned down to the catwalk. Emi and Tane were stuck between them and Silver and Tane held their only chance at getting out of this in his hand, literally. Maxx tried to fade out but his body only shimmered for a second. He remained firmly in the agent's grasp.

"Nice try, Fragg," Agent Case said as he applied extra pressure.

"Worth a shot," Maxx grimaced.

Tane looked at Maxx. He took Emi's hand and smiled at her. "There's always plan B."

"What's plan B?" Emi asked.

"This!" Tane shouted.

He pushed Emi aside and lunged at the agent holding Maxx down. Tane caught him by surprise in a giant bear hug and the two of them toppled over the railing, crashing towards the floor below. Case activated a set of boot thrusters but Tane held on and his added weight sent them crashing across the laboratory floor. They slammed into the far wall with a deafening thud. Case tried to get up but Tane held on tight.

He screamed up to his friends. "What are you waiting for? Run!"

Maxx grabbed Emi's hand and they sprinted toward the door. Emi leaned over the railing as they ran, searching for Tane in the darkened laboratory below.

"We can't just leave him," she said.

Maxx yanked her through the lab door leading out into the hall. "We don't have a choice. If we don't get out, then none of us do. Come on!"

***

Silver's smile faded as he watched the two of them run out the laboratory doors. He snapped open the radio strapped to his side and barked orders into it.

"They've escaped. I want all exits sealed. I need agents up here immediately. The boy and girl do not leave this building. Block all fading into or out of the city until you hear otherwise from me. Yes. All of it."

Silver looked down at Agent Case, who was still wrestling with Tane on the floor.

"Would you please neutralize that buffoon?"

Case nodded to his employer and pinned Tane down. The spark coursing across his chest energized and surged, sending waves of energy through Tane's body. Tane convulsed and shook on the ground.

"I got him, sir."

The charge fluctuated across Tane's chest. He reached for the agent's leg, whispering before losing consciousness.

"Might like a fan, wuss."

***

Maxx kicked open the door. He and Emi sprinted up ten flights of stairs before stopping. Maxx leaned against the wall.

"I can't believe he did that. He sacrificed himself for me...for us." Maxx put his hands on his knees and tried to catch his breath.

Between gasps of air, Emi asked, "Do you think we should go back?"

Maxx looked down over the railing. "We can't. The best thing we can do to help him is get out of this place."

Emi joined him at the rail. Maxx felt her heart beating wild as she leaned against him.

He held his breath. "Listen. Someone's coming up."

The sound of footsteps and voices echoed below them. Pin points of lights swarmed against the walls several floors down. Maxx made out a few words as the men gained ground.

"Make sure someone tells Silver that an immediate response would be a lot easier if he didn't shut down all the elevators."

"Why don't you tell him when we get up there?"

"I can't wait to get my hands on Fragg again."

Maxx recognized the last voice as Agent Ketchall's and motioned for Emi to follow him.

"It looks like we're going up again," Maxx said.

They sprinted up the steps two at a time for the next six floors before they had to slow down.

Emi grabbed the railing as they turned the next platform. "I know this question is getting old but do you have any idea how we're getting out of this building from the roof?"

"Not really but I'm working on it," Maxx said.

"Well you better think fast," she said. "It looks like we made it to the top."

They stopped on a small landing in front of a metal fire door. Maxx pushed the center bar and it opened out.

He ran outside and stopped. "Wow."

He felt Emi come up beside him.

They stared out into the city's night line. The O.S. Headquarters was the tallest building in the city and from that vantage the entirety of the virtual landscape spread out before them.

"It's beautiful," Emi said.

Maxx felt an unexpected peace. He felt the warmth of Emi's touch as she held his hand. The suddenness of the moment made it all the more special and he was glad it was her by his side to share it with. He wanted to stay there with her on the rooftop and forget everything else, no crazy blue ghosts, no agents with a grudge, no Other Syde, just the two of them.

"I think someone's up on the roof!"

Maxx let go of Emi and shut the access door, bracing a metal bar between it and a nearby ventilation shaft. He pulled Emi over to the roof's ledge and peered down the hundred floor drop to the street.

"You sure know how to woo a girl. Any luck with fading yet?" Emi asked.

Maxx tossed a pebble over the side and watched it fall. "I've tried. Whatever tech O.S. is using to keep us here applies to the roof too. If what Silver said is true, there might not be any place to fade from."

Following the stone's course down the side of the building, Emi said, "So we're trapped, again. This is becoming a recurring theme here.

Everything we've been through tonight and we get stuck on the roof. Really?"

The door handle turned. They both spun around. It cracked open an inch. Someone forced a shoulder into it.

"Something's jamming it from the outside. Blast through it."

A burst of energy blew the handle off. It skidded across the roof. An armored hand poked through the hole and felt around the outside of the door.

Emi brushed her hair back. "It looks like this is our last stand, Sundance. Just make sure you write me in prison. I hope it's not like in the-"

"Do you trust me?" Maxx stared into her eyes.

"What?" Emi asked.

"You heard me." Maxx squeezed her hand.

"Of course I do…I mean other than getting me into this mess," she said. "What's the plan?"

Another blast blew the top hinges off the door.

"We jump." Maxx waited for her reaction. "I have a plan."

"Are you crazy?" Emi protested but stepped up on the roof ledge with him.

She wrapped her arms around his waist and closed her eyes. "I hate you, Maxx."

"I know."

He jumped off the ledge, holding Emi in his arms.

She screamed as they plummeted down the side of the skyscraper.

A dozen O.S. Agents filtered through the smoking doorway, searching the rooftop. One of them spoke into a transmitter on his wrist.

"Roof is clear. There's no sign of anyone up here." He turned to the others. "I could've sworn I heard voices."

CHAPTER 29

"You have to do exactly what I say! Got it?"

Maxx squeezed Emi tight in his arms. They were free falling a thousand feet from the roof of O.S. Headquarters, plummeting towards the street.

Emi buried her head in his chest. "This is a hell of a time to be giving instructions!"

Maxx saw their reflections racing passed the building's tinted windows, adding a degree of surrealism to their situation.

He shouted in her ear. "Just hold on to me. Right before we hit the ground, I'm going to fade us out and then back in. It'll feel a little weird. Don't worry. I've done it before."

"But you said we couldn't fade- "

"Not now!" Maxx concentrated on the fast approaching pavement. This may have been his craziest stunt to date. Maxx knew the standing rule was no one could actually get hurt inside O.S. but with Talbot's appearance and O.S. Corporation pulling their strings, he wasn't so sure anymore. Emi squeezed tighter. She put her faith in him. He hoped it wasn't a mistake.

"7...6...5...4...3...2..."

Both of their images blurred and then vanished ten feet above the sidewalk. They re-emerged a split second later and several feet lower. Their momentum reset, they dropped the rest of the way down. It didn't work as well as it should but hopefully enough. Maxx took the brunt of the impact, landing feet first and then falling backwards with Emi on top of him. Tumbling across the sidewalk, they rolled out into the street and stopped. Maxx ended up on top of Emi, her back against the pavement and her eyes closed tight.

"You can look now, Butch," he said.

Emi opened one eye, gazing suspiciously around. "We're not road pizza? Huh, go figure."

She made it up to one knee when an air horn blared behind them. Maxx grabbed her and yanked her back onto the sidewalk. A stretch limousine whisked passed, blowing Emi's hair in its wake.

Maxx helped her to her feet. "After all that and you want to get taken out while jay walking. Some city mouse you turned out to be."

They ran across the street, passed the front of the O.S. headquarters, and rounded the corner into an alley.

"You sure know how to entertain a girl," she said. "This beats my back of the van pizza and soda by a mile. I thought we couldn't fade anymore?"

Maxx rubbed his head and sat on a metal box. "We can't fade out of the program but I figured we could do it enough to reset our synselves. I hoped the half second or so would be enough."

"You hoped? You mean you weren't sure?"

"I was pretty sure."

Emi laughed softly. "Okay, what now? We still need to figure a way out of here."

"I know. I'm working on it. Since we can't fade out of O.S., we need to find Daniels inside the program and show him what his former employer is up to. The only problem is that Tane had the coordinates and thumb drive with him. I'm kind of at a loss."

"You mean these?" Emi reached into the waistband of her jumpsuit and produced a glowing red square and metal rectangle.

"How?" Maxx took the items from her. The jump drive was cracked into two pieces but the digital map seemed intact.

Emi noticed the ruined drive. "It must have broken when we landed. Sorry. Tane slipped them to me when he took my hand back in the lab." Emi caught her reflection in a window in the alley. "Oh my god, I'm a virtual virtual mess." She swiped a finger across each eye to wipe away the smeared makeup.

Maxx tucked the pieces of the portable drive into his pocket and unfolded the digital map. Maybe he really did underestimate Tane. He'd been surprising him a lot lately. "It's okay. The information isn't any good without Tane. He's the only one that can access his encrypted account. I'll take what I can get at this point. Okay, this looks easy enough. It shouldn't take long to get there."

He tugged Emi away from the glass while she worked on her hair.

"Okay, just promise me that was the last one hundred story sky dive." Emi ran her hand over her bangs.

A man walked up to them as they exited the alley. In his twenties and dressed in jeans and a long black overcoat, he faded and re-appeared every few steps. He stopped in front of them, sweat dripping from his forehead.

His eyes were blood shot and his voice cracked. "I can't get out of here. The computer won't let me leave. I need to get out of here. I have to take my shot."

He continued fading in and out while he spoke. Maxx tried to touch the man's shoulder but he wouldn't stay corporeal long enough to make contact.

"I don't know. Why don't you quit trying for a little while?" Maxx gave his best reassuring smile. "Maybe they're just having a glitch in the system. Give it ten or fifteen minutes. I'm sure they'll have it worked out."

The man focused on Maxx's words and they appeared to calm him. Nodding, he stopped trying to fade.

"Yeah, you're right. Of course you are. I'm going to get a coffee until they get it fixed. I'm sure they're working on it. Thanks." He half-heartedly waved at Maxx as he crossed the street.

"This is not good," Emi said. "They can't keep everyone trapped in here. People are going to start freaking out."

"Yeah, I know. We better get moving since we're travelling by foot power," Maxx said.

They started down the sidewalk as a car alarm caught their attention. A black luxury sedan smashed into a lamp post a few feet away.

The driver screamed at some guy. "You walked right into the street. I thought you were fading but you came right back in. Do you know how much this is going to cost me?"

The errant pedestrian turned to the driver, raising his hand up to his face, which faded out and then reset. He was totally oblivious to the man arguing with him. Maxx noticed small groups gathering all around them on the street. People randomly faded and came right back. Most of the conversations centered on the programming problems. This had the potential to turn into total chaos and fast. Maxx knew they needed to get off the streets.

A voice echoed down from above. All conversations stopped.

"Attention. Your attention, please. We here at the Other Syde Corporation would like to apologize for the service interruption you are currently experiencing. This is a temporary inconvenience that we'll have resolved shortly. We will be running random large scale bio scans over the city. Please, do not be alarmed. We are trying to identify the perceived problem and make the correct adjustments. If you need to immediately exit the Other Syde, go directly to an Other Syde Corporation substation and you will be accommodated as best as we're able at this time. Thank you for your continued confidence in the Other Syde Corporation and our software. Again, this is a temporary situation that we will resolve shortly."

Emi stared up at the sky. "I've never been called a perceived problem before. Have you?"

"There's a first time for everything, I guess," Maxx said. "Let's just hope we don't get correctly adjusted."

Looking around, Emi headed toward the street. "I think we need a faster means of transportation than the shoelace express."

"What?" Maxx followed her but kept staring up at the sky, searching for the voice from above.

Waves of red light beamed down, washing over entire sections of the city. They were slowly moving their way. He heard Emi talking to someone.

"Sir, this is official Other Syde business. We need to commandeer your vehicle." Emi had morphed her clothing to imitate an O.S. Security Agent's armor and pointed to a yellow convertible parked next to them.

"What do you need my car for? Can't you fly?" The man rubbed the hood of his vehicle, like he was soothing a frightened child.

"Sir, in case you haven't noticed." Emi pointed out into the street. "We've got a bit of a situation going on here. One of our main processors crashed and the man behind me is the only person who can fix it."

Maxx waved at the baffled motorist. "She's right, sir. The name's Jeff Henson." Maxx shook his hand. "I pretty much built Lucy, that's what I call her, from the ground up. I can get her up and running in no time."

Maxx moved towards the driver's door but Emi stopped him. She gave him a polite shove and pointed at the passenger seat. Maxx thought about arguing with her but didn't want to steal her thunder.

The man asked, "Why don't you carry him and fly?"

Emi settled in behind the steering wheel and closed the door. "Why? He...um."

"Air sick. I get terribly air sick. I've been that way ever since I was four. As soon as my feet leave the ground, my lunch leaves my stomach. Nasty stuff." Maxx shut the car door and held his hand up to his mouth, pretending to dry heave.

Emi put the car in drive and waved as they pulled from the curb.

"Your cooperation will be noted, Citizen."

The man stood dumbfounded in the middle of the road before he called after them.

"Hey! How do I get my car back?"

Emi sped away, blowing through the next intersection. She morphed back into her jumpsuit and adjusted the seat.

She looked over at Maxx. "Am I going the right way?"

Maxx laughed and leaned back. "Yeah, Citizen, you're good. Stay on this road for the next three blocks and then hang a right. At this rate, we'll be there in a couple minutes. That was a nice touch with the security armor."

"I know, right. That was pretty good. Maybe I should switch from dance to drama?" Emi gunned the engine.

Maxx watched her behind the wheel, her hair whipping in the wind as she roared down the street. It was nice to see her smile.

Emi hit the brakes as she made a sharp right at the next intersection. The back wheels screeched as they rounded the corner.

Maxx braced his hands against the dash. "You know the whole plan is kind of contingent on us getting there in one piece. You need to make the next left."

"Sorry, this is the most fun I've had since we got here. I got a little carried away." Emi let off the gas and made the next turn less aggressively.

She slowed down and cruised the next stretch of road. Maxx appreciated the small break from the insanity unfolding around them. He pinned all his hopes on finding Daniels and getting some answers. It was a gamble but he had no other cards to play.

Maxx pointed. "It should be right here. Look for number 1010."

Emi slowed down and watched the numbers on the passing buildings until she stopped in front of a small iron gate. A one story bungalow wedged itself between two skyscrapers. The siding was bright yellow with brown wooden shutters. Potted plants spread across the front steps and porch. The windows were all closed and the drapes drawn shut.

Emi stopped at the curb. "I'm guessing this is it."

"It's what Tane's map says." Maxx got out and started for the gate.

He heard a car alarm chirp. Turning around, Emi pointed the remote at their stolen vehicle. The headlights flashed.

She pocketed the keys. "What? We might still need it. I don't want some criminal stealing our ride."

"You mean like us?" Maxx asked.

They crossed the small yard, complete with ornamental fish pond. It reminded Maxx of one of the cabins they used to stay in at the lake. The porch steps creaked in protest under Maxx's weight.

"You don't find many creaky boards in O.S.," he said.

A brass knocker hung on the door, the name Daniels engraved into it.

"Look." Emi pointed back to the street.

Maxx saw the waves of red light washing over the buildings a few blocks away.

"It looks like they're stepping up the hunt. Let's hope this works." He tapped the door striker against the plate.

It didn't take long. Maxx heard footsteps approaching and the inside door chain unlatch, followed by several other chains and locks releasing.

"I guess you can't be too careful," Maxx said.

"I guess not," Emi answered.

The door swung open. A woman in her early forties wearing a yellow sun dress greeted them. "May I help you?"

Maxx hadn't expected that. Her straight blond hair curtained an inviting smile and vivid blue eyes.

He couldn't help but smile back. "Ma'am, we're here to see Mr. Daniels. Would he be in?"

She stood in the door, motionless. She took time to look both of them over from head to toe, never losing her grin. Maxx looked behind them, half expecting to see a couple O.S. Agents land in the yard. Turning back, they stood in mutual silence for what seemed like an eternity.

Maxx grabbed the back of Emi's shirt, getting ready to run in case the woman sounded some kind of alarm.

Instead, she twirled and walked back into the living room, stopping mid-way and waving them in.

"Come in, please. He's in his den. You two have a seat on the couch and I'll go and fetch him."

Maxx took a careful step inside, waiting for the giant cage to drop from the ceiling or a blast of knock-out gas to hit them. Emi nudged his shoulder.

"What are you waiting for?" she asked.

"Booby traps."

"I only see one boob here." She pushed passed him into the living room.

Maxx moved a couple throw pillows to make room for him and Emi on the floral print couch. He noticed a newspaper on a coffee table.

Flipping it over, he read the top. "October thirty first, two thousand ten? That's a little bit creepy. That's around when Daniels disappeared. Why would he keep a paper with that date on it?"

"Let's just keep on our toes," Emi said. "We don't know what we're walking into yet." Emi punched him in the arm. "Shhh, she's coming back."

Maxx tossed the paper down just as their host came back. She stood in the doorway for just a moment before moving to the side. Behind her stood a man, maybe early forties, dressed in a sweater and trousers.

He welcomed his visitors. "Good evening, kids. My wife said you needed to see me?"

Daniels produced a smoking pipe and casually lit it.

Maxx stood up and offered his hand. "Mr. Daniels, my name is Maxx Fragnelli. It's a real honor to meet you, sir."

Daniels remained still, puffing at his pipe. He stared at Maxx's outstretched hand and then over at Emi, who was still on the couch. Rings of smoke slowly dissipated between the two of them. He turned and walked away.

"I'd appreciate it if you and your girlfriend could please show yourselves out." Daniels paused at the threshold to the next room.

Maxx persisted. "Mr. Daniels, I know it's you. I've seen your picture a hundred times. You're something of a personal hero of mine. Look, we just need a couple minutes to talk. Our friend Tane is in trouble. Those slime balls at O.S. Corp have him hostage. They're trying to take over-"

"I don't care. It's not my problem. Not anymore." Daniels disappeared into the next room.

Maxx followed. "But...my friend needs help."

"There's nothing I can do." Daniels crossed a small sitting room with Maxx a few paces behind. "Please, respect my privacy."

"They're going to have us arrested."

"That's too bad." Daniels moved toward another room.

"I saw my dead brother."

Daniels stopped.

Maxx almost bumped into him and realized he hit a nerve. "It works. They figured out how to make it work. My brother died six months ago and I saw him here inside O.S. We saw the pentagram thing at the O.S. building. They're bringing ghosts into the program, Mr. Daniels. It works."

Daniels kept his back to Maxx. He took off his glasses and gently folded them, placing them in a shirt pocket.

"You've been in the research and development lab?" Daniels asked.

Maxx nodded. "It's on the eighty-ninth floor."

Daniels opened a set of carved glass patio doors. "Let's go outside and talk. Why don't you tell your girlfriend to come along?" He motioned towards the living room, where Emi stood next to the couch.

Maxx waved for her to join them. "Thank you, sir. This means a lot to us…but she's not my girlfriend."

Daniels smiled. "Ah…to be young again."

CHAPTER 30

"And they have my body where?" Daniels repacked his pipe with fresh tobacco.

Maxx, Emi, and Daniels sat at a circular glass table on a small cement patio. Maxx stared up at the sky as hover crafts scanned the buildings nearby.

Maxx answered with a question. "Are you're sure we're safe here? The scans won't pick us up?"

Daniels comforted him with a wry smile. "This is my house, son. If you created software this advanced, how many back doors would you have programmed? I assure you we're so far under the radar that O.S. thinks this place is a laundry mat."

The last comment caught Emi's curiosity and she looked up from the table. "Then how did we find it so easy?"

Daniels chuckled. "A bright girl you have here, Maxx. I hid it from the prying eyes of my former employers. I never expected this cult following that has developed around me. You really found my location from a teenage Asian girl posing as a night club owner?"

"We did. Where she got it, I couldn't tell you." Maxx scouted the streets around them one last time. "And yes, your body is in a private room in some third rate nursing home back in Newton City. You're hooked up to more medical gadgets than we could count."

Daniels shuffled a wooden coaster along the table with his finger. "That's not right. It wasn't the deal I cut with corporate when I left. They promised me expert medical care for the remainder of my natural life and in the event of any life threatening illness or the onset of old age, they were to transfer my body into a cryogenic chamber to prolong my existence here in-world. They got to keep the programming and I got my life back."

"Well, if you do decide to go back, you need to be prepared," Maxx said. "Your real world self is pretty frail. I doubt if you could even make it out of bed on your own. They seem to keep you pretty medicated."

"Those bastards. They were just going to let me die and fade away here in-world." Daniels smacked the table with his hand. The glass splintered.

Emi pulled her hands away. "Sir, we're sorry about what they did to you but we really need your help."

Daniels seemed oblivious to Emi's words. "And they've modified my technology for accessing the afterlife? You've seen it?"

Maxx nodded. "Yeah, they definitely got the ghost program working. My brother, Jason, is in here somewhere. He spoke to me. I ran across someone else, the person who killed Jason. He's here too and whatever damage he does to our virtual bodies carries back to the real world. I don't know how but it does. Look." Maxx lifted his shirt and showed Daniels his wound.

"That's incredible. But how?" Daniels studied the cuts and reached towards Maxx's stomach.

Maxx pulled away and fixed his shirt. "I don't know but he's still after me. I need to figure out how to stop him and find my brother." Maxx watched as the building next to them was drenched in red light.

The same woman who let them in came out on the patio with a pitcher of lemonade and glasses on a platter.

"Who wants lemonade?" she asked. "It's always the quickest way to cheer me up. Kids?"

Maxx leaned back as she placed the tray on the table. "That would be great. Thanks…uh?"

She handed him a glass. "Clarissa."

She repeated the gesture to Emi, who accepted it and smiled. "Thank you."

"You're welcome. It's so rare for us to get visitors here. I have brownies in the oven. They should be done in ten minutes. You're staying aren't you?" Mrs. Daniels beamed.

"Who can say no to brownies?" Maxx sipped his drink.

Clarissa turned to go back inside. Her husband grabbed her around the waist and pulled her close.

"Don't worry. I made some for you too, sweetums. Now don't embarrass the children." She pulled away but Daniels held her hand.

He stared into her eyes and said, "I love you."

"And I love you." She vanished back in the house.

Daniels waited until he was sure she was gone.

"It's not her." He finally turned toward them. "As much as I wanted her to be, she isn't my Clarissa. When I gave up on bringing her back, I decided to do the next best thing and make another. It sounds so silly now."

Daniels took a long drink and swirled the glass in his hand, watching the ice cubes dance sporadically inside.

"I added everything I could remember. I wrote forward thinking analytic code and random drift response equations. I downloaded pictures and programmed memories. It took months for me to get it just right. I thought I won. I thought I'd have her back." He placed the cup on the table. "I was wrong. *My* Clarissa loved making up words to fit into the crossword puzzles I obsess over. Any chance she had, she'd sneak them away from me and fill in the blanks with nonsense words and then I'd have to go back and find them. It drove me crazy. She said she did it to remind me that the world doesn't always make sense and needed a little gibberish at times."

The cubes in his glass floated to the bottom.

Maxx tried to bring him back from his memories. "Sir, I'm sorry for your loss."

Daniels didn't miss a beat. "Clarissa was a painter. She'd mix colors into such amazing montages and sit in front of the canvass and wait for it to speak to her. She found meaning where I saw only splotches and explained it to me so vividly that I had no doubt it was there but beyond my perceptions. I always envied her that."

Daniels twisted the wedding band on his finger, making small rotations as he looked at the intricate detail of the jewelry's craftsmanship.

Maxx touched Emi's arm to get her attention and leaned close. "I think he's had one too many lemonades."

Emi pushed him away in embarrassment.

"I heard that." Daniels looked straight at Maxx. "And you're right, I'm babbling. This ring is important to both of us, Maxx. It's special in more than the obvious ways. Clarissa made it for me. I worked for days to make her one in return and came up with a simple gold band that was crooked and ill fitting. She loved it all the same. This Clarissa has no spontaneity. When she paints, she can reproduce any image down to the smallest of details but there's no passion. Her color stays within the form. I look into her eyes and see only my memories."

"Mr. Daniels, I'm sorry," Emi said.

An explosion erupted across the street. The sidewalks were lined with people unsuccessfully attempting to fade out of the program. Each face carried varied degrees of panic and fear. A guy in a tuxedo kicked another man on the ground.

He screamed with each strike. "I have to go home! You can't keep me here!"

A woman in a leather jacket argued into her phone. "I'll sue. I'm married to an attorney. I'll own this whole place."

Someone in a chipmunk costume repeatedly rammed their head into a mailbox and shouted, "Come on! Die! Die!"

Mrs. Daniels came back out to the patio but Daniels stopped her. "Why don't you go back inside for a little bit, dear? We're almost done out here. The kids are getting ready to leave. We can do some crosswords when I come in."

"But the brownies..." She paused, disappointment filled her eyes. It only lasted a few seconds and her smile returned. She blew Daniels a kiss. "Okay. Don't be long. I love you."

"Love you..." Daniels' words hung in the air with palpable despair. "They've destroyed my world. It's been corrupted into something it was never meant to be. Now, they're trying to commercialize death. I can't let that happen. It's not what I wanted." Daniels grabbed Maxx's arm. "You have to stop this. Shut down the portal and expose the company for what they are."

"Okay...but how?" Maxx asked, surprised by Daniels surge of emotion. "Tane's the only one who can access the information he sent from their headquarters and they have him hostage."

"With this." Daniels removed his wedding band and spun it on the glass table top.

Maxx followed the ring's revolutions. "Come again?"

Daniels cupped his hand over the ring. "You need Clarissa's ring. It can close the portal. I had to use a personal object to open the rift. If it passes back through, it will close on itself."

Maxx hesitated, not wanting to offend his idol with his answer. "But, you know the ring isn't real."

Daniels slapped Maxx lightly on the head. "Not this ring. You're going to have to get it from my real house. I'll give you the address and where I have it hidden."

Emi watched the chaos unfolding out in the street. Two men on motorcycles were competing in an impromptu joust using broken street signs. She turned to Daniels. "But we're stuck here, Mr. Daniels. We can't fade back into the real world."

Daniels folded his arms across his chest. "Didn't I say this old dog is full of tricks? This is a virtual safe house. There's nothing those fool programmers spew that has any effect inside of my walls. You can both transfer back to the real world whenever you wish."

Maxx and Emi exchanged surprised looks.

Daniels continued. "I've already sent my address and pertinent information to your cell phone."

"How'd you know my cell phone..." Maxx started to ask but stopped when Daniels raised his brow.

"You think I can build the most sophisticated virtual world of this generation and initiate code to bridge the gap between the real and after lives but I can't hack your profile for personal information?" He diverted a laugh toward Emi.

"Come with us, Mr. Daniels," Emi said. "You can help."

"I'm sorry, dear. If what you're telling me is true, and I've been verifying that since you two arrived, then I can't return. If I go back then I'll find myself as an invalid. I'm much more useful in this realm. You two have to get Clarissa's ring and sneak into the real Other Syde Headquarters. It's surprisingly similar in layout to the virtual offices that the two of you just escaped from."

Maxx interrupted him. "But how do you expect us to actually break into the real O.S. H.Q.? It's a little more complicated than the virtual games we play here. We're talking about actual criminal trespassing."

"I sent you another back door code to use. They've blocked the Clarissa password after your friend used it for the first download. The code will work in the real world just as effectively. You'll need to download another set of files from the lab and get out. I've already tried to access that information from here but they've taken extra precautions and cut off remote entry. Send the information to me and I'll contact the authorities myself. They'll have no choice but to release your friend, Bane."

"Tane," Maxx corrected.

"They'll let Tane go free and I'll ensure all of your records are expunged from their files. I'll extract my own revenge from there."

Maxx rubbed the back of his neck. "What about the security?"

"They still think the two of you are trapped in here. No one will be expecting you to show up there. Security will be light at this time and I'll disrupt their surveillance cameras." Daniels ran his finger over the fresh cracks in the table, spider webbing away from where he struck it.

"How do we get to Newton City?" Maxx asked.

"We'll take my van," Emi said. "With no traffic, it should only take a little over an hour."

Maxx tried to sum up the running plan. "Okay, so we get the ring from your house, break into O.S. Headquarters, shut down the portal, download the files, and send them back here to you. No problem. Do you want us to look into the whole global warming problem while we're at it?"

Daniels patted him on the shoulder. "You remind me a lot of myself in my younger days. You can do this, Maxx. It's a good plan."

"It's the best one we've got anyway. Are you ready for this?" Maxx asked Emi.

"Nowhere even close but we don't have a choice," she answered.

"Should I remind you it was your idea to come along tonight?" Maxx grinned.

"That thought's only crossed my mind a thousand times in the last hour." She looked at Daniels. "Thank you for helping us."

"I've always had a soft spot for young love. Be careful." Daniels turned as Clarissa called from inside.

"Snookums, I have today's crossword. I need a six letter word for desert hallucination."

Daniels answered, "I'll be there in a moment, dear."

Maxx shook his hand. "Mr. Daniels, will we see you again? I had so many more questions I wanted to ask."

"The randomness of life is something even I was never able to replicate. I hope we do." Daniels waved and walked back into the house.

Maxx looked at Emi. "You ready for all this?"

She took his hand. "Just stay close and hope we don't run into any more surprises."

"What could go wrong?" Maxx smiled.

They both faded from the patio.

CHAPTER 31

Emi stared at the light above her. It brightened and dimmed intermittently. It wasn't very large but it gave her something to focus on. Her whole body shook. She wondered if it was an after effect of coming out of the virtual world. Her arms and fingers tingled like the circulation had been cut off.

She felt the ground shake and wondered if they were still trapped in the program somehow. Mr. Daniels promised they could fade back but maybe he'd been out of the loop too long. It was hot, much hotter than she remembered it being back in Maxx's room. She tried to pull her hand up to wipe her face but her arm didn't seem to want to cooperate. That's when she realized someone had tied her arm down to her side. It's also when the panic kicked in.

She wasn't in Maxx's bedroom. That was for sure. The space was small, like a storage container. Wires ran from the small light above her across the metal roof and out of sight. Some more feeling returned and she turned her head to get a better look around. That was right before someone clamped their hand down over her mouth.

"Mmmmmmm!" She tried to sit up but she was pulled back down. She tried to fight only to realize that both her hands and feet were held tight. Feeling their filthy fingers across her face, she bit down into whatever flesh she could manage.

"Ow. Ow. Ow. Would you be quiet already?" Maxx whispered in her ear.

He was crouched down beside her. The room swayed and felt almost fluid. Something rumbled underneath of them and they jerked forward. Maxx relaxed his grip.

"What's going on?" she asked. "Where are we?"

Maxx lowered his voice. "They're moving us. We're in the back of some kind of cargo van. I came to quicker than you. It's normal after your first time. Tane's here too."

He pointed to a cot fastened to the floor next to them. Tane's body was still, an oxygen mask strapped over his face.

Tears welled up in Emi's eyes. "Tane?"

Maxx rubbed her hand as he worked at untying her. "He's okay. I already checked him out. He's just sleeping. The mask is feeding him some kind of anesthetic. He's still stuck in the program. I think they're taking us into the city, back to their headquarters."

Emi felt a tingle in the back of her neck as Maxx pulled off the adhesive patch. She saw the wires running along the floor, leading from her cot to a computer tower fastened against the van wall.

Maxx pointed to the front of the dimly lit cab. A glass window separated them from the driving compartment. The glass was embedded with thick meshed wire. Emi turned to her side and saw another cot beside hers. A blanket was pulled up over the head.

"Who is that?" Emi asked.

"That's me. I wadded up my blankets and pillows to make it look like I was still lying there. I don't see any cameras back here but I didn't want to take any chances."

"They kidnapped us?" Emi rubbed her wrists.

"Something like that, I'm sure they couldn't just call the cops since they don't know where Tane sent that information. They probably want to keep our bodies secure until they can find us in O.S. and kick us back here to give us a proper interrogation. I don't know how they got us out of my house." Maxx looked around the back of the van. "I need to get up to that window and see where we're at."

"And then what? What are they going to do to us?" Emi asked, though she wasn't sure she wanted to hear the answer. Having people chasing after her in Maxx's computer world unhinged her nerves, but to be in trouble in the real world took it to a whole other level.

"Then we bail out of this crate before they get us inside the building. We were headed to the city anyhow, right? I need you to stay put and keep quiet. I'll be right back." Maxx snuck along the wall of the van.

Other than the three cots, the space was empty. Emi watched Maxx make his way to the front and peered through the window's corner. The truck swung a hard turn and Maxx flew across the cabin and smashed into the wall with a thud. Emi froze, lying against the cot, and waited for eyes to appear in the glass. Maxx threw himself on the floor and they both watched the window. The outline of a head filled the center of the glass. It remained there a moment before vanishing. Maxx crawled back to Emi on his hands and knees.

"That hurt," Maxx said.

"Well, did you see anything?" she asked.

"Thanks for the concern. Yeah, it looks like we're about ten minutes out of the city. I saw an overpass sign through the windshield. These guys are hauling some serious butt. He's got it pegged at over ninety." Maxx rubbed the side of his head.

"Sorry, are you okay?" She brushed her hand against his cheek. Everything was happening way too fast but she needed to get her wits together. If there was one thing she learned from spending so much time with Maxx was that you had to deal with the situation you found yourself in.

Maxx pulled himself under Emi's cot to hide. "I'm okay. We need to think of a way to get out of here when we get closer to town. You don't happen to have a flashlight do you?"

"I must have left it in my other cot," she said.

Maxx pulled his phone out of his pocket. He shielded the screen with his hand before turning it on. The glow illuminated the lower half of his face.

"I can't believe they didn't confiscate this. They really must have been in a hurry. Maybe these guys are just the muscle. Stay here a minute." Maxx crawled back out from under the cot.

"Where do you think I'm going to go?" Emi twisted on her stomach.

Maxx made his way to the back and checked the doors before the light on his phone timed out and the van went dark. He crawled back to her, passing Tane as he went. Emi watched Tane's chest crest and fall as their friend started to softly snore. She hoped he was all right and that sacrificing himself back at the virtual lab didn't turn out to be a waste of time.

"I can't see a way out of here." Maxx popped up beside her.

Emi jumped, nearly falling out of her makeshift bed. "Real nice, super ninja, you scared the crap out of me."

"You were expecting someone else?" Maxx laid his head next to hers on the pillow.

"Only you could get me into this kind of mess, Maxx." She stroked his hair where he hit his head. If they weren't in the process of being kidnapped, trapped on a cot in the back of the van speeding down a dark highway heading who knows where, she may have wanted to stay there with Maxx a few hours more. Tane's snoring cut her thoughts short and she looked over at him. "I wonder why they didn't gas us like they did Tane."

"Yeah, I was thinking about that. Since they think we're still stuck in O.S., they didn't need to worry about us fading out of the program. My guess is they have Tane sedated somehow inside the program too. I still can't believe he did that back in the lab."

Emi smiled. "He's a good friend, Maxx." She looked around the cab. "So how do we get out? And what are we going to do about Tane?"

"I've got an idea and Tane will have to stay here."

"What?" Emi pulled her head up.

"Look, I know. I don't like it any more than you but we can't lug him around like that and I don't know what will happen if we try to wake him up and force him back from O.S. It might do some kind of neurological damage. They're not going to do anything to him as long as we have the files on their secret project."

Emi just stared at him, giving him *the look*.

"C'mon Emi, I don't want to leave him here either. He's my best friend. It's the only thing I can think of. I just need you to trust me."

Emi lowered her head back on the pillow. "That account is starting to run empty."

***

"Help! Somebody get him off me!"

Emi's screams bounced off the walls of the van. The vehicle slowed and the silhouette appeared in the tiny window up front again.

Emi thrashed on the cot and threw her blanket in the air. "Help! It hurts! Please! Help!"

The brakes locked and the cots skidded forward before being held in place by straps attached to the legs. A man cursed and two doors slammed. The metal latch at the back of the truck clanked and the door slid open, filling the compartment with the light. Two men crawled into the bay area of the truck, searching with flashlights until they stopped on Emi.

"Sonufabitch." One of the men rushed over to her. Emi was sprawled across the floor with her head propped against Tane's cot. Tane's arm wrapped under Emi's shoulder and his hand clenched her throat. She had both hands locked around his.

"He's crazy. He said it's my fault." Emi coughed her words.

"Get him off of her before he kills her." The man at the back of the van snapped.

His partner pulled Emi away and Tane's arm fell limp against the floor. They flashed their lights toward Maxx's cot and saw him motionless under the blanket.

Emi hugged her reluctant rescuer, wrapping her arms around him. "He must have passed out. Thank you. I don't know what came over him. I just…now!"

Emi thrust her knee up and connected with the man's groin. He grunted and crumbled to the ground.

"Bllarrrgghh!" Maxx jumped up from his cot, rushing toward the other man. He knew he only had a couple seconds to pull this off.

His threw the blanket in the air, distracting his target. The man turned as Maxx tackled him. They hit harder than Maxx expected, rolling around the floor of the van. Maxx struggled to get the upper hand. He saw a flash of silver as the man pulled a knife from his waistband.

Maxx pushed away and scrambled across the floor. The man raised the blade and came after him. A blur came down beside them as a metal flashlight slammed into the man's head. Maxx spun around as Emi raised the light to deliver a second blow.

"I think that's enough." He grabbed Emi's hand. She had a crazy look in her eye but after she realized the guy was out, she dropped the light.

The victim of her groin strike still rolled around in pain.

"Come on, thumper. It's time to go." Maxx pulled Emi to the back of the truck and they jumped out onto the road. A streetlight glared above them. Maxx shielded his eyes, adjusting to being outside.

He looked back into the van. Tane was motionless on the cot. Grabbing Emi, they jumped over the guard rail and stumbled down a grass embankment. It wasn't the smoothest of escapes but he was making it up as they went. Emi held onto Maxx's arm to keep her balance.

"Blargh? That was your battle cry?" She asked as they slid down the hill.

"It was a high pressure situation. It worked didn't it?" Maxx looked over his shoulder to see if anyone was chasing them.

Emi tripped and pulled Maxx down with her and they tumbled end over end down the hill, stopping on the berm of the lower road. A flashlight shined down and circled around until it rested on Maxx. A loud crack pierced the night air. The asphalt beside Maxx exploded.

Maxx felt the sting of small rocks striking his skin. "They're shooting at us! Run for it!"

They sprinted for a nearby underpass. The beam of light followed them but the thick brush along the road provided cover until they reached the protection of a cement tunnel. Hugging the wall, Maxx waited to see someone run down the bank after them.

"Oh my God, I can't believe he was shooting at us. This is serious, Maxx." Emi's breaths were labored and she fished around in her pockets for her inhaler.

Her movements were frantic until her fingers found the small canister. She depressed the top and took a long draw.

"Are you okay?" Maxx asked.

She held out her hand.

"I'm fine. That was just pretty intense. Let's keep moving." Emi looked back at the hillside. No traces of roving flashlights.

"Intense is right. I thought you were going to bash that guy's head in. Were you going to keep swinging until you saw brains?" Maxx tried to lighten the mood.

"Sorry, I don't know how many times to knock someone in the head until they're unconscious. They forgot to teach us that in dance class."

"Fair enough. I think we're safe." Maxx looked around.

They were just inside the city limits and stood at an intersection. Traffic was light, even in Newton City at that time of night. Maxx figured the guys from the van would have to make it to the next off-ramp and double back to get to them. They had a few minutes at least to get moving.

"Which way?" Emi stood beside him on the sidewalk.

Maxx checked his email from his phone. He found a new message from Clarissa99.

"I'll give it to Daniels. He keeps his word. The address to his house is right here. Let me punch it in through GPS," Maxx said.

Maxx worked at typing in the information as they continued down the side of the road. A car drove by. Maxx looked up to make sure it wasn't their friends from the over-pass.

Emi pointed to a nearby alley. "Let's at least get off the road. We're way too open out here."

She led them through the intersection. "Stay close."

Maxx worked on his phone, looking up mid-way through into the alley. It was a lot darker than he expected without the street lights. They passed an old dumpster. The smell of last night's rotting leftovers made Emi cover her nose.

"Maybe this wasn't the best idea," Emi said.

Something crashed behind them and Maxx grabbed Emi by the arm, rushing her out to the next street. He looked back to see a set of emerald eyes following them. Maxx moved it up to a slow jog before the eyes vanished in the dark.

"Okay, maybe we'll stay on the road from here on out," Maxx said. "It looks like we're not far away. We should be there in like ten minutes." Maxx made a mental map of the route. "The O.S. offices are only a couple blocks from there, looks like Daniels liked to live close to where he worked."

"Before you put your phone away, you better call your mother," Emi said. "She's probably freaking out."

"Yeah, you're right." Maxx touched a picture of his mom on his phone and waited.

"Mom?" He immediately yanked the phone away from his ear.

A woman's voice raged on the other end of the line. Maxx waited until the voice died down before raising it back to his face.

"Mom! Listen! We're fine. I know they took us. Emi's with me. What did they tell you?" Maxx asked.

"They what? No. We're not sick. No, the machines didn't rot our brain. They were lying to you. Yes, they were. I'm in the city. I'm with Emi. Don't call the police. No! Do not! We're fine. Tane? He's with us too. We're all fine." Maxx pulled the phone away again and raised his eyebrows at Emi.

"Be nice. She's worried." Emi shook her finger at him.

Maxx nodded. "Is Dad okay? Tell him I'm sorry. It was some guys I know. They hired those people to pull a practical joke and take us. Yeah, like with college fraternities. I'm fine. No, I'm not lying. I'm staying at Tane's tonight. We're working on something. I know they looked real. Okay, Mom. I need to go. I'll be home in the morning. I promise. Okay. I love you too. Okay. Good night."

Maxx put his phone away.

"Do you really think she bought that?" Emi asked.

"I doubt it. She said it all happened pretty fast and she was half asleep. Those butt nuggets just broke in and carted us out. She'll call Tane's house and figure out I'm not there but at least she heard my voice and knows I'm alive. I'll have a ton of explaining to do when we get back. I am so toast." Maxx paused. "Hey, what if those goons go back to my house looking for us?"

"I don't think they'll go back in," Emi said. "They may watch the house from outside. We need to get that ring."

"Yeah, we're close to Daniels' place. Let's just hope it's still there. It's been a while since he actually lived there. What if someone else moved in? We didn't even think about that," Maxx said.

"We'll deal with it. Let's just get there," she said.

Maxx's phone vibrated and he saw the incoming number was his mother. It took less time than he figured for her to catch him lying. He hated doing that to her and even more not answering. Hitting the ignore key, he put away his phone.

The streets were vacant except for the occasional prostitute or vagrant. They walked in silence. Retaining enough street savvy to steer clear of those urban obstacles, they cast enough stares to keep track of their surrounding but not so many to draw attention.

Maxx kept them on path and concentrated on the pavement below when he spoke. "I'm sorry."

"What?"

"I'm sorry I got you into this. I never thought it would go this far. It wasn't supposed to spin this out of control. We're fugitives. My best friend is comatose and in the back of a van going who knows where. My mom almost had an aneurism because two goons broke into our house. I got you shot at. I even got Jason involved in this mess. How pathetic can I get? I'm in way over my head." Maxx's shoulders slumped and his feet shuffled across the sidewalk.

"Maxx, no one expected all this. It's not your fault." Emi stopped and turned him around to face her.

"Yeah, it is. If I hadn't been trying to scam everyone in O.S. they would never know I existed. I drug Tane into this just because he was my friend...my only one. I've been a screw up my whole life. It's all because of me. You, Tane, my family, my brother..."

Emi lifted his chin. "It wasn't your fault then and it's not your fault now. Look, I wasn't there with what happened to your brother but I know what you've told me and what I've heard. There was nothing you could have done to avoid it. If it wouldn't have been you, it would've been someone else that night or another night. You can't control the world, as much as you try."

Maxx looked down and smiled. "Yeah, I think that point has been pretty much bashed into my head in the last twenty-four hours."

"We have to save Tane. We have to get all those people out of O.S. Who knows what's going on in there? They need you," Emi said. "If your brother is stuck in there with that crazy ghost, then he needs your help. And…I need you. I can't do this alone."

Maxx took a long breath. "Okay. You're right. The pity party's over. Let's bury those butt heads."

"Now there's the Maxx I know and love."

"And what?" Maxx asked.

"Nothing. Come on. We're close."

"And what?"

CHAPTER 32

"Well, I guess no one moved in." Emi pushed open the broken gate.

Maxx searched for a sidewalk between the over grown grass and weeds. The front yard leading to Daniels' house was a shambles of broken lawn ornaments and the remnants of a decayed garden.

Maxx stopped at the porch. "This is amazing. It's an exact duplicate of his house in O.S., right down to the door knocker."

Emi checked the mailbox, removing the lone postcard inside.

She flipped it over and laughed. "I guess this is someone's idea of a joke."

Handing it to Maxx, he read it out loud. "Don't get left out. Join the exciting new world of tomorrow. Register at OtherSyde today. Your only limit is your own imagination." Maxx dropped the card to the ground. "Nice."

The door handle was completely broken off. Maxx pushed against the door and it swung open.

"Maybe you should stay out here," Maxx said.

Emi nudged him forward. "No thanks, I'll take my chances in there with you. Just stay close."

"Hold on to me," Maxx said.

The smell of mildew caught him by surprise and he pulled his shirt over his nose. Leading them into the living room by the light of his phone, he looked back at Emi, who covered her nose with her arm.

He pointed to a mass of clothing piled on the floor. "You think anyone is squatting in here? It looks like Daniels' house has become a hobo Hilton."

"We better keep an eye out. Where did he say the stairs were again?" Emi pulled in close behind Maxx. He felt her trying to match his stride as they moved across the room.

"It looks like they're down the hall." Maxx tested the knob before opening it. Something darted out between their legs and scurried down the hall.

Emi screamed, "Something touched my feet!"

Maxx caught sight of the fleeing rodent. "Sorry, that was a closet. I think it's the next one."

"I'll give you sorry. It something else jumps out, I'm climbing up your back." Emi cinched her grip on his shirt.

Maxx tried the next door but it wouldn't budge.

Emi peaked over his shoulder. "Are you supposed to push or pull?"

"I know how to open a door. It's wedged in the frame, probably warped. Grab my waist and help me pull," he said.

Maxx wrapped both hands around the knob while Emi grabbed around his waist. He braced his foot against the wall and yanked with Emi pulling behind him. The door creaked and slid out maybe an inch.

He re-gripped the handle. "It's moving. Another pull should do it."

Putting his weight and Emi's into it, Maxx threw himself backwards. The door snapped open and they both fell against the wall. Maxx ended up in Emi's lap.

Wiping his hand on the carpet, Maxx stood up. "I think I stuck my hand in cat poop."

He reached down to help Emi up.

"That better be the clean hand and you better hope it was a cat." She looked up the stairwell.

"Thanks for that visual," Maxx said.

The staircase was narrow, leading up to another door. Thankfully, the top door wasn't stuck. Maxx didn't feel like tumbling down a flight of stairs. Turning left, they stopped at the first room they came to. The door had been removed from its hinges and was lying in the hall.

"It looks like we're not the first ones to come here looking," Maxx said.

A small desk sat in the corner, its contents strewn across the floor. Several filing cabinets lined the other wall. Multi colored folders were scattered everywhere.

Maxx picked one up. "I can't believe they left all of his notes. Why wouldn't they take this stuff?"

"Maybe they were looking for something specific." Emi jumped as the window blind blew open. Broken glass littered the floor beneath it. "Maybe they didn't know this place existed and this is all from scavengers."

"Maybe." Maxx found a calendar on the wall.

A smiling Jack O'Lantern leered back at him. He bent down on one knee.

"This is where Daniels said it would be." Maxx pointed to the floor.

He felt around against the floor boards until one of them jiggled. Clawing at the edge of the wood, he pried one of the planks loose.

"Is it in there?" she asked.

"There's a cigar box." Maxx pressed his face against the hole.

He fished his arm into the opening, retrieving the box. The top was sealed tight with duct tape. Finding a seam, he ripped it loose and pulled out a small plastic bag. A gold wedding band settled into the corner.

"We have a winner." He held the ring between his thumb and finger. "Let's hope this works like Daniels said it would."

Maxx searched through the rest of the box. Emi moved over to the window as he shuffled through some papers.

"Uh, Maxx, I think we have company." She pointed to the street and parted two of the window slats. "A black sedan just pulled up. It looks like two guys in suits. Is there another way out of here?"

"I don't think we have time to find out." Maxx looked out the window. A large black car with tinted windows was parked along the curb. Two large framed men in black suits stood in front of the headlights, both of them looking down at a piece of paper. One of them pointed towards the house before they started across the yard.

"Come on. I have an idea," Maxx said, rushing out of the room.

"Wait up." Emi ran after him.

They raced back down the stairs and into the living room. Maxx pointed to the pile of dirty clothes stacked on the floor. He dove into the middle of the pile and reached back for Emi. "In here, let's go."

Emi didn't budge. "You've got to be kidding. There's no way I'm getting in there."

Maxx wiggled his fingers, waving for her to follow. "Let's go, princess. You need to start putting some of this on."

He lunged towards her, pulling her into the mass of fabric. The clothes shifted and bulged as they both disappeared into the pile.

"It smells worse than your hand in here," Emi said.

"Shhh."

***

The boards on the front porch creaked and the doorbell buzzed for only a second before dying out.

"What? You waiting for the butler to let us in?"

The door flew open, coming completely off its hinges and skidded along the floor. Two large and angry looking men stood in the doorway.

"Do you really think they'd come here?"

"The boss said to check it out, so that's what we're doing. Some of them club kids said Fragg and his friends were looking for Daniels. The punk and his girl jumped out of the van not far from here, so who knows."

Stepping over the remains of the door, the men crossed the living room and stopped.

"They said check everything."

Maxx held Emi close under the rumpled mound of clothes. He pulled his finger to his lips and whispered. "Shhh."

Someone kicked at the pile of clothes. Maxx saw Emi's eyes widen. She cupped her hand over her mouth.

The next kick struck Maxx in the side and he groaned. It felt like his kidney just ruptured but he wrestled the pain back trying to remain motionless.

"What the hell was that?" One of the men said to his partner.

Maxx heard the distinct sound of a round being chambered into a pistol. Emi clenched her hand tighter over her face. He had to do something. Hiding wasn't going to cut it with these two. He needed to protect Emi. Maxx's side was on fire but he stumbled to his feet, rumpled and ripped clothes loosely clinging to him. He limped towards the men. A hooded sweatshirt covered his head and red jogging pants several sizes too large slumped around his waist. He stretched his hand out near one of their faces.

Deepening his voice, Maxx asked, "Got anything to spare?"

The man crinkled his nose and stepped back. "Uh, his hand smells like shit. Get the hell away from me."

Maxx turned towards the other guy, reaching for the lapel on his suit jacket. A second jumble of rags rose up from the pile behind him, looking like a dirty laundry ghost.

The man pushed him away. "Get out of here, you bums. Who knows what kind of diseases you got?"

Maxx staggered towards the door. "Sorry. Don't want no trouble."

He looked back to make sure Emi followed. They shuffled outside and down the steps to the yard. When they hit the sidewalk, they broke into a slight jog until they made it to the road.

"You never fail to impress me, Maxx."

"I know."

"You're like a secret agent."

"I know."

"These clothes really smell horrible."

"I know."

CHAPTER 33

"Are you sure you're using cold water?" Emi hovered next to Maxx as he dispensed another glob of soap into his hands.

"I think I know the difference between an *h* and *c*. It's just not working." Maxx scrubbed his hands together in the sink.

"Why'd you put it on your finger anyway?" Emi asked.

Maxx was glad she politely left stupid off the end of her question.

"Those goons were coming in. It was the only safe place I could think to put it." Maxx tugged at the gold band around his finger.

He ran his soap covered hands under the faucet, twisting and pulling at the band. Emi washed her face and neck in the next sink, drying off with a paper towel.

Running her fingers through her hair, she said, "At least I smell less like a hobo now."

She peeked out into the hall. "I can't believe this place is exactly like the virtual O.S. Headquarters."

Maxx gave up trying to get the ring off. "I think my finger's actually swelling. It makes sense really. If the people who work here also work at the virtual O.S. offices, it would be easier to have to same layout. How am I going to get this thing off?"

Emi twisted the ring a couple times. "Let the redness go down. Maybe we can find a kitchen and some butter or something in an employee lounge. Do you remember how to get back to the lab?"

"Just because I'm wearing a woman's wedding band, doesn't make me an idiot." Maxx snuck back out into the hall and held the door for Emi.

"I'm not touching that comment." She smiled.

Even with the dimmed lights and lack of employees, they stayed close to the walls and kept an eye out for security and cleaning people until they found the elevator.

As the doors slid open, Emi said, "I can't believe no one else is here."

"Everyone is probably on notice to help look for us." Maxx pressed the button for Research and Development. "We sneak into the lab. I toss the ring through the portal and shut it down. We download a new set of files and send them to Daniels after we get out. What could go wrong?"

"Uh, they tie us up and keep us hostage here forever," Emi said.

"Yeah but they don't know who else we sent the files to. They can't take that chance."

"What about Jason?" Emi looked up at the ceiling.

"Yeah, I thought about that. I mean, if we don't close the portal than we could still bargain with them. Maybe I could force them to let me back in and find him but…what they're doing is wrong. Like Mr. Daniels said, they want to commercialize death. That's not what Jason is about. As much as I want to see him again, I don't want to see him exploited either. Did I tell you I talked to Jason back in my bedroom?"

Emi turned. "In your bedroom?"

"Yeah, it was a dream. I know that. Maybe it was my subconscious, but it still felt like my brother and he always knew the right thing to do."

Emi touched his shoulder. "I think you're right, Maxx. I'm proud of you."

The doors opened. Emi followed him down the hall towards to the lab. The same red security lights they saw back in the virtual building circled overhead in timed revolutions.

"Do you think Tane's here somewhere?" Emi asked. "I'm worried about him."

"Yeah, I am too. The sooner we get this done, the quicker we can get him out of here. He's probably still snoring."

Maxx did his best to sound confident but that was getting harder to do the deeper they got into this mess. They were in totally over their heads but his friends needed him and he was seeing this through.

"I hope so," Emi said.

Maxx squeezed her hand.

"Let's get this over with." Maxx pushed the lab door open.

Even with the lights off, Maxx could feel the expanse of the room. He fumbled along the wall for a switch. "I don't remember it being this dark before."

"Maybe they're conserving energy," Emi said. "Be careful."

"Just stay close. Here, I found it." Maxx slid his hand up the wall and flipped the switch.

Maxx searched for the pentagram somewhere below them. He saw its outline under the catwalk.

"Mr. Fragnelli. We meet…again."

Maxx spun around. The voice sounded almost artificial and at first, Maxx thought someone was using an intercom. A group of O.S. Agents stood behind them, gathered on the catwalk. They surrounded a man in a wheelchair. An IV bag hung from a pole attached to the chair. To his right, a smaller man with thinning brown hair grinned at them. His stomach slumped over his utility belt. Maxx noticed the yellow Taser strapped to his side.

"The mighty Maxx Fragg, we're finally face to face, for real." The man's hand hovered over the Taser. "Are you still planning to kick my ass?"

"Agent Ketchup?" Maxx asked.

"What's the matter, Fragg? Don't you recognize me? Ha, you look like the same snot nosed kid to me."

"Yeah but you look like a shrinky dink that was left in the oven too long," Maxx said. He was really sick of getting ambushed every time they turned around. They wouldn't take the chance of just waiting for him in the lab. How would they know he'd come?

"You little sh-" Ketchall reached for his weapon.

The man in the wheelchair held him back.

The mechanized chair engaged as he came closer to Maxx and Emi. "I'm surprised that I didn't leave a more memorable impression on you, lad. Though I'm sure the voice modulator makes it difficult."

Maxx caught Emi's attention and nodded towards the light switch on the wall.

"Get ready," he said.

Maxx lunged for the wall and hit the switch. The room went dark. Pulling Emi behind him, Maxx ran straight for the exit. He slammed face first into the door. A split second later, Emi did the same thing.

"My head," she cried.

The lights came back on. Agent Ketchall was standing next to the light switch. Maxx kicked the door but it didn't budge.

The man in the wheelchair applauded. "Well played, son. It won't be that easy, I'm afraid. I control everything that happens in this building. I'm hurt you don't know who-"

"I know who you are, Silver." Maxx felt his face flush with anger. "I was just hoping you'd keel over and die before you finished your introductions. Where's Tane?"

Maxx mentally inventoried his surroundings. He had no weapons, no other way out, and no sign of his friend. The pentagram that stood inside the virtual O.S. lab softly glowed on the level below them.

"Oh, I assure you he's close by." A mechanical wheeze substituted for Silver's cough. "He's being closely monitored, just like the two of you are."

"What are talking about? We got away from those jerks in the van on our own," Maxx said. "There's no way you set that up."

Silver stopped his wheelchair. "You're right, we didn't expect you to make your way out of the program on your own, let alone overpower two of our agents. But I didn't get where I am today by being sloppy. I plan for all contingencies. We've been following you ever since you escaped the transport van and then to Daniels' old home and even in the employee's restroom on the third floor. Be a dear and pull down the back of your boyfriend's collar."

Emi hesitated but Maxx gave her a reassuring nod. She pulled down his t-shirt and gasped.

"Maxx, there's a transmitter sewn into it."

Maxx craned his neck to try and see. Emi grabbed her own shirt, twisting around to find her own tracker.

The group of agents around her laughed. Ketchall pointed and said, "She looks like a puppy chasing her tail."

Even Silver smiled. "I assure you, dear. There's one on your collar also. We have been watching your every move since we took you from your home. That was quite clever, the trick with the dirty clothes. I did enjoy that. Those agents have already been terminated. You are an intelligent lad. It's a pity you're more trouble than good or we may have found a position for you here."

Maxx fixed his shirt. "I don't want to work for your corrupt company. I just want my friend back. Do you want to negotiate for the information we took or not?"

Silver edged closer to them. "So you're the gallant knight, storming the castle to save his friend. How noble that is." Silver's smile faded. "It doesn't work that way, son. We're a multi-billion dollar international corporation funded by a dozen governments and private institutions. This company is about to unleash a technological renaissance the likes of which the world has never seen and you think that I'm about to negotiate with a smart mouthed boy and his little trollop?"

Maxx eased Emi back towards the wall. "Then why not just get rid of us back at my house and turn us over to the cops? I think you're bluffing, old man."

He continued his tactical retreat with Emi in tow.

Silver slammed his arm against his chair rail. "You have no idea what I am capable of."

Seeing an opening in Silver's guard, Maxx stopped.

"I know one thing. You can't cheat death. That's what you're trying to do. Isn't it?" Maxx stepped towards Silver with every few words. "You don't have much time left in this world but you think you can leave a window open to get back in. You found a couple glitches that you weren't expecting didn't you? There are things a lot bigger than you and your corporation out there."

Maxx stopped directly in front of Silver. He looked back. Emily was still by the wall.

"We'll see, pup. Go ahead and fry this one," Silver snapped. "We'll get the information from the red headed fool."

Agent Ketchall drew his Taser. "With pleasure." A green dot appeared on the grating and travelled up Maxx's leg.

"Maxx!" Emi cried.

Maxx fell backwards, extending both arms. He bladed his body to the side just as Ketchall fired. He learned that from a reality cop series. One of the prongs pierced his chest, just above his rib cage. The other missed its mark and sailed past Maxx, extending the length of its cord before falling to the floor.

The electrical current soared through the lines. Every muscle in Maxx's body spasmed. Even though he was only hit by one of the prongs, it felt like Maxx's chest exploded. Half out of instinct, half in desperation, he flung himself over the railing of the catwalk.

Maxx screamed as he fell, "Emi! Run!"

Dropping nearly fifteen feet, Maxx hit the floor hard. He tumbled along the ground, turning side over side until finally stopping flat on his stomach. The prong that was embedded near his ribs tore free during his fall. Blood soaked through the side of his shirt. Between the jolt of electricity and the drop, Maxx's head throbbed. The lab spun around him.

People were running across the catwalk above him. He hoped Emi listened and was trying to find a way out. His arm twitched, an after effect of the Taser he guessed. Slowly pulling himself up, Maxx stumbled toward a set of spiral stairs leading back up the platform. He hit the first step and stopped. The pentagram. It was their only hope. Turning, he watched the swirling green mists circling inside the mechanical gate behind him. Maxx ran for the machine.

"Hey, Silver! Any last words before I shut your project down?" Maxx shouted up through the grating.

"Forget the girl. Stop the boy," Silver said.

Ketchall shouted his own commands. "You three go to the other end of the catwalk. You two come with me. I want everyone to transition to live ammo."

Maxx's heart skipped a beat at the mention of live rounds. He stopped at the edge of the portal.

"You just had to put it on your finger, Fragnelli." Maxx twisted and pulled at the band.

A muffled cry echoed from the portal. "Maxx."

Maxx stopped fighting with the ring and bent down.

"Jason?" Maxx listened for the voice again.

"Maxx."

Maxx realized that instead of coming from inside the mists, it came from around the corner, on the opposite side of the pentagram. Someone was strapped down to a gurney, hidden in the shadows.

"Tane!" Maxx ran over to him.

He tore the gag from his friend's mouth.

"Ow." Tane drew a deep breath and drowsily looked around the chamber. His hands and feet were fastened to the cart by leather straps.

"Maxx? Is that you?" Tane tried to get up but the straps held him in place. "You've got to get out of here. There konna gill you. Where's Emi?"

Maxx worked at freeing one of his arms. "She's here somewhere. Silver and Ketchup are here too. We need to shut the machine down. We found Daniels and he told us how. I need to get this ring through the portal."

Maxx showed him the ring on his finger. He freed one of Tane's arms and then started on the other.

"What are you waiting for?" Tane asked. "Throw it in!"

"I can't. It's stuck."

"Why'd you put it on your finger?"

"I don't know! Okay. It was a spur of the moment thing."

Two shots erupted above them. Maxx dropped for cover beside Tane's gurney. The bullets struck the wall behind them.

"Stay down." Maxx searched the room. The echo from the gun blasts rang in his ears. He felt Tane trying to pull his other arm free. Three sets of laser sights poured down from the stairwell across the room. Turning, Maxx saw more targeting lights searching the opposite side of the lab as another group of agents made their way down the stairs.

Maxx wrenched at the ring, tearing his fingernails into his skin. Blood dripped down his hand. Another shot blasted down from the catwalk.

Tane shouted, "Give them what they want, Maxx. It's not worth it. It's over."

Maxx watched the lights closing in and stared down at his bloodied finger. There were six armed men closing in on him, ready to plant a bullet in his head. Tane was barely conscious. Emi was running for her life somewhere above him. His options were limited.

"This one's for you, Jason."

Maxx ran towards the glowing machine.

A set of laser sights flashed over his shoulder right before his arm exploded in pain. Maxx's vision blurred and he felt his knees buckle. Stumbling, he spun around as another shot flew inches past his face. His shoulder on fire, Maxx turned and jumped into the swirling green mists.

"I hope this works!"

CHAPTER 34

Maxx's face felt numb. The veins in his forehead throbbed against the cold tile floor. His shoulder pulsed with each beat of his heart. Rolling on his side, he looked back at the portal. The swirling mists had all but vanished, the last traces of green fading away. Maxx touched his shoulder and a new wave of pain shot through him. He saw the blood on his fingers. He'd never been shot before. It wasn't exactly something on his bucket list.

The room was quiet. He didn't see any laser sights slicing through the darkened lab. He shook his head to try to regain his bearings.

"Tane?"

The gurney beside the pentagram was gone.

"Where did everyone go?" Maxx saw the bloodied ring still on his finger.

He tore off a piece of his shirt and wrapped it around his shoulder, the blood soaked through the makeshift bandage.

"Silver?" Maxx pulled himself up. He could see the catwalk above him. "Ketchup?" Staggering over to the nearest staircase, he listened for footsteps. "Emi?"

The pain in Maxx's shoulder spread down his side with every step he took as he made his way back to the center of the lab. The ring went through portal, just not the way he planned it. The gateway should be closed. He won.

A blue pinhole of light appeared near the pentagram. Maxx watched as the glow divided into four separate small spheres. Each of them expanded and morphed, slowing forming the outlines of people.

As their details sharpened, one of the figures spoke.

"I knew it. As impossible as it seemed, I knew we'd find him here."

Silver stepped away from the portal. He was back to his younger self, the same form Maxx saw back at the virtual O.S. laboratory, only Silver's wheelchair was replaced with a cane. Agent Ketchum and two other security agents flanked him, dressed again in their suits of meshed armor. Ketchum also transformed back to his younger and much slimmer self.

Silver could barely contain his excitement. "When you disappeared from the lab, I thought perhaps you crossed over, but I had to find out for myself. This is our greatest break through yet."

Maxx looked down at his hands. "No way. It's impossible. I can't be in the program. How?"

"My boy, I don't have a clue," he said. "But do you know what this means? The gateway, it works both ways. Just imagine the possibilities. This takes the entire project somewhere entirely new."

Maxx stumbled backwards. "You have no right…"

Silver motioned for the agents to surround Maxx.

Agent Ketchall grabbed him by the wrist. "Give us the ring, Fragg. Make it easy or we'll just take the whole finger."

Maxx pulled his hand behind his back. "What ring? I don't know what you're talking about."

Silver laughed, not a cheery kind of laugh but one that made the hairs on Maxx's neck stand up straight. "Don't insult me, son."

Ketchall activated a laser knife he held in his hand. The other two agents grabbed Maxx's arms, wrenching his shoulder. Maxx saw dark spots as the pain clouded his vision. He struggled but he couldn't move.

"Bring him over here." Silver waved.

Grabbing Maxx's wrist, they dragged him across the room, forcing his hand in the air.

Silver admired Daniels' ring. "You have no idea how long we've been looking for this. We knew Daniels mixed the occult with our technology. His research notes told us that. What we didn't have was the personal item he used to open the portal. That is, until you brought it to us."

Silver patted Maxx on the cheek. He would have spit on the old geezer but he was having a hard time concentrating on anything but the pain.

"This will hurt a great deal I'm afraid but sacrifices must be made." Silver nodded to Ketchall. "Take the finger, agent. We can work with the ring here just as easily as in the real world."

Ketchall twisted Maxx's wrist and brought it up near his chest. He held the glowing knife near Maxx's face. Maxx could feel the heat of the blade on his cheek.

"Don't worry, kid. It'll cauterize as soon as I cut through. Still gonna hurt like a sunnavabitch though." Ketchall lingered the knife just above Maxx's finger.

"Go to hell, Ketchup." Maxx fought back the tears and the searing pain in his shoulder.

"Guess I'll see you there. You might feel a pinch," Ketchall laughed as he lowered the blade.

Maxx closed his eyes. He felt his skin burning and smelled his flesh cooking. He tried to pull free but then the pain just stopped. Maxx figured his finger was gone, cut off below the knuckle. He listened for the sound of the ring clanking off the metal floor. Opening his eyes, he saw the fresh burn mark on his finger but it was still attached to his hand. Ketchup stood in front of him, his mouth gaped opened. Maxx stared at the agent, who stood silent, a vacant look in his eyes.

"Ketchup?"

Maxx waited for him to say something. Instead, Ketchall's face contorted in pain and blood dripped from the corner of his mouth.

Maxx looked down at the agent's chest. A claw-tipped blue finger wiggled from inside his chest. The glowing finger disappeared back inside of him. He fell helplessly to the floor.

Instead of Agent Ketchall, Maxx was face to face with a raging mad Warren Talbot, mangled hair flowing in the air as he admired his blood soaked hand. Talbot turned and casually wiped the blood on Silver's suit jacket. The man, who a moment before exuded nothing but confidence, stood there in stunned silence. Talbot sneered at him before turning back to Maxx, the madness welling in his eyes.

"I was afraid you forgot about me. I'm glad you're back so we can finish this once and for all," Talbot snarled.

The agents holding Maxx's arms let go.

Maxx realized Ketchall still had a hold on his wrist and he yanked it free. "What do you want, you lunatic?" Maxx asked. "You ran into me, remember?"

Maxx swung at him and missed.

Laughing, Talbot placed his hand on Maxx's shoulder. "What I've always wanted, boy? I want your heart to be as dark as they made mine."

Silver regained some composure. He retreated back towards the closet set of stairs while barking out commands. "Kill that thing and get me the ring! That's an order!"

The remaining agents drew their Tasers and took up positions on either side of Talbot. He glanced at each of them but turned his focus to Silver. The men fired their weapons. The energized cords passed straight through Talbot, striking each other instead. Their armored circuitry sizzled and shorted out, sparks flying from their suits. Talbot grabbed the electrified strands.

Yanking the agents toward him, he laughed. "That was almost Vaudevillian. You need to hire better guards, old man."

Grabbing one of the agents by the neck, Talbot heaved him across the room. The flailing man struck the far wall, sliding down head first. His neck made a cracking noise as it hit the floor. The other agent let go of his weapon and swung at Talbot. His fist passed through the cyber-ghost's head. Talbot grabbed him by his chest plate, the metal crinkling under his grip. The mad ghost heaved the man up into the air. His head embedded into the metal grating of the catwalk above them. His legs convulsed as he thrashed against the metal webbing until they finally stopped and he hung motionless. Silver made it half way across the lab before Talbot turned, pouncing on him. Forcing him to the floor, droplets of blue ooze hissed from the corners of Talbot's mouth, the glowing saliva smearing down Silver's face.

"Now, you were saying something about a ring," Talbot said.

"The...the...ring? It's nothing." Silver writhed against the floor.

Talbot ran a claw down Silver's cheek. Tears formed in the old man's eyes. His body shuddered and faded but remained trapped under Talbot's hold.

"Having a little trouble trying to find your way back to your own world?" Talbot hissed. "Join the club. I've learned a few new tricks here." Talbot released a blast of energy from his hand and Silver transformed back into his older, frailer self. "From the looks of it, you're about a step away from death anyway. It's not worth wasting any more energy on you but I'll be sure to look you up when you cross over to my side of the tracks." Talbot pulled him closer. "Tell me about the ring, old man."

Maxx saw the sweat pouring over Silver's face. He dropped his cane against the floor. "The ring is the key. It can open and shut the portal if the wearer knows how it works. It's the passport between worlds."

Talbot dropped Silver, who crumpled into a ball on the floor. Maxx couldn't help but feeling sorry for the man, even if he was straight up evil. Talbot had cut him down like a weed from a garden.

Turning back to Maxx, Talbot eyed the ring on his finger. "A way back to the physical world?"

Crap. Silver just gave the lunatic another reason to want to take Maxx apart.

Leaping into the air, Talbot soared across the room, flying towards Maxx with his arms outstretched. He tried to run but Talbot was on him in a flash, tackling him to the floor.

He pinned Maxx's arms down. He couldn't believe how strong Talbot was but it felt two vices pinning him against the floor. His touch felt like ice cold water flowing across his skin, down into his veins, working its way to his heart.

Talbot smiled, enjoying seeing Maxx in that much pain, but he then he paused, looking stunned himself.

"It's you...in the flesh. You're real." Talbot's unnaturally wide smile returned. "This ring is more powerful than I'd dared to hope."

Talbot tore the ring from Maxx's finger, peeling away large amounts of skin in the process.

Maxx screamed, pulling his hand up to his chest. If felt like Talbot ripped his finger off. Holding his hand against his stomach, Maxx tried to put some distance between them. "You can't go back, you know? You're dead."

Talbot held the ring up to the ceiling admiring his prize. "First I take the power of this talisman and then I kill you, boy. Then we'll see what I can and can't do. You took away my life so now I get to take yours. An eye for an eye is how the saying goes, right?"

Talbot placed the ring on the tip of his finger, slowly savoring the process. Maxx pushed farther away, still trying to process it all. The portal should have closed. How could Maxx be in the virtual world, *really* in the virtual world?

"When I get back to the physical world, maybe I'll pay that pretty little girlfriend of yours a visit. She seemed very...healthy."

"Leave Emi out of this, you pervert!"

"Oh, come one, Maxx. She'll need someone to comfort her. Ironic, isn't it? I'll be back in your world and you'll be stuck here in this cruel joke of existence." Talbot pushed the ring passed his first knuckle.

"I'm going to knock that smirk right off your face." Maxx felt the rush of anger-fueled adrenalin flood over him. His hand tightened into a fist.

"You have no power here, boy." A bolt of energy crackled around Talbot's hands, shooting out and striking Maxx in the chest.

Maxx collapsed. It felt like he'd been tasered again. He could barely lift his arm off the ground.

"You can't..."

A rush of air blew passed Maxx. Something crashed into Talbot, as they both skidded across the lab. The ring flew off Talbot's finger, bouncing across the laboratory floor.

"Get the ring, Maxx." Jason wrestled Talbot to the ground. "I'll take care of Talbot."

Jason was covered in the same orange glow that Maxx saw back at the virtual dating service. Maxx could only watch, transfixed by Jason and Talbot fighting for the upper hand. Talbot pinned Jason on his back, trying to wrap his hands around Jason's throat.

"Jason!" Maxx ran to him. He wasn't going to lose him again.

"No, Maxx! Find the ring." Jason let go of Talbot's wrist and waved Maxx away. "He's too powerful. I'll hold him off."

Jason locked arms with the cybergeist. Pulling up his legs, he kicked Talbot in the chest, sending him flying across the lab.

Talbot bounced up and rushed Jason. "You can't stop me. My hate gives me twice the power you possess." Crashing into Jason, Talbot tossed him into a bank of computers. "Let's find out if someone can die twice."

Maxx needed to help his brother but he knew Jason was right about finding the ring. He heard it hit the ground when Jason tackled Talbot but he didn't see where it landed. Crawling on his knees, Maxx felt along the ground, stopping as Talbot rammed Jason's head into the wall.

Talbot's voice cracked as he slammed him back again and again. "Die! Die! Die!"

"Find the ring, Maxx," Jason yelled.

"I'm not losing you again," Maxx said.

Jason pried Talbot's arm from his throat and twisted him around, forcing his face into the wall as blue ooze splattered like a bomb going off.

"We can't let him back in your world, Maxx. Think of Mom and Dad. What about Tane and Emi?" Jason pleaded.

Sparks exploded from the damaged machinery as Talbot broke free.

Maxx swept his arms along the floor, searching for the ring. He bumped into Silver in the dark, who mumbled to himself over and over.

"No…no…no. Not like this. Not like this."

Maxx thought about slapping the old fool for causing all this trouble but figured in his condition he probably wouldn't even notice. Maxx tried a new direction, stopping to check on his brother. Talbot had pinned Jason to the floor and morphed his arm into a glowing blue ax.

Maxx screamed, "No!"

Jason slipped free and wrapped Talbot in a bear hug. "I believe in you, Maxx."

Images filtered through Maxx's head. He thought of his parents and Jason's funeral, his grandmother lying helpless in that nursing home, Tane strapped down to a gurney in the O.S. Headquarters, and

Emi running from a pack of O.S. Security Agents. The world weighed on his shoulders and all he could do was thrash around in the dark for answers. The back of his hand hit something. He heard the metallic tings as it bounced across the tiles. He scrambled to follow the sound, brushing him arms wide across the floor. His fingers closed around the smooth golden band.

"I got it! Jason, I got it!" Maxx held it up like a trophy.

Jason twisted Talbot's bladed arm behind his back and braced him against the floor.

Jason fought to keep him down. "Take it back through the gate. Get out of here, Maxx."

Maxx jumped up and ran for the portal. His side ached more with every step as he crossed the lab. He stopped just before the gate, ready to jump back through. He looked over at his brother and Talbot. They both quit fighting and watched Maxx standing in front of the machine. Maxx pulled back his arm.

"Throw that ring and you'll be stuck in this world. Stuck with me!" Talbot shrieked.

Maxx rubbed his fingers across the band. "At least I'll be here with my brother. I'll have more than you."

Jason pushed away from Talbot. "That's not an option here, Maxx. I'd like nothing better than to get to hang out with you but that's not up to us."

"Then who is it up to, Jason?" Maxx asked. His hands trembled. "Why did I have to lose you in the first place? It isn't fair."

"Fair? Maxx, this isn't about fair. It's about fate and what's meant to be. There wasn't anything you could do to avoid the accident that day, any more than I could have, or even Mr. Talbot."

"I'll rip both of your hearts right out of your chests." Talbot crawled on all fours and rocked back and forth, eyeing the ring in Maxx's hand. His wild blue hair covered most of his face, making him look more like an animal than a man.

"Is that what you want to end up like, Maxx?" Jason pointed at him. "Letting fear and anger consume you? You're better than that."

"But I don't want to lose you again."

Jason grinned. "You didn't lose me in the first place. I'm right here. I always have been. No one can take that away from us."

Maxx looked at the ring. "I'm not leaving you."

Tossing the ring into the pentagram, Maxx watched it hover in mid-air in the center of the portal. Time stood still as his brother and Talbot watched it floating inside the gate. The green mists returned, slowly circling inside the void until they covered the tiny ring and it dissolved back into the portal.

"No!" Talbot screamed.

He rocketed across the laboratory, dragging Jason with him as they careened towards Maxx. The impact knocked him into the base of the pentagram, his head cracking against metal foundation.

Jason rushed over to him.

"Maxx! I can't believe you did that. It was your only way home."

Maxx felt the warmth of his brother's touch, the complete opposite of Talbot's ice cold grip. He looked up at his brother.

"Looks like you're stuck with me, bro."

"You always were the stubborn one," Jason said.

Talbot appeared behind Jason and grabbed him by the waist. Hoisting him over his head, Talbot looked down at Maxx.

"Two can play that game."

He heaved Jason's body head first into the swirling mists of the portal. Jason disappeared into the abyss.

"No," Maxx cried, reaching out for his brother.

Talbot grabbed Maxx by the leg and flung him across the lab like a rag doll. He crashed into the wall and slid down to the floor. He was pretty sure at least a few ribs were broken.

The room spun around him as Maxx staggered to get up. He was close to one of the staircases leading up to the catwalk above them. Stumbling towards it, he needed to put some distance between him and Talbot until he could figure something out. Something slammed into his back and he collapsed against the stairs. Talbot flipped him over on his back. His hair whipped across his face like a tornado.

"No more rings, no more brothers, no more armored idiots, Fragg. Your game just ended," he said.

CHAPTER 35

Maxx couldn't tell what was worse, losing his brother…again, or the stench of Talbot's breath inches away from his face.

"Don't they make breath mints in the after-life?" Maxx sounded a lot braver than he felt. His ribs ached, his head and shoulder throbbed, and he had no idea how to get home. If Talbot had his way, Maxx didn't expect that to be a problem much longer.

"Always with the jokes, huh, boy? Quite a barbed tongue you have there." Talbot stretched out his own tongue and it morphed into a thin two-pronged blade.

It speared towards Maxx's face. He twisted to his side and it bounced off the metal steps.

"Ewww. That's just sick," Maxx said.

He jabbed at Talbot, striking him square on the nose. Talbot reeled back, grabbing his face.

"That's impossible." Talbot pulled his hand away, green blood dripping down his lip.

Maxx was as surprised as him. He pulled himself up, adding bruised knuckles to his growing list.

"Looks like the rules changed when I jumped through the portal with the ring." Maxx looked down at his hand and concentrated. It morphed into the working end of a sledge hammer.

"Let's finish this," Maxx said.

Maxx swung hard, connecting with Talbot's chest. He flew across the room, tumbling end over end. It felt better than Maxx expected. He raced toward Talbot, not wanting to give up his advantage. Talbot stumbled to his feet just as Maxx got within reach. He slammed his new hammer-fist down into Talbot's back, driving him back down.

"That was for messing up my ghost hunting gig in O.S."

Talbot crawled along the floor, trying to get away. Maxx grabbed his ankle and tossed him into a wall.

"That one was for getting my friends involved in this crap."

"But, I didn't have anything to do with-"

"I don't care!" Maxx swung again, smashing into his side. The sound of ribs cracking was like music to his ears.

Talbot tried to lash out but Maxx dodged it, pinning his arm to the ground with a giant glowing hook.

"That should hold you," he said.

Maxx wailed away at the man. With each strike, he felt more anger rising in him. He jumped on Talbot's chest and wrapped his fingers around his throat.

"And this, you blue piece of shit, is for my brother."

He felt Talbot's ice cold flesh under his grip. He squeezed with every ounce of hate he could find. He wanted to twist that monster's head right off his body. Talbot thrashed, his hand finding Maxx's face. He raked his claws down Maxx's cheek, the skin bubbling as they carved his flesh. It felt like Maxx's face was on fire. He didn't care about right or wrong. It didn't matter whether his brother would approve. Maxx's life had become a symphony of pain and guilt since the accident and he needed to make the noise stop.

Talbot's eyes rolled back in his head. His hair quit flowing and fell limp, forming a pool of green around his head. He arms fell to the side.

Maxx bounced his head off the floor and let go. He sat there, straddling his tormentor's chest, and snarled.

"I hate you."

He morphed his hand into a battle ax and raised it above his head.

"Try coming back from this," Maxx said.

One shot. That's all he needed to end this, to wipe this un-living abomination completely out of his life. The only chance he had for any kind of future, one with his friends, with Tane…with Emi. Maxx pictured her there in the lab, beside him, watching as he beat Talbot to near death and then plunging his blade into his skull. He could see the terror in her eyes, the pain.

Maxx reached for her as tears filled her eyes.

He saw his reflection in the side of his ax. His hair swirled around him, the spikes extended and flowing like blackened vipers biting the air. Maxx's eyes glowed like they were on fire, simmering in each socket. He looked like…Talbot, every bit as full of hate.

Maxx dropped his hand to the floor with a clang. Slowly, he climbed off Talbot, his chest heaving with each labored breath. He sat there, on the floor, in an imaginary lab, in an imaginary world. He looked over at Talbot's still bleeding body.

"I'm not you," he said.

He stood up and limped over to the portal. His hand transformed back to normal. Standing at the base of the pentagram, he fell to his knees and rested his head against the base.

"What am I going to do now, Jason?"

He anger was gone. Maybe it found its own way back through the gate. He didn't know, and really didn't care. He was just tired of feeling that way, tired of fighting the world. Look at where it got him. He almost became the same kind of psychopath as Talbot. He didn't hate the man anymore. He felt sorry for him, so wrapped up in an emotion that he couldn't move on.

"Emi." Maxx's whole body felt numb as he pulled himself up to look inside the darkened center of the pentagram. "I'm sorry."

Maxx felt something sting his side. He looked down. The tip of a sword jutted out of from his stomach. It almost seemed surreal. There was no pain, only confusion. When the blade vanished, back into his body, he saw the blood flow, soaking into his shirt.

Dumbfounded he slowly turned around.

"You idiot! You can't kill a ghost. I'm already dead." Talbot laughed, blood dripping from the edge of his sword.

The words barely registered as Maxx toppled over, clutching at his shirt.

"Let's keep it simple this time," Talbot said, holding his sword-hand above Maxx's neck. "Goodbye, kid."

Maxx didn't have the strength to even try to stop him.

"Warren! Stop!"

The voice echoed across the lab. Talbot froze, his arm still lingering above his head.

"Warren."

Maxx and Talbot both turned towards the pentagram. A new fog formed inside of it, the haze swirling in concentric circles, twirling faster and brighter.

"Who said that?" Talbot asked.

The vapors turned into a vortex and burned bright green. From the center of the whirlwind, two figures appeared.

Talbot cried, backing away. "No! That's impossible. You're playing some kind of trick."

Maxx didn't understand. All he could see were their outlines. Talbot fell to his knees, holding his hands out in front of him like he was trying to protect himself from whatever it was coming through the portal.

When Maxx looked back at the gate, Jason stood on the ledge next to a small boy. The child, maybe ten years old, wore cut-off knee length jeans and a red t-shirt. He brushed back a tangle of brown hair and waved at them.

"Warren, it's me. It's Gil." The boy stepped down and reached for Talbot. He recoiled from his grasp, like one touch would destroy him.

Stumbling across the room, Talbot crashed into the damaged computer towers. He wiped the glowing hair from his face.

"Gilbert?" Talbot stared in disbelief. "But…I killed you."

Jason walked over to Maxx, bending down next to him. "Are you okay?"

"I never thought I'd see you again." Maxx grabbed his hand. "Talbot tossed you through the portal and you were gone."

Jason hugged him and Maxx never wanted to let go.

Jason sat next to him on the floor. "It looked like we could use some help, so I brought reinforcements."

"But who is he?" Maxx asked.

"Just watch." Jason pointed over to the mismatched duo.

"Don't hurt me!" Talbot screamed.

The boy rested his hand on Talbot's quivering shoulder. "It wasn't your fault."

Talbot's arm transformed back to normal. Covering his face with his hands, he sobbed. "But I was supposed to watch you. That was my one job at the lake, to keep an eye on my little brother. I didn't mean to fall asleep."

Gilbert pulled Talbot's hands away. Blue tears streamed down his brother's cheeks.

The boy wiped them away. "You were twelve, Warren. I'd forgiven you a long time ago, so has Mom and Dad. You just never found a way to do that yourself."

Talbot looked up at him. "I never wanted this, Gil. It was different after you were gone. I was sad but then angry, so angry. I lost my childhood because we lost you and I hated anyone that grew up normal." He buried his head in his little brother's shoulder and wept.

Gil stroked his hair. "Loss is a part of life. You can't have one without the other. You're still a brother...and a son. Mom and Dad are waiting. They miss you. Why don't you come with me?"

Jason leaned into Maxx. "Sound familiar?"

"How'd you find Talbot's brother? Dial-a-ghost?" Maxx sat, astonished by the scene unfolding in front of them.

"Always the smart ass." Jason slapped his brother across the back of the head. "Let's just say he reached out to *me*."

Taking his hand, Gilbert pulled his brother up and they stared at one another, stared for a long time, until Gilbert wrapped his arms around his brother's waist.

"I forgive you," he said. "I always have."

Walking arm in arm towards the portal, Maxx couldn't help but chuckle at the site of the pair, a six foot glowing monstrosity in tattered rags and a small child.

Gilbert turned to Talbot as they crossed into the gate. "There's a whole side that you haven't seen. Just wait. And Warren?"

"Yeah, Gil." Talbot smiled at him with rows of crooked teeth.

"You really need a haircut."

They disappeared into the portal, quietly fading away, and the room fell quiet.

Maxx turned towards his brother only to realize he was gone.

"Jason?"

"I'm still here." Jason knelt down beside him, putting his hand on Maxx's shoulder. They stayed like that, watching the glowing mists of the portal until Maxx finally spoke.

"I just wanted to say I'm sor-"

"Don't. There's no need. I know, Maxx. I know everything." Jason squeezed his shoulder. "You've had one hell of a day. You did good. You helped a lot of people. How does it feel?"

Maxx looked at his wounded shoulder and blood covered shirt.

"Other than the gun hole, stab wound, Taser holes, concussion, and multiple bruises? I'm good. Did I save them? I mean, Tane and Emi, are they safe?" Maxx asked.

Jason shrugged. "I don't know. You did everything you could. I know that."

Maxx looked around the laboratory. Silver was gone, so were the injured agents.

He looked at the pentagram. "How am I going to get home? I mean, I jumped through the portal to shut it down. If I jump through after Talbot and his brother, where's it going to take me?"

Maxx's vision blurred and he felt the fatigue overtaking him.

"Faith, little bro. Sometimes, it's all we have." Jason stroked Maxx's hair and rested his head in his lap.

Between the shock, the flood of emotions, and the blood loss, Maxx's body finally took over and his world went black.

CHAPTER 36

Maxx opened his eyes. He was in the back seat of a convertible speeding down a deserted dirt road in the middle of the night. Emi was sitting next to him. He felt her fingers wrapped in his. The wind blew her hair back.

She leaned in and whispered, "I love you, Maxx."

She smelled like fresh baked bread and flowers. Behind him, Maxx saw the trails of dust spraying out from the rear tires. Above him, a single star shined down in an otherwise clear night sky.

Tane was sitting up front. He leaned over the seat and said something but Maxx couldn't hear it. The radio was on full blast, playing a song Maxx knew but somehow he couldn't make out the lyrics. Jason was driving and made eye contact with him in the rear view mirror. They exchanged a smile until his brother's face changed from joy to concern. Maxx turned in his seat. Three pinpoints of light raced down from the sky. It looked like they were chasing the car. As the orbs gained on them, Maxx recognized the outlines inside, O.S. Agents. He tried to scream a warning but nothing came out.

Jason drove faster, weaving dangerously down the narrow road. The dirt bit into Maxx's face, blinding him as they raced faster and faster. He could hear the agents closing in behind them.

"There's no place to run, Fragnelli. End of the line."

Maxx felt the car jerk. He saw the dust blurred image of Agent Ketchall hanging onto the car's bumper.

"Looks like your ticket is about to get punched, Fragg."

Ketchall pointed to something up ahead of them, off in the distance.

Two red lights blinked intermittently. Maxx heard the warning signal blare as two wooden crossing barriers lowered in front of them, blocking their path. He saw the railroad tracks stretching out to either side right before the headlights shut off.

Someone grabbed Maxx's shoulder. The hand was ice cold but it burned into his skin. The skeletal visage of Johan Silver, dressed in one of his agent's metal suits, laughed in his face.

"Fate is a cruel mistress, Mr. Fragnelli."

Maxx tried to pull free, the train signal cutting into his brain. He saw a light racing towards them along the tracks. As the engine barreled closer, Maxx saw Warren Talbot wearing a conductor's hat and hanging outside the window. He screamed into the night as he yanked on the chord of the train's whistle.

There was no way they were going to stop in time. Maxx looked at Jason, who seemed oblivious to the fact they were about to die.

Maxx found his voice. "Stop! Jason, please, you have to stop."

The car rammed through the barricades. Maxx lunged for the steering wheel an instant before the train rammed into the side of the car. Time slowed. Maxx was thrown from the car, hurtling helplessly through the night. He saw his brother, spinning in circles above him, being carried away in a swirling tornado of dirt and twisted metal. Maxx felt weightless, like he could just let go, drift up and become lost in the black expanse above them.

Something ripped into his leg, pulling him back down. Talbot's mess of wild blue hair violently whipped across his calf, each strand cutting deeper into his flesh. Talbot looked up and tipped his hat.

"We still got business, boy."

Suddenly, Agent Ketchall was beside him, twisting one of his arms.

"...snot nosed punk."

A zombified Johan Silver clawed at his other leg, biting into his ankle.

Jason was still spinning helplessly in the air above him. He reached out for his brother but he was too far away. The wind carried them higher into the spinning vortex. The ground below vanished. Maxx felt like he was being torn apart. He twisted and kicked but they held on tight, tearing away small bits of him as their collective weight dragged him farther away from his brother.

"Tane! Emi!" he screamed but his friends weren't there, only him and his nightmares.

Maybe that was the way it was supposed to end all along, alone and consumed by his own emotions. Maybe it was what he deserved and he should quit fighting and give in to fate.

Someone grabbed his free hand, wrapping their fingers around his wrist. Jason looked down at him.

"Be more than an obstacle, Maxx."

A blast of light flared down from above them, smothering Maxx. The roaring winds stopped and the pain melted away. He felt nothing, not cold, not warmth, not weight, only light. Talbot, Ketchall, and Silver were gone. So was Jason. Maxx drifted higher into the void as thoughts of his family flooded through him, his mom and dad, memories of his brother. He could almost picture Tane looking at him there, hanging helplessly in thin air, and telling him to quit fooling around and get down from there. He thought about Emi, how she made him feel when he was with her and how he wanted her in his life.

It was time to let the world back in, the good *and* the bad.

He looked down at his shoulder. The bullet wound from back at the lab was still there. He forced his finger into the hole in his shirt. Pain shot through his arm and he screamed. It felt like his whole side was on fire but in a way it felt good too, better than the numbness. Maxx stopped rising. He hung there suspended in mid-air, trapped between the light and the pain. He pressed down on his shoulder again and cried out as he plummeted towards the ground.

"Jason!"

***

"Easy, Maxx. I've got you. You're okay."

Maxx felt someone's hands on his shoulders, pushing him down. He opened his eyes. His dad was standing over him, guiding him gently back down into a bed. He was in a hospital room. A tube flowed from up from his arm. He followed it to an intravenous bag dripping fluids from a pole. His mom hovered behind his dad, her face filled with concern.

She wrapped her arms around Maxx and squeezed. "Oh thank god, Maxx. We thought we lost you."

"Uh, Mom? Choking. Need to breath." It didn't even sound like his own voice. It was course and weak, like someone sapped every ounce of strength out of him. He tried to sit up in the bed but he couldn't. He was sore in places that he didn't realize could be sore.

Tears gushed down his mom's cheeks. "Those awful men broke into our house and took you away. We didn't know what to think. And then you called and said everything was alright but I knew it wasn't. A mother knows these things, Maxx. I knew it wasn't right. We called Tane and Emi's parents and went to the police station and reported you all kidnapped. Emi's father tracked her with some kind of chip. When the police realized where they took you, they called in the F.B.I."

"You brought in the Feds?" Maxx shot up and instantly realized his mistake when the room started spinning.

His dad pulled her away. "Easy, hon, the boy just woke up. They tracked the GPS in Emi's phone and found her in that Other Syde Headquarters. Newton City Police and their swat team stormed the building. It seems Emi's dad has some connections there. They lost the signal right before they busted in. They found Tane in the parking garage strapped to a gurney in a van and Emi was being chased by a bunch of security guards. You were in some lab upstairs, lying on the floor beside some glowing machine. No one knows how you got there but you've been sleeping for two days."

Maxx looked around the room. The curtains were drawn. A crumpled pillow and blanket rested on a recliner in the corner.

"Where are Tane and Emi? Are they okay?" Maxx asked.

His mom motioned to the door. "They're fine. They're waiting in the hall. They've been here since the ambulance brought you in. They told us what happened but they didn't know who shot you."

Maxx gingerly touched his bandaged shoulder. "I don't know either, Mom. It all happened so fast. I can't remember."

She kissed his forehead. "I'll accept that. For now. I'm just glad you're okay."

"I told you that computer junk was no good. You could've got yourself killed," his dad said.

"Not now, Harold." She pulled back the curtain. Sunlight streamed in from the window. She opened the door to the hall. "Okay, you two."

Emi rushed in, throwing her arms around Maxx. "I thought I lost you. Those goon agents chased me all over the building." Emi let go and sat on the edge of the bed. "What happened in the lab?"

Tane stood behind Emi, grinning ear to ear.

"Good to have you back, buddy."

"Thanks, Tane. It's good to see you not strapped down," Maxx said.

Emi nudged Maxx's arm. "What happened? Tane said you jumped through the gate and vanished."

"I did. I went...somewhere else. It was the virtual world but I was real, if that makes sense. Talbot was there and so was-"

"Talbot?" His dad interrupted. "You mean Warren Talbot? The man from Jason's accident?"

Maxx looked at his parents. "Yeah, it was him. It sounds crazy, I know. Jason was there too. He saved me."

His dad rested his hand on Maxx's shoulder. "Son, you were shot and stabbed. They kidnapped you, drugged you, and did who knows what to your head while you were in that cyber world. It wasn't really Jason, Maxx. It couldn't be."

Maxx just smiled, meeting their collective stares.

"Sometimes you've just got to have faith."

His mom cried and Tane put his arm around her.

His father patted him on the leg. "Okay. Get some rest. We'll talk later."

He took Maxx's mom by the hand and led her out of the room.

"Dad," Maxx said.

He stopped at the door.

"Maybe we could tackle the garage when I get out of here? You and me?"

He grinned. "That sounds good. I'll look forward to it."

When the door closed behind them, Maxx sat up, slower that time, and asked, "What happened to Silver? Did the police find him inside?"

Tane pulled up a chair. "Oh yeah, they found him all right. I didn't see it but a bunch of the cops were talking. He was still hooked into synskin and babbling about deen greamons and dattered shreams. They said he was pretty much mental toast."

"What about Agent Ketchup? I mean he was a jerk and all but..."

Tane slowly shook his head.

"Crap." Maxx turned to Emi. "Are you okay?"

"I'm getting there but I think I've had my fill of virtual worlds." She pulled Maxx's blankets higher on his chest.

Maxx laughed. "I don't blame you. Did your dad freak out?"

"Freak out? Yeah, you could say that. I had to threaten to move in with my mom for him to let me come here. He's in the waiting room, by the way. He can't wait to meet you. We decided it was best not to tell my mom about this."

"Maybe we can postpone meeting your dad. I don't think I can take being attacked again," Maxx said.

"I'll tell him you're still in a coma." Emi laughed.

"Thanks."

Maxx's mom poked her head back in the room. "The doctor wants to take a look at him now that he's awake. Does he remember anything else?"

"Okay, Mrs. Fragnelli," Tane said.

Emi smiled at her. "You know your son. He's the Fort Knox of secrets but I did learn a few pleasant surprises about him. He's brave when he needs to be and pretty smooth in a pinch. Now we just have to work on that ridiculously rich part."

"Ouch. I'm a total bust on that end. They took all of our money, remember?" Maxx looked at Tane. "You didn't get a chance to hack into the vaults while you had access to the O.S. programming?"

Tane stood up. "Same old Maxx. Yeah, he's definitely back. I was too busy trying to save our butts, buddy. Besides, the whole O.S. site is down. I checked it the day we got back. They're closed indefinitely for service updates. With the feds and other agencies swarming all over their real world headquarters, I don't think they'll be up and running again anytime soon."

Maxx stared out the window. "What's that mean for Jason?"

Tane shrugged. "I don't know. It was all over the news. They kept like twenty thousand people trapped in there for over six hours. At least four people died while they were stuck in there. No one's very happy with the Other Syde Corporation."

Maxx dropped his legs over the side and tried to get up. He wobbled and fell back into the bed.

"Easy, Maxx." Tane reached into his shoulder bag and pulled out a laptop, handing it to him. "Here, I grabbed it from your room. I figured you'd be jonesing for an internet fix."

Maxx set the computer on the bed beside him. "That's okay. I think I've had my fill of virtual living, for a while at least."

Tane waited for Emi at the door.

She hugged Maxx and kissed his cheek. "We'll be right down the hall. Do you want anything from the cafeteria?"

"Cheeseburger and fries?" Maxx asked.

Smiling, she joined Tane at the door. "I'll get extra pickles."

The door closed and Maxx leaned back on his pillows. He eyed the laptop sitting at the foot of the bed. Listening for footsteps outside, he powered up the computer. Resting it in his lap, he brought up the HeadRoom site and navigated to Jason's profile.

"Jason, what can I say? You saved my butt again. Another adventure for the Fragnelli boys. I still wish the accident never happened. I miss you but I know you're still with me. You're the best brother anyone could ask for and I'm glad we had the time together that we did. Thanks, for everything. I love you. I'll talk to you soon."

Maxx watched the cursor blink under his post. He closed the lid and set the laptop on the table beside him. He remembered something his brother told him that day at the air strip, something he forgot about until just then. They'd just won another heat and Maxx was all about rubbing it into the loser's face. He felt Jason's hand on his shoulder and he said to Maxx, "It's not about the winning, little brother. What matters is how you run the race."

Jason was still teaching him lessons. Maxx's life wasn't perfect, not by a long shot, but he smiled, thinking about how lucky he was to have the family and friends that he did. The sun streamed into his room and he could feel the warmth on his face. His life may not be perfect but it was his and he wouldn't have it any other way.

www.ingramcontent.com/pod-product-compliance
Lightning Source LLC
Chambersburg PA
CBHW020749250626
47155CB00003B/987